P9-CRG-142

SHATTERED

MIRROR

ALSO BY SARAH PRICE

An Empty Cup
An Amish Buggy Ride
Secret Sister: An Amish Christmas Tale
The Faded Photo
Heavenly Blues

The Plain Fame Series

Plain Fame
Plain Change
Plain Again
Plain Return
Plain Choice
Plain Christmas

The Amish of Lancaster Series

Fields of Corn
Hills of Wheat
Pastures of Faith
Valley of Hope

The Amish of Ephrata Series

The Tomato Patch
The Quilting Bee
The Hope Chest
The Clothes Line

The Amish Classics Series

For a complete listing of books, please visit the author's website at www.sarahpriceauthor.com.

SHATTERED

MIRROR

SARAH PRICE

Waterfall
PRESS

This is a work of fiction. Names, characters, organizations, places, events, and incidents are either products of the author's imagination or are used fictitiously. Any resemblance to actual persons, living or dead, or actual events is purely coincidental.

Text copyright © 2018 by Price Publishing, LLC
All rights reserved.

Scripture quotations are from the ESV® Bible (The Holy Bible, English Standard Version®), copyright © 2001 by Crossway, a publishing ministry of Good News Publishers. Used by permission. All rights reserved.

No part of this book may be reproduced, or stored in a retrieval system, or transmitted in any form or by any means, electronic, mechanical, photocopying, recording, or otherwise, without express written permission of the publisher.

Published by Waterfall Press, Grand Haven, MI

www.brilliancepublishing.com

Amazon, the Amazon logo, and Waterfall Press are trademarks of Amazon.com, Inc., or its affiliates.

ISBN-13: 9781503942882
ISBN-10: 1503942880

Cover design by Shasti O'Leary Soudant

Printed in the United States of America

SHATTERED

MIRROR

PROLOGUE

Kelly hadn't been home for fifteen minutes when the first argument began. She stood in the kitchen, the brown bags of groceries on the counter waiting to be emptied and Fiona crying at the table. Her coloring book was open, and her yellow box of crayons lay empty, the contents spread over the tabletop. The five-year-old held half of a purple crayon in her hand as big tears rolled down her cheeks.

Kelly was deciding between putting away the groceries and consoling her daughter when her husband walked in from the garage and stopped in the doorway.

Todd's bulky frame filled the opening, and he frowned. "What's going on here?"

Kelly sighed and ran her fingers through her shoulder-length brown hair. After a long day of work, she was exhausted and felt certain that she looked it. She hadn't had time to freshen up, something she liked to do before Todd came home.

"Zach broke her new crayons." She glanced at Fiona, her coloring book opened to the page of elephants. Fiona loved elephants and, when Kelly had picked her up from school, her daughter proudly showed off the new coloring book that her preschool teacher had just given her for a belated birthday present.

"Could you talk to him?"

Todd frowned, the steely-blue irises barely visible behind his puffy eyes. "About what?"

Count to ten, Kelly told herself. She had never wanted to be the kind of wife who greeted her husband with problems instead of a big smile and warm hug after a long day at work. Parenthood, however, seemed to have knocked that routine off course. Gone were the leisurely dinners, sometimes with candles and a shared bottle of wine, when they talked about work and the news and dreamed about the idyllic family they would have someday.

The reality of children and different parenting styles had killed those romantic evenings, or, at least, put them on hold for the time being.

"About being nicer to his little sister."

Todd scoffed and set his laptop case on the floor near the water cooler. "Oh come on, Kell. That's what big brothers do. Torture their sisters."

She felt her pulse quicken. "Zach damaged her things, Todd!"

Todd practically laughed, which made her wonder if she *was* making a mountain out of broken crayon. "He's nine!" After shrugging off his jacket, he flung it over the nearest chair. "What do you expect?"

A dozen different answers to that question popped into her mind, but she tried to control her temper. It was always the same thing with Todd. Zachary could simply do no wrong as far as his father was concerned. And Kelly could foresee where that attitude would take her son in the future. "How about a little support from his father in disciplining him?"

He mumbled something under his breath.

"I mean it, Todd. This boy needs to be disciplined, taught respect for other people and their things." She could see the flash of anger in her husband's eyes. *Easy does it,* she warned herself. The last thing she wanted was a full-blown confrontation on a Friday night when neither of them could escape the aftermath the next day.

"I think you do enough of that."

"Because you don't do *any* of it."

"Why should I when you have that corner of parenting covered so well?" His sarcasm did not go unnoticed, and Kelly found herself clenching her fist. "Look, he's just a little boy. He's probably trying to get your attention. You're always so busy with other things."

"Other things?"

"Yeah. Like work and . . ." He glanced at Fiona, who was sniffling as she tried to peel back the paper wrapper to the broken purple crayon. ". . . With her."

Kelly stared at him, her mouth suddenly dry and her rage in full throttle. *Her.* That's what he always called Fiona. *Her.*

No, Todd Martin had never wanted a daughter, only sons. Perhaps it was because he had been the youngest of four boys; he had definitely been the most spoiled. Even his mother had made a snide comment about having a granddaughter, the first in the Martin family for two generations.

The contrast in Todd's behavior after Zachary's birth and after Fiona's had stunned Kelly. For Zachary, she hadn't been able to get Todd to leave the hospital or return to work. He had taken paternity leave to help her with "his" son. For Fiona, he had spent most of the delivery time on his BlackBerry until the nurse finally confiscated it. And afterward? Todd had returned to work the very next day. Working as a liaison for a high-level government contractor was too demanding to take time off, he had claimed.

But Kelly had seen through that ruse.

"She has a name," Kelly said in a stiff voice. "It's Fiona, and it wouldn't kill you to use it once in a while."

Todd leaned against the counter and crossed his arms. That was his defensive stance, the one he took when he was ready to engage in full-blown battle. "I don't know what you're talking about."

Sarah Price

Kelly glanced over at Fiona, who, thankfully, was oblivious to their discussion. Unlike Zachary, Fiona seemed to live in a world of rainbows and unicorns. She didn't seem to notice—or maybe she just didn't mind—that her father favored her older brother. In fact, as far as Kelly could tell, Fiona preferred it that way. And sometimes, truth be told, so did Kelly. Fiona was so much easier to entertain. She loved visiting the historical farms in Morristown, especially if there were animals to see. Fosterfields Living Historical Museum was her favorite because of the pigs, sheep, and mules. Fiona could spend an entire day watching the newborn piglets nursing or the little lambs playing in the paddock. Neither Todd nor Zachary would have spent more than five minutes there before declaring it boring and rushing the small girl back to the car.

Fiona was just different.

And Todd didn't know what to do with that.

"Look," Kelly said, willing herself to calm down. "Zachary's almost ten. He's too rough with Fiona. He needs to learn some respect, Todd. And responsibility. He has yet to learn anything about accountability."

This time, Todd laughed. "Accountability? What is he? An adult?"

"No, but he will be one day. If we don't start now"—Kelly fought the urge to roll her eyes—"when do you expect to flip the switch? At fourteen? Sixteen? When he's driving? When he's leaving for college?"

"You're ridiculous!" He shoved off from the counter and crossed the room. When he reached the other side, he opened a cabinet and pulled out a bottle of gin. "He's just a kid."

"You don't even make him pick up after himself!" Kelly watched as Todd poured a healthy gin and tonic into a tall glass. *Great,* she thought, knowing that the evening would rapidly head south. "Could you take it easy on that, please?"

Shoving the bottle back into the cabinet and slamming the door shut, Todd glared at her. "Don't start that again!"

4

Before she could respond, the sound of feet running down the staircase followed by a cheerful "Daddy!" abruptly ended the conversation. Zachary raced into the room and hurried to embrace his father. "Wanna go throw the football?"

Todd laughed and ruffled his son's dirty-blond hair. "You bet, son. But let me change first."

"Todd . . ." When he glanced at Kelly, she gestured toward Fiona.

"What's this I hear about you breaking your sister's crayons?"

Ignoring the question, Zachary tugged at his father's hand. "Go get changed!"

To his credit, Todd set down his drink and held firm. For a moment, Kelly held out hope that, for once, her husband would discipline their son. "I want an answer first, Zach," Todd said.

"It was an accident, Daddy." Zach glanced over his shoulder at his mother. "I told Mommy that."

Todd followed Zachary's gaze. "See? He didn't mean to break them."

Kelly's mouth opened but no words came out.

CHAPTER 1

Every morning when Kelly stood at the door to Zach's bedroom, trying to get him up for high school, she said a silent prayer that she wouldn't find him hanging from the ceiling fan.

Today was no different.

Downstairs, the dogs barked in the kitchen as Fiona tried to feed them. Even for a thirteen-year-old, that was no mean effort with four rambunctious canines eager for their breakfast. Kelly sighed, the noise of their sharp barking grating on her nerves. Why had she agreed to more dogs? Didn't she have enough going on, dealing with Zachary? But Fiona's eyes, so full of hope and love, had swung the balance in the favor of insanity.

So, despite already having too much on her very small plate, Kelly had said yes. After all, what were two more, right?

Now that those two small pups were a year old, Kelly regretted falling victim to loving her daughter so much that, once again, she had found it too hard to refuse.

"Zach?" she called out. No response. Her heart began to race, and she felt her palms grow sweaty. Was today the day?

As always, she rapped her knuckles on the door twice before opening it. *Privacy,* she always reminded herself. A teenage boy needed privacy. But the truth was that she needed those few extra seconds to brace herself for whatever was in store for her on the other side of the door.

"Zach?"

Kelly placed her hand on the doorknob, the metal cold beneath her fingers, and, after turning it, she slowly pushed open the door.

As usual, the room was dark.

And it stank.

Despite forbidding him to smoke in the house, Kelly could smell the stale scent of cigarettes. The ashtray—a used can of Red Bull—on his nightstand added insult to injury. He wasn't even trying to hide it anymore. When she saw Zach sprawled across the bed, sleeping, she breathed a sigh of relief. It crossed her mind that such relief, something she'd have found shocking and confusing just a few years ago, was now part of her new normal.

His curly blond hair hung over his face, covering his eyes. She had been begging him to get a haircut for two months now. As usual, Zach refused. She noticed that he wore the same dirty blue gym shorts and ripped red T-shirt that he had worn the previous day and the day before that. In fact, Kelly couldn't remember the last time she *hadn't* seen him wearing that shirt.

His lack of attention to his personal hygiene was just one more indicator that her son was depressed.

Crossing the room, Kelly opened the curtains. Bright light streamed in, and Zach grumbled, rolling over and covering his face with his pillow.

"Come on, Zach. You have to go to school."

"Not going," he mumbled.

Kelly sat down on the edge of the bed and placed her hand on his shoulder. "Come on, sweetheart."

None too gently, he pushed her hand away. He made no effort to get up.

"Look, this isn't a game, Zach. It's the law." Kelly forced herself to stay calm. It was like this every morning, the constant battle to get her seventeen-year-old son to school. It was his senior year, and Kelly found herself counting down the days until he graduated and, hopefully, got a job or joined the military—or did anything at all that forced him to leave the house. For good.

After silently counting to ten and realizing that, once again, Zach had no intention of getting up, Kelly sighed. "Zach, you *have* to go to school."

Outside the doorway, the sound of paws pounding on the stairs announced the impending arrival of dogs. Within seconds, two of them dashed into the room, jumped onto the bed, and began licking Zach's face. Their bodies wiggled and their tails wagged as they, too, tried to get him up.

A muffled "get off" followed by a kick sent both dogs scurrying.

"Zach being a jerk again?"

Quickly, Kelly turned to the door. "Fiona!" She pressed her hand against her chest, uncertain if her heart palpitated because Fiona had snuck up on her or simply because she was on edge. Maybe both.

Fiona was dressed and ready for school, her dark hair, cut in a stacked bob, neatly combed and tucked behind her ears. For as much as Zach broke every rule possible, Kelly's daughter never felt above the law.

Fiona glanced over Kelly's shoulder at her older brother, still in bed. Fiona made a face and shrugged. "He's such a loser."

"That doesn't help!"

Fiona rolled her hazel eyes and disappeared toward her own bedroom.

Reluctantly, Kelly stood up and walked over to Zach's dresser. Every day was like this. And she didn't understand how it had happened. It wasn't as if Zach went out with friends. He didn't have many. For the most part, he stayed home and slept. Sometimes Kelly heard him wandering around downstairs at odd hours and then, come morning, he'd refuse to get up.

Standing in front of the dresser, Kelly glanced over her shoulder to make certain Zach hadn't stirred. Then she opened the top drawer as quietly as she could. Long ago she had given up on organizing his drawers; he only messed them up without any consideration for her efforts. So she wasn't surprised that everything was in complete disarray.

She tried to poke around without making any noise. But she didn't have to look hard to find it. A metal tin for mints that, without even opening it, Kelly knew didn't contain any candies. She picked it up and carefully pushed back the lid. She lifted the tin to her nose and inhaled. The sweet, semipungent odor was easy to identify.

Marijuana.

She hadn't really needed to inhale to know what it was. It was obvious just from looking at the tiny dried leaves. But she had *needed* the confirmation. She didn't know why, exactly; perhaps just so she could be sure that she wasn't losing her mind.

Once again, she glanced at the bed. He hadn't stirred.

Gone were the days of her brilliant young son attending advanced classes in elementary school and taking online summer courses at Stanford.

Everyone knew—just knew!—that Zach was going to get a football scholarship to any college of his choosing. He began playing when he was in kindergarten and, by the time he reached high school, he was the only freshman on the varsity team. Even more impressive, he played both offense and defense. Zachary Martin was one of those kids who never sat on the bench.

But that was all over now. A tangible dream that had literally gone up in smoke. She wasn't certain which had come first: the depression or the drug abuse. Either way, she knew that somewhere along the line, one fed the other.

Kelly shut the lid, carried the box out of the room and to the bathroom. Within seconds, the dark-green and brown dried leaves circled clockwise in the water before disappearing from the toilet and her life. At least for now.

"More pot?"

Kelly shut the toilet lid and turned to face her daughter. "You should really be a detective when you get older, you know that?"

"I may just do that." Fiona gave her a big grin, her freckled nose wrinkling just a little and her face lighting up. "Bust all those stupid drug dealers in town."

Despite the heavy feeling of weariness that coursed through her veins, Kelly gave her daughter a soft smile. How Fiona could be so unaffected by the chaos that reigned in the house was beyond her. Some days, Kelly wondered if Fiona wasn't suppressing her true emotions about how Zach was single-handedly destroying the family. Other days, Kelly wondered if Fiona was just a super resilient child. After all, she had survived her parents getting divorced with few, if any, scars.

Kelly said in a soft voice, "Wouldn't that be nice?"

Leaving the mint tin on the counter, Kelly walked to the door, waiting for Fiona to step aside.

"Guess this means another rehab for him, huh?" She said it so casually, as if it were the most normal thing in the world. Perhaps in Fiona's world it was, Kelly thought. After all, their family's sense of normal was quite different from other families'. "Think Dad will agree again?"

Doubtful, Kelly thought, but she kept it to herself. She didn't need to disparage Todd to her daughter. Fiona already knew, without being told, that her father lacked proficiency in many departments. Being a decent father to his children was one of them.

As for Zach, how many times could she keep fighting to send him to the same places? He'd already been to Treatment Power once and Dynamic Point twice, not to mention that God-awful inpatient center in upstate New York. In addition to the fact that treatment was expensive and insurance didn't cover all of it, she had to battle Todd each and every time. It was as if Todd didn't want Zach to get better or, perhaps, he simply couldn't admit the truth. Either way, Kelly wasn't certain if she was up for another court battle.

"Maybe," she said to Fiona. "But for now, let's get you breakfast and to school."

"Aw man!" Fiona's big hazel eyes darted in the direction of Zach's open door. Kelly could see Fiona staring at the lumpy form of her big brother stretched out on the bed, wearing those dirty, rumpled clothes. A look of disgust crossed the girl's face. "He gets to stay home again? So not fair!"

Kelly gave a half-hearted laugh. She placed her hand on Fiona's shoulder and guided her down the staircase. "Getting a good education might seem like the short end of the stick, Fi, but trust me, you're miles ahead."

CHAPTER 2

"What do you mean, he didn't go to school again?"

Kelly bit her lower lip as she stared out the kitchen window. Why had she answered her cell phone? The display had all but screamed "DON'T ANSWER THIS" when it flashed the name "Jackie." Perhaps a better question was why she had mentioned anything about Zach and school when her sister inquired about the current state of her household.

"You don't understand. It's not like that—"

"Don't tell me that I don't understand, Kelly!" The hostility in her sister's voice as she interrupted her threw Kelly for a loop. Jackie always sounded angry, especially if it concerned Zach and Fiona. But Kelly could never figure out why. "March up there, yank him out of bed, and get him to school!"

She knew Jackie wouldn't listen, but still, Kelly felt the need to explain herself. "Jackie—"

"You're the mother, Kelly," Jackie interrupted again. "Not a babysitter. How many times do I have to tell you that? No one swoops in at midnight to rescue you from this."

For a moment, Kelly contemplated hanging up. Did Jackie really just say that? As if anyone *could* rescue her! What did *her sister* know about substance abuse anyway? Jackie's picture-perfect life did not include the ugly realities of divorce or failing grades or drug abuse. And yet, her sister always felt the need to tell her what to do. The freedom with which people gave unsought advice irritated Kelly, especially when it came from her younger sister.

"Tell me again why, exactly, you called?" Kelly heard herself ask.

Silence.

Unfortunately, it didn't last for long.

"Look, Kelly, you need to get it together, girl. Your marriage fell apart, your son's falling apart, half the time I think *you* are falling apart." Jackie paused, giving Kelly enough time to catch her breath. Oblivious to the damage caused by her words, Jackie continued talking as if she hadn't already poured enough salt on the open, gaping wound that was Kelly's bleeding heart. "Thank God that Fiona has some common sense. So far, anyway."

Defeated, Kelly tried to ignore the insinuation that Fiona was destined to follow in her mother's footsteps. And despite the fact that she should have been accustomed to her sister's style, Kelly still felt the hint of tears stinging at the corners of her eyes. "This isn't helping, Jackie," she managed to say as she held the phone against her ear. But she stopped trying to explain. There was no point.

If Jackie heard her, she didn't acknowledge Kelly's words. "You know what you need to do? You need to call that God-awful high school and get that Michael Stevens thrown out!"

Kelly cringed, knowing what was coming next.

"This is *exactly* why I pulled Heather out of public school." Short pause. "You can say that I overprotect her, but at least I have a say in the matter. Besides, I'd rather have her sheltered for a few more years in private school, even if it does cost an arm and a leg."

An arm and a leg that I couldn't afford, Kelly added silently. *Even when I was married.*

"You know that's not an option for me," Kelly said quietly.

"Todd can help pay."

Kelly almost laughed. "Right."

There was a moment of silence before Jackie said slowly, "Mom would pay for it, Kelly."

Stunned, Kelly blinked twice. She would no sooner ask to borrow money from her mother than she would take out a second mortgage. After their father died, their mother had managed to finish raising her three children on a very limited income. And, to her credit, she had invested her money and managed to save a small nest egg.

No, Kelly would never ask her mother for financial assistance. "You know I won't take money from Mom."

Jackie clucked her tongue. "You don't have to sound so proud."

"Mom needs what she has," Kelly countered. "It's not as if she's rolling in money, Jackie."

"Oh please." Jackie gave a soft but sinister laugh. "Dad left her enough money, and she's doing a lot better than you think. Believe me, if you asked, she'd do it in a heartbeat."

Kelly frowned. How would Jackie know that anyway? Was that how Jackie afforded private school? "I don't care what you think. Not everyone, including Mom, has the luxury of an endless amount of blank checks, Jackie."

Jackie caught her breath. "You make it sound like I do!"

Kelly wondered if she had finally hit a nerve with her sister. Maybe their mother *was* helping to fund Heather's prestigious education after all. If that was the case, her sister should be ashamed of herself. Kelly made a mental note to find the right time to discuss this with their mother. She didn't want Jackie taking advantage of their mother just so that she could keep up with the Joneses.

As quick as she made the slip, Jackie recovered. "Jason works his tail off, Kelly. Maybe if Todd had worked harder and drank a little less, you would've had choices, too!"

Kelly sighed. "What do you want, Jackie?"

"I want you to straighten out your son."

"I meant what do you want right now. With this call." Did she really have to spell that out? Even Jackie couldn't be so far removed from reality to not realize that her belittling grew old after a while.

Her sister paused as if trying to remember why, exactly, she had called Kelly in the first place. "Oh. Right."

For some reason, Kelly felt a small sense of satisfaction for throwing Jackie off her game. It didn't happen often, but when it did, it felt good.

"Heather's birthday."

Inwardly, Kelly groaned, and she hoped her sister didn't hear. Was it October already? Every year it was the same thing, and she knew what was coming.

"We're having a small party here. Well, you know, we wanted to see if Fiona could come."

"Uh . . ." As always, her sister did the right thing on the surface, even though she never dove deeper to do the right thing by Fiona. Cousins by blood, but not friends by choice. How could Kelly protect her daughter from such an invitation without looking like the bad guy? She could hear the conversation Jackie would undoubtedly have with their mother if Fiona didn't show up:

I invited Fiona, Mom. I don't understand why she didn't come.
Poor Heather. I'm sure her feelings were hurt, Jackie.

Kelly shut her eyes and shook her head. Fiona was going to fight her on this one, but she would have to make an appearance. "When is it? I mean, I have to check her schedule."

"Of course. But I wanted to let you know about it." Something jingled in the background. It sounded like the bells over a store's door. Had Jackie been discussing all of this while out shopping? "A week from Saturday. Nothing fancy or anything. Just a few of Heather's friends, pizza, movie, stuff like that."

"Sure. Sounds great." A small lie. The last thing Fiona would want to do is spend a night at Jackie's house with Heather's clique of friends. She was two years younger than Heather and had nothing in common with her. Heather was into boys already, and Fiona showed no interest in that yet. In fact, on social media, Heather's Instagram photos had recently begun to look like an account mirroring one of the Kardashians'. Between the clothes and the makeup mixed with the provocative poses, Kelly didn't want her daughter hanging around those girls. "Let me check with her and get back to you."

"Perfect."

They hung up. What Jackie thought was perfect was anything but. Kelly set down her phone and resumed staring out the window. Despite the blue skies and green trees, she felt gray inside. No. Nothing was perfect at all.

CHAPTER 3

"I just don't know what to do anymore."

It was Tuesday, just after noon. The sun warmed the air, lending a bit of comfort to the early October weather. Kelly sat on the front porch, staring into the tree-lined street. Despite being the middle of the day, the neighborhood appeared empty, except for one neighbor who walked his dog on the other side of the street. That was how Kelly felt: empty. She watched the dog happily trotting a few feet behind its owner, and Kelly found herself wishing that someone would lead her down the road, too.

"You have no idea what it's like, Charlotte."

Her friend, seated beside her on the steps, shook her head, compassion etched into her face. "I can't imagine."

"Some days I wonder what I did wrong," Kelly said, willing herself not to cry. "I mean, why does everything fall apart for me? My marriage, my kid." She glanced up at the sky, blinking rapidly. It didn't help. A tear fell and she swiped at it. "My life."

Charlotte wrapped her arm around Kelly's shoulders and pulled her into a loose embrace. The gesture surprised Kelly. She couldn't remember the last time Charlotte had demonstrated physical affection with anyone, never mind her.

"Sometimes bad things happen to good people."

"I'm not sure that helps." Kelly managed a small laugh. "But if that's the case, I must be darn great."

Charlotte pulled back and smiled. "I sure think so. Fiona thinks so."

Kelly exhaled through her mouth. Somehow *that* didn't make her feel better. "That's a small list."

Charlotte gave her a gentle nudge. "Come on. It's time to get off the pity-party wagon."

There she was. The real Charlotte. The one who was always the voice of reason, the one who set her straight. But today Kelly wasn't buying it. "I think I should be allowed to ride the wagon a bit longer, Char. After yesterday's phone call with Jackie—"

Charlotte bristled at the mention of Kelly's sister. "I don't want to hear it."

Kelly ignored her. "She's so superior and full of herself. Her perfect life. It makes me sick."

"You have no idea what goes on behind her closed doors. Trust me."

Glancing at her, Kelly saw the disdain on Charlotte's face. It made her friend look older and angry. "Then why is she so pompous?"

Charlotte took a deep breath and stared straight ahead. "I'm not here to talk about your sister. Or your brother, either, for that matter." She paused and turned her head to look at Kelly. "I suspect he hasn't been in touch, right?"

"I thought you didn't want to talk about him."

Charlotte refocused her gaze on the street. "That's what I thought," she mumbled. "He didn't call after the divorce, either. What's *wrong* with your family?" The question came out in a rapid breath and, as if an afterthought, she immediately held up her hand. "No, don't answer that. I already know."

Kelly almost smiled.

"Besides, let's focus on the problem at hand. Zach."

Zach. Somehow Kelly had managed to get him to school that morning. He arrived late, and only after Kelly threatened to call the police again. That had motivated him enough to drag himself from bed and get dressed. A small victory.

"Look, Kelly, the bottom line is you need to get him help. And fast. He's depressed and self-medicating."

Kelly glanced at her. Leave it to Charlotte to cut through the extraneous information and put it out there. It was Charlotte's greatest attribute but also her greatest flaw. Sometimes Kelly just needed to vent, to complain and talk. Sometimes she just needed Charlotte to listen and empathize. But that wasn't how Charlotte operated. Everything was cut-and-dried: fix it or forget it.

Still, Kelly knew that she spoke the truth. "You're right. I know you're right. But how?"

"Just get him into rehab again."

Kelly gave a half-hearted laugh. "You make it sound so easy."

"It should be. Call your doctor for suggestions and just take him there."

"Oh Charlotte! Please." This time, Kelly gave her a stern look of disbelief. "How can you even say that? It isn't like Todd would just *applaud* the effort."

"Deal with him later, then."

But Kelly knew the truth. How many times had she taken Zach in what she suspected was a drug-induced state to the hospital? Twice? Maybe three times? Every single time, the hospital had suggested that she send Zach to a detox center and a proper inpatient rehab, not like the one in New York that he had attended two winters ago. And then in swooped Todd to the rescue. At least that was how Zach had viewed it. After all, students sent away to rehab during the football training season didn't get to play on the team. That was *always* Todd's argument when Kelly confronted him about why he signed Zach out of the hospital without her consent. In her ex-husband's eyes, playing football trumped attending rehab. In Kelly's eyes, it was just Todd denying the truth.

No one wanted to admit the truth about addiction, especially when it entered a second generation.

"He needs more than just rehab. He needs psychiatric help, too. And that's more complicated. Dual diagnosis, they call it. Because he's a minor, Todd has to sign off on treatment for any medical care, including psychiatric. And we both know how he feels about *that*."

"What if he doesn't sign off?"

"I'd have to go back to court and *that* could take months before I get to speak to a judge. The system isn't exactly rigged in my favor," Kelly said with a mournful sigh. In a divorce, there were three parents: the mother, the father, and the courts. And she had learned long ago that the court system didn't really care about what was right, only what was lawful. "Or Zach's, either, for that matter."

"Look," Charlotte said, pointing a well-manicured finger at her. "If it means you have to go to court again, then do it. Even if it does take months. But you *have* to get custody yanked away from that miscreant ex-husband of yours. I mean, seriously, that's the blind leading the blind."

If it hadn't been so painfully true, Kelly would have laughed.

"He can't admit his son is an addict because he'd have to look in the mirror and see the truth on that one," Charlotte continued, shaking her head. "Getting rid of that narcissistic hypocrite was the best thing you ever did. However, not demanding full custody was your biggest mistake."

How many times would Charlotte remind her of that? "You know he'd never have agreed to that! Besides, New Jersey leans toward joint custody anyway."

"All you had to do was drag out his own rehab records, Kelly. Any judge with half a brain would have seen through Todd Martin. Even now, you could fight for custody. The courts will have to agree that you can't have an addict father raising an addict son."

Kelly didn't reply. There was no reason to. After all, there was little point in rehashing should'ves and could'ves, she told herself. Yes, she knew that she hadn't fought hard enough for the children. She could have brought up Todd's history during the divorce. But she hadn't because she thought he'd keep his drinking under control after the divorce, for the children's sake, anyway. In hindsight, Kelly realized that had been a silly presumption; if he wouldn't control his drinking for their marriage, why would he control it for his children?

Still, she wished that Charlotte would give her credit for having tried after the divorce. How many times had Youth Services been called in for help when Kelly learned that Todd had been drinking during his parenting time with the children? For berating Fiona to the point that she had returned to Kelly in tears? For letting their underage son sneak out of the house and wander through Morristown during the night? Surely Kelly had called them enough that Todd *should've* been on their radar.

However, the department had their own reasons for basically turning a blind eye to the excessive drinking, emotional abuse, and general neglect. They claimed that they had more important cases to focus on. *Real abuse,* the one responder claimed. But Kelly suspected that it had something to do with the color of her and Todd's skin as well as the neighborhoods they lived in. Neither matched the stereotype of a typical victim or perpetrator, and the Youth Services counselors closed the case. Her children had become collateral damage to the state's limited definition of abuse.

Regardless, Kelly didn't need Charlotte's constant reminders that she had failed. She reminded herself about *that* every single day without help from anyone else, thank you very much. Whenever she argued with Zach or saw sadness in Fiona's eyes, Kelly felt the harsh embrace of failure cover her.

Yes, she knew all too well that, by not protecting her children, she had failed them.

Besides, Zach favored his father, and Kelly hadn't the heart to sever their relationship. Had she tried, she surely would've failed, because the court system told her point-blank that children needed both parents. Eventually, the court succeeded in achieving what they had set out to do—"if neither party is happy, then we did our job." It made little sense to Kelly. Even though the court was supposed to follow the law, what law said that both parties in a divorce must suffer in order to be fair?

She knew that she'd never marry again. Not just because her first marriage had brought her to her knees and pulling herself back to an upright position was the hardest thing she had ever done. No. That wasn't it. The reason she knew—just knew!—that her first marriage definitely would be her last was that she had realized that no matter how much she thought she knew Todd, he'd turned out to be a complete stranger. And that had terrified her.

The realization had hit her one morning when she had woken up extra early. Todd lay beside her in bed, sound asleep and snoring. He hadn't changed out of his clothes from the day before, and he reeked of cigarettes and gin. On the nightstand next to him was a bottle of prescription pills, which was odd because Kelly hadn't known he was taking any medication.

Quietly, she had stolen from the bed and tiptoed over to look at the bottle. It was a prescription for Percocet. And the person's name on the label was not Todd's.

That had been the moment when her first major panic attack struck. Besides living with an alcoholic, now she had to deal with him taking drugs? She had no idea who this man was and felt violated by years of deceit.

The divorce had only proved her to be painfully correct.

"Well, that's all over with now," Kelly said to Charlotte. "The most important thing is to get this kid help, just like you said. But how? If Todd agrees at all, he'll just push for one of those useless outpatient rehab centers that insurance *will* cover. And we both know how *that* turned out the last few times." If those outpatient rehabs *had* worked, perhaps Zach would have cleaned up his act and stayed sober. If Todd had stopped being so darn frugal and invested as much in his own son as he did in *his* addictions, Zach might have had a chance. But focusing on the what-ifs never got anyone anywhere.

"So what're you going to do?" Charlotte asked.

"I don't know." It was painful to admit, but Kelly wasn't one to pretend that she had the answer. "Maybe ride it out a little bit. See if I can survive the rest of the school year. I mean, once he's eighteen and finished school, I'm done, right?"

Charlotte shook her head. "College."

"Ha!"

"OK, then. But he still has to live somewhere. You can't just toss him onto the streets."

Oh yes I can, Kelly thought. But she didn't want to have *that* discussion with Charlotte again. Kelly knew that catering to Zach's poor behavior and using kid gloves with him were exactly what had created the problem in the first place.

"Kids just don't come with instruction manuals," Kelly said at last.

Charlotte laughed. "True." Something vibrated and she dug into her purse for her cell phone. "Gotta take this call, Kelly. Maybe I better go, anyway. I have to show a house in an hour." Before answering the phone, Charlotte leaned over and kissed Kelly's cheek. And then, just like that, Charlotte stood up, began talking on her cell, and walked to her car, which was parked in the driveway.

Visit over.

CHAPTER 4

"I'm not so sure that's a good idea."

It was Wednesday afternoon, and Kelly stood at the kitchen counter, her back to the stove, where tomato sauce simmered next to large pot of boiling water. The kitchen smelled of garlic and meat, a warm and welcoming scent that always accompanied her spaghetti sauce—Fiona's favorite. But Fiona hadn't even noticed. Instead, she was focused on the question at hand. "Come on, Mom!" The pleading in her voice and look of despair in her hazel eyes broke Kelly's heart. "I never get to have *anyone* over!"

And that was the crux of the problem: Fiona was right.

Kelly couldn't remember the last time anyone had visited. Period. The days of endless summer sleepovers and busy weekends with kids just showing up at the house for a Friday or Saturday night had stopped years ago. When her children needed support the most, it vanished upon the announcement that Kelly and Todd were divorcing. Poof. Just like that. Gone were the invitations to birthday parties or movie nights. And if Fiona asked friends over, the parents would politely decline, some claiming that their child was busy, while others outright admitted that they'd prefer to wait until "things calmed down."

Kelly shouldn't have been surprised. She, too, had experienced a shunning from society. No invitations to summer gatherings, weekend barbecues, or even the annual tailgating parties held in Peapack during their autumn steeplechase races. And at Christmas, when she used to attend half a dozen parties and Debbie Weaver's infamous cookie swap, she was invited to none.

The biggest insult, however, came in the form of holiday cards. Or, rather, the lack thereof. In the past, Kelly had taped their Christmas cards to a ribbon hung over the kitchen doorway. Sometimes she needed two or even three ribbons. That first Christmas after the divorce, she received just three cards. Knowing that most people typed the addresses into a program to print labels, Kelly realized they must have made a conscious decision to delete her name from the list. Embarrassed, she had removed the ribbon and never put it up again. And, after two Christmases, Kelly had finally culled her own holiday card list to zero. Like the sleepovers and holiday cards, Kelly's Christmas spirit had vaporized.

Apparently, however, enough time had passed that parents no longer feared their children being exposed to the reality of the dreaded disease called "divorce." Was three years the unspoken incubation period?

Still, the thought of having a bunch of girls in the house for a sleepover was daunting. Ever since Monday, things had been calm on the Zachary front, but Kelly didn't want to take any chances. Weekends were always the worst. And she didn't fancy the idea of catering to a herd of teenage girls. What would they eat? Drink? Want to do? No. Kelly was way out of practice and wasn't certain she wanted to make the effort.

"I don't know . . . ," she started again, letting her voice trail off.

"Why not, Mom? I never get to have anyone over."

On the surface, it seemed like such a simple question. *Yeah Mom, why not?* But there were so many layers to the answer. Besides entertaining strange girls for twelve or so hours, she had other concerns. Namely her son. What if Zach misbehaved? What if the girls told their parents about Zach? What if the parents talked? The privacy of her home provided the last sanctuary for Kelly. A place where she didn't have to pretend that everything was great. A place where she could hide in her room when things got ugly on the other side of her bedroom door.

"Fiona . . . ," Kelly started. How could she explain this to her thirteen-year-old? "I just don't know if this is the right time with Zach—"

"So this is all because of him?" Her face twisted into a grimace and, in frustration, Fiona raised her hands to the sides of her head. "It's so not fair! He ruins everything!"

As her daughter's eyes filled with tears, Kelly suddenly felt her heart break. Something about Fiona's words echoed in the back of Kelly's memory. Words that she'd heard so many times over the last few years. A chill flooded her body at the wave of recollections that engulfed her in both guilt and resentment.

It *wasn't* fair. For almost four years, Zach had been ruining a lot of "everythings": birthdays, holidays, family dinners, vacations. And somehow, they had managed to cope, to try to live a normal life in spite of Zachary and his issues with substance abuse. How many holidays had been shattered, splintering the family, that one year when Zach had been at the inpatient rehab? And then the numerous outpatient rehabs had fractured the family even more. Kelly had to drive Zach both ways, every day. For months.

No. It wasn't easy.

And, of course, it wasn't fair.

Life and fair didn't go together. Kelly had learned that long ago. If life *were* fair, Todd would have stopped drinking. If life *were* fair, their family would still be intact. If life *were* fair, Zach wouldn't be a drug addict.

The fantasy of fair had blown up long ago for Kelly. Having a younger sister who married better, lived better, and simply *was* better had started the big reveal. How could anyone live in the shadows of a smarter, more successful younger sibling? Especially when she did everything in her power to remind Kelly of that fact as frequently as possible.

And then there was Todd. Such a charming young man who had pursued her, wooed her, and finally won her. The man who used to whisk her off to New York City for dinners at quaint restaurants in SoHo. Afterward, they'd stop at jazz bars, listening to the musicians as they nursed an after-dinner drink.

On their one-year anniversary of dating, he surprised her with a trip to the city and splurged on a carriage ride through Central Park. Later, they dined at the Tavern on the Green, seated outdoors under the twinkling lights that hung from branches overhead. When the champagne arrived, he got down on one knee. He had promised her the world.

How could any woman refuse?

But deception comes in many forms. In Todd's case, shortly after the wedding, he removed the sheep's clothing and revealed the wolf underneath in the form of a clear glass bottle that he kept hidden in the freezer behind the ice cream Kelly never ate. Gin.

Finally, along came Zach. In the beginning, Kelly had tried to bond with her son. But so had Todd. He had always wanted a son, and he did everything in his power to get in between Kelly and Zach. After all, *he* was the one who had always wanted a boy, a son who would grow up to be just like him.

And Todd had certainly won in that regard.

No, life wasn't fair at all.

Kelly knew that, and most of the world knew that. But her thirteen-year-old child? Did *she need* to know that so soon? Fiona would have plenty of time to make that discovery. For now, Kelly wanted to wrap her arms around her daughter and protect her from that inevitable realization as long as possible.

Staring at Fiona, who simply wanted to have a normal Friday-night sleepover, Kelly couldn't help but wonder how much she could expect her daughter to give up before she, too, became collateral damage to Zach's addiction. Perhaps it wouldn't hurt, just for once, to let Fiona have a bit of normal. Too much of it had been stolen from her.

"On one condition," she heard herself say, hoping that Fiona didn't pick up on the reluctance in her voice.

"Anything, Mom!"

"Heather's birthday," Kelly said. "You have to at least make an appearance at her party."

There, she thought. Might as well kill two birds with one stone.

If Kelly suspected that Fiona might fuss over that last request, she was pleasantly surprised by her daughter's willingness. "Fine. Whatever."

Fiona didn't appear thrilled about having to attend, but she wasn't fighting her mother, either. Relieved, Kelly sighed. That solved *that* problem. "OK then. But just three girls."

Fiona whooped and ran over to her mother. Tossing her arms around Kelly's neck, Fiona gave her a warm embrace. The feeling of her daughter's lithe body pressed against hers caused Kelly a moment of surprise. How long had it been since anyone had hugged her? *Really* hugged her? Kelly couldn't remember. The feel of a human's touch, one with deep emotion and genuine joy, sent a shock wave through her. If nothing else, *this* was worth whatever trouble she might endure with Zach in a household of young girls.

"Thanks, Mom! You're the best!"

Savoring the moment, Kelly tightened her hold on Fiona. If only she could keep Fiona close, to protect her from the outside world and all of the horrors that awaited her at the local high school. She didn't want her youngest exposed to the dark side of life. No, she wanted to keep Fiona just like this . . . sweet, innocent, and excited about something as simple as having a few friends over for a Friday-night sleepover.

CHAPTER 5

Later that evening, Kelly heard Zach prowling around on the second floor. She was downstairs, sitting at the kitchen table with her laptop before her. She had been grading papers for one of the online courses that she taught. Earlier in her career, Kelly had been an English instructor at a nearby college, but after Zach's second stint with an outpatient rehabilitation, Kelly realized that she needed more flexibility in her schedule. That was when she began teaching English full-time for an online university. She needed to be home for Fiona, as well as to drive Zach back and forth to the treatment center. While she missed the intellectual interaction with her colleagues, she had come to enjoy the freedom that her new situation allowed.

Now, as Kelly tried to get caught up grading her students' assignments, she could hear Zach upstairs. Doors opened and slammed shut. Drawers yanked out and banged close. One of the drawers must have fallen out, and a dog barked at the noise.

Finally, she heard the inevitable: Zach's heavy footsteps on the hardwood floor of the hallway before he called out for her.

"Mom!"

Give me strength, Kelly prayed.

Apparently she didn't respond fast enough as, seconds later, she heard him running down the stairs. He flew around the corner, his hair disheveled and long overdue for a washing. When was the last time he had showered? And his gray eyes? They were wide and bloodshot. The fullness of his face, the skin covered in those telltale red pimples, which she had learned was common among heavier drug users, made him look far older than his seventeen years. Kelly was alarmed at how much weight he had gained. How had she not noticed that before?

When was the last time she had actually looked at her son? Just as quickly as she thought that, she pushed away the guilt. Her son had disappeared long ago, replaced by this complete stranger who was clearly enraged.

"What's up?" she asked, hoping that she sounded casual and not slightly alarmed that, after several days of not seeing much of Zach, he now loomed before her with a dark scowl upon his face.

"What'd you do with it?" His voice was loud and harsh.

Ah, she thought. *The pot.* But she didn't want to give in so easily. If Zach wanted answers, he needed to work harder at it. "What are you talking about?"

"Don't play stupid with me!" He withdrew his hand from behind his back. She saw the metal mint tin in his palm and, just as quick as she recognized it, he threw it at her, hitting her in the arm.

"Zachary!"

His eyes narrowed, full of rage. His entire face appeared to contort as he morphed into a whole new person, one that Kelly did not recognize.

"Where is it?"

Her heart raced as she rubbed her arm. "How dare you throw that at me!"

"Where. Is. It?" He enunciated each word.

Lifting her chin, she faced the stranger who stood before her, swallowing the fear she felt. He looked like an animal, a fierce, ferocious beast. She knew that animals could smell fear, so she did all she could to present a calm exterior. The last thing she wanted was to let him know just how frightened she was. Kelly jutted out her jaw and met his gaze. "If you mean the pot, I flushed it."

"You what?"

"It's my house and I don't want illegal drugs in it. You know the rules, even if you continue to break them. So I flushed it down the toilet."

For a second, Kelly thought he might charge at her. She steeled herself, bracing for the moment when she would have to decide whether to engage in a fight or choose the alternative: flight. But the attack never came. At least not at her. He struggled, his face and neck shaking as he clenched his fist. Through gritted teeth, he mumbled several expletives, and then, suddenly, he spun around, raised his fist, and punched the wall.

The Sheetrock crumbled beneath the force, leaving an almost perfectly round hole staring back at her.

The suddenness of the strike, along with the loudness of his voice, frightened her to a whole new level. He was a large boy, and if he turned his anger on her, she knew that she couldn't defend herself. Three years of high school football had left him broad shouldered and stronger than most seventeen-year-olds.

Still, Kelly reminded herself that *she* was the mother and this was *her* home. Surely she didn't have to live like this?

"Knock it off, Zach!"

"Shut up! Just shut up!" He glared at her. "That wasn't even mine!" Once again, he slammed his fist into the wall, leaving a second hole directly above the first one.

"Look what you're doing!" Knowing it wasn't the smartest thing, she reached for his arm, hoping to stop him from damaging her house and hurting himself, but he yanked it free. For a moment that seemed suspended in time, they stared at each other, frozen just long enough for her mind to flash to another image.

She held him in her arms, his chubby toddler legs, poking out of his blue-and-white-striped shorts, wrapped around her ribs as she carried him over the grass and to the black fence. His dirty-blond hair, thin and not fully grown in yet, caught the breeze and blew onto his forehead. Kelly reached up and brushed it aside. She wanted to see his eyes, so light blue that they looked almost gray.

"Is that a horsey?" She pointed to the large animal that lingered in the shade of the oak tree.

Zach clapped his hands twice and then reached out as if to touch the horse.

"Careful, Kelly!"

Ignoring her husband, Kelly moved closer so that Zach could reach the animal. It seemed as curious about Zach as the boy was about it. The large creature inched closer and extended its neck. Zach's fingers spread apart as he leaned over and ran his hand on the horse's nose.

"My God, Kelly! Are you insane? It could bite him!"

But even Todd's irritation couldn't ruin this moment. Kelly looked into Zach's face, that cherubic little face, and knew that she could never love anyone as much as she loved her son at that moment. He was her firstborn, her baby, her true love.

"Zach," Kelly whispered, the image of that sweet and innocent face slowly fading away as she returned to the present. "Please. Please stop."

For a split second, she thought she saw something soften in his eyes. It was so quick, a nanosecond or less. But in that moment, she saw it. Then they hardened again. And in that instant, Kelly felt a glimmer of hope, the first one she had felt in almost four years. Her son, that sweet baby boy whom she had loved and doted on for so many years, was still in there. He might be buried deep, beneath too many memories of being bullied and disappointed at school and at home. But he was there!

Zach narrowed his eyes and turned, spitting on the hardwood floor before walking back upstairs to his bedroom and slamming the door shut. Every fight ended in the same way. A slammed door. The stomping of feet. And usually the sound of a fist hitting the drywall.

Years ago, she had labored over that bedroom, painting the walls a pale shade of blue and decorating it with blue-and-beige-plaid curtains and bedding. On the walls, she had hung printed and framed inspirational Scripture verses including her favorite from Isaiah: "All your children shall be taught by the Lord, and great shall be the peace of your children." She had decorated the room with love in her heart and hope in her soul.

Now, the room looked more like a crack den: broken shades, torn curtains, and an abundant number of holes in the wall. Just the previous week, Zach had etched vulgarities in the headboard of his bed with a pocket knife that his father had given him the previous Christmas, the same knife that he had used for carving up his arms on more than one occasion.

Last year, she had given up trying to patch the holes or replace the window shades. That was just throwing good money after bad.

Somewhere in the deep recesses of her memory resided the image of her sleeping newborn, his little arms tossed over his head as he lay on his back, his little hands clenched into fists. Seventeen years ago, she never would have imagined those fists being raised against her or punching walls. No. Back then, she spent hours gazing at the little miracle of life that napped in a brown sleigh crib with a blue plaid bumper carefully tied around the sides in order to protect Zach from injury. It was all that a mother could do: to dream of protecting her child. She never imagined that the dangers that jeopardized him would come from within. And how could any mother protect a child from that?

CHAPTER 6

"That's a terrible idea!"

The next morning, as Kelly leaned against the kitchen counter, she was glad that her sister was on the other end of the phone and not standing in front of her. While she knew that Jackie was probably correct, hearing it didn't make the situation any better. Kelly couldn't go back on her word to Fiona. "Fiona deserves some normalcy in her life." The words came out far too fast and with a sharp edge to Kelly's voice. She knew that it was a risk having all those girls stay overnight. If Zach came home and acted up . . .

She pushed that thought out of her mind. She would talk to Zach, explain to him that he needed to behave. Just once. For his sister.

If only Jackie would consider doing the same for *her*.

Instead, what had initially been a phone call to let Jackie know that Fiona would attend Heather's birthday party was changing into another one of *those* discussions. And with Jackie, the one person in the family who never held back her true feelings, that spelled disaster.

Finally, Jackie spoke. "What will their mothers think if they find out?"

And there it was.

Shaking her head, Kelly knew that she shouldn't be surprised. Her sister always focused on social appearances—what other people *might* think. Just once Kelly wished her sister would offer some moral support, perhaps a shoulder to cry on. Kelly had never given up hoping that, beneath the Michael Kors dresses and Dries Van Noten shoes, there lingered a shred of compassion.

But she was always disappointed.

When Kelly had filed for divorce, her sister all but turned her back on her. In Jackie's world, people simply did not get divorced. Period. Jackie never asked why Kelly left Todd or whether she needed support. For Jackie, the embarrassment of divorce trumped the familial relationship. So, instead of providing sisterly empathy, Jackie had merely disappeared, probably into high society, which, like Jackie, didn't want to be associated with the dirty business of divorce.

"She doesn't ask for much, you know that, Jackie. As for other people and what they might think, I don't care."

"Yes you do."

Kelly shook her head, even though her sister couldn't see her. Why did everyone get this wrong? Why did they shield the rest of the world from the realities of life behind closed doors? Did they really think they were fooling people? "If more people *talked* about addiction," Kelly replied carefully, "maybe people could actually *do* something about it."

Her sister scoffed. "That's the most ridiculous thing I've ever heard!"

Kelly cringed. She felt her nerves twitch.

"Everyone pretends it's not happening in their own homes," Kelly managed to retort, somehow finding the wherewithal to stand up for herself. The exhaustion of battling addiction alone, without a support system that understood—or at least tried to—taxed her nerves. "But I can assure you that those television advertisements and highway billboards aren't there just for *my* son."

"Well, I *know* that, Kelly," Jackie snapped. "I'm not ignorant."

But Kelly wasn't so certain. After all, what did her sister know about drug addiction? What did either of them? Their own teenage years had been spent surrounded in the protective cocoon of the 1970s and '80s, when most mothers stayed home, and families were more inclined to stay together. Thanks to their father's success, their mother hadn't needed to work, and the children came home to a house that smelled of Lysol and lavender. Unlike many of their peers, their parents were actually happy, their mother a bit strict but in a loving way. There hadn't been any opportunity—or need—to experiment with the dark side of under-age drinking or high school drugs, not in the Parkers' rigid household.

Which, of course, made the chaos of Kelly's disheveled life leave question marks dangling over everyone's heads.

Kelly, however, suspected that a far different truth was hidden beneath the surface of public dismay.

"Then who do you think those advertisements are targeting?" Like so many other parents, as soon as someone else's kid was known to be a drug abuser, they started handing out judgment. "They aren't just low-income kids, Jackie. Addiction isn't picky about who it ensnares."

There was a moment of silence on the other end of the phone. Kelly waited, hoping that her sister had, for once, actually listened to her.

"Well, Zach *does* come from a broken family, Kelly. What did you expect?"

Another reminder of her sister's inability to forgive her for divorcing Todd and creating a stain on the otherwise pristine Parker family name. While neither of her parents had been particularly fond of Todd Martin, they had welcomed him into the family. It wasn't until *after* the honeymoon ended that Kelly learned the truth about his addiction to alcohol. Her mother had chosen to ignore Todd's problems and, when Kelly finally announced her intentions to divorce Todd, commented that Kelly always demonstrated a weak constitution when it came to life's challenges.

"Jackie." Kelly shut her eyes as her shoulders weakened. "Please."

"I'm just glad Dad isn't here to see any of this."

Kelly took a deep breath. She tried counting: *one, two, three . . .* But she found that her breathing was coming in short, brisk gulps.

41

Mentioning her father was always the last blow, the one that made Kelly's knees weak and her breath labored. Yes, she, too, was glad that her father wasn't there to see the implosion of her own life and family.

Finally, with a heavy sigh, her sister relented. "I can see you are set upon doing this, Kelly, but I still think it's a bad idea to have all of those girls over." She paused before she added, "Maybe Zach could stay at his father's."

"What!"

Jackie sounded surprised. "I mean, Todd *is* his father, right?"

"You want to talk about terrible ideas?" For a long time, despite their custody arrangement, neither Fiona nor Zach had stayed at Todd's. They just didn't want to spend time with him. Frankly, Kelly hadn't fought them on it. She knew that Todd would drink his nightly bottle of gin and pass out, leaving Zach free to wander the streets of Morristown with that terrible boy, Michael Stevens. "No, everything will be fine here. But I was hoping that you could swing by for a little bit." She hesitated before adding, "You know, to keep me company? It's not like we see each other all that often and, well, it might be nice for a change."

A long pause.

With each delay in her sister's response, Kelly's blood simmered. Why did she still hold out hope that she might one day have a better relationship with her sister? And why did Jackie fight her so hard? It wasn't as if Kelly was asking for all that much; her sister lived just one town away, in Mendham. Despite the fact that Jackie didn't work, her husband earning enough money from his Wall Street job, she rarely made her way to Morristown. She was too busy with charity work or driving Heather all over Morris County. And then, of course, there was the Mendham Golf and Tennis Club.

On any given day of the week, Jackie could be found making the rounds with her friends on the eighteen-hole course. When they had first joined it, Jackie had said it was for Jason.

"The best business deals are made on the greens," Jackie always said.

Now, however, it was usually *Jackie* making the best deals: lunch dates, charity obligations, party invitations. To each his own, Kelly had thought. It wasn't the type of life she would have wanted to live, even if she could.

But, then again, neither was this one.

"I really can't, Kelly," Jackie said, interrupting Kelly's thoughts. "Heather already has plans with some friends, and I promised to drive them." Jackie paused as if thinking of something. "Maybe you could ask Mom? You know she's always looking for invitations."

Why do I keep trying? Kelly thought. Other women had loving and warm relationships with their sisters. No matter how hard Kelly tried or how much she needed her sister, Jackie always had an excuse. If the shoe were on the other foot, however, Kelly would have cancelled any plans to help her brother or sister. Of course, she also knew that, even if the shoe *were* on the other foot, her sister would never admit it anyway. As for her brother, the oldest of the three siblings, Eddie lived farther away and seemed to have voluntarily cut himself off from the family. Kelly knew that *he'd* never help.

"Fine," Kelly said, trying to mask the hurt. Once again, in a moment of need, she had reached out to her sister, and once again she had been shot down. "I'll see if Mom can come over."

After she hung up the phone, Kelly sat in the chair and stared at the empty wall, her mind reeling as she tried to identify the exact moment when her younger sister had become such a perfect model of pretension and arrogance. When her husband had been promoted? When they had moved to Mendham? Kelly couldn't be certain. The one thing she *could* be certain of was that the divide between her and Jackie continued to widen. And as far as Kelly could tell, there was no bridge that would cross that chasm.

CHAPTER 7

"Hi, Ms. Martin."

At the sound of her name, Kelly looked up and smiled at Molly Weaver, one of Fiona's friends, who had just shut the front door behind herself. "Hey you! Haven't seen you in a while. How's school?"

Molly tossed her backpack onto the floor near the bottom of the stairs and ran over to hug her. "Mom said to give that to you."

I bet, Kelly thought.

Molly's mother, Debbie Weaver, hadn't been handing out too many hugs during the initial years after Kelly and Todd divorced. In fact, Debbie had been the first of many who disappeared once word spread that the Martins were divorcing. No more invites to cookie swaps. No more invites to Girls' Nights Out. And certainly no more invites to the annual after-party following the hoity-toity steeplechase races each October.

One of the things that Kelly had quickly learned during her divorce was that, apparently, happily married couples harbored a secret fear that divorce was contagious and, therefore, they avoided people going through a divorce at all costs. It had been Kelly's first eye-opening lesson about the fragility of so-called adult friendships.

When she shared this observation with Charlotte one night when they were out to dinner in Morristown, her friend—only *remaining* friend at that time—had laughed at her for being so naive.

"Of course Debbie wouldn't want you around! You've shifted from friend to foe. It's not as if her husband doesn't have eyes, Kelly. And you know those Wall Street types . . . Fidelity is only an investment bank in their mind."

Kelly had made a face at her. "Oh please! Ryan has never said more than two words to me!"

"Maybe *he* doesn't want you around, either," Charlotte had said as she lifted her glass of wine to her lips. "It's not like Debbie and Ryan have the greatest relationship. Those men don't want a divorce pandemic hitting their social circle. Kills their wallets."

But now, three years later, all of that was superficial water under the bridge. Enough time had passed to eradicate the fear of Kelly and Todd's divorce. Somehow Fiona and Molly had reconnected the previous year when Debbie pulled her out of her private school and enrolled her in the Morris School District. An unlikely friendship bloomed, something that neither Kelly nor Debbie managed to nip in the bud. Kelly knew there was no reason to punish the child for the mother's sins.

"Well, you make certain to send my best regards to your mother." It was the polite thing to say, even if it wasn't true.

The front door opened again, and two more girls practically bounced into the foyer. One of them was unknown to Kelly.

Fiona ran down the stairs, and the girls squealed in delight, giving each other overly dramatic hugs as if they hadn't seen each other at school just hours earlier.

After the squeals and selfies ended, the four girls ran upstairs. Kelly listened to the happy little thumping as they ascended the staircase. She heard the bedroom door open and then shut. *Maybe this won't be so bad after all,* Kelly thought with renewed hope.

"Knock, knock!"

Kelly looked up, surprised to see Charlotte saunter through the open door. "Hey you! What are you doing here?"

Charlotte kicked off her pumps. "Just stopping in to say hi." She walked over and gave Kelly a quick kiss on the cheek. "I've got a hot date tonight," she said, grinning mischievously.

"Oh?"

"Gotta love Tinder."

Kelly laughed. "Aren't you too old for Tinder?"

"Honey, online *everyone's* twenty-nine."

Leave it to Charlotte to immediately lighten her mood. Kelly smiled. "Well, good date or bad date, it'll be better than my night," Kelly said in a low tone. "Fiona has three girls for a sleepover."

Charlotte followed Kelly into the kitchen and leaned against the counter, dropping her purse on the floor. "Yikes. And Zach?"

"I don't know where he is right now, frankly."

After refusing to go to school and having slept all day again, Zach had left the house around two in the afternoon; Kelly presumed he'd gone to watch a football game at school. Secretly, she hoped that Todd would text her, telling her that Zach had walked to his house and planned to stay overnight. While she knew that Todd's house was a horrible environment for Zach, she'd had second thoughts about exposing the other girls to his behavior. The lesser of two evils, she thought.

"Hey," Kelly said, lowering her voice once again. "Guess who's here?" She didn't wait for Charlotte to respond. "Debbie Weaver's daughter."

Dramatically, Charlotte coughed and patted herself above her breastbone in an exaggerated gesture. "Excuse me?"

Kelly nodded. "Can you believe it?"

"When did *that* friendship happen?"

Kelly rolled her eyes and shrugged. "Probably when Debbie moved her kids to the public school system."

"Ah yes, I forgot about that. After all those years proclaiming the inferiority of public school, she had to take it on the chin and enroll her daughters there." Charlotte chuckled to herself. "I bet that hurt."

"No kidding."

Kelly remembered only too well one holiday party at Debbie's house when she had been standing with a group of women from Debbie's precious country club, and the conversation had turned to the public schools. One of the women, a recent addition to the country club scene, had remarked that her children went to the public school, and a polite pandemonium broke out with Debbie's friends educating the newcomer about the benefits of private education. Kelly had remained quiet, knowing far too well that she and Todd couldn't afford anything other than public school.

"Well, anyway, Molly appears to be doing fine, I suppose." Kelly couldn't think of anything else to say as a segue to a different topic.

Charlotte sniffed disdainfully. "That's right. Good things never happen to good people."

For a moment, Kelly wondered what Charlotte meant. But then she remembered that Debbie had abandoned Charlotte, too, during *her* horrible divorce. There was no love lost between Charlotte and the Debbie Weavers of the world.

And Kelly understood that.

"So tell me about this date?" Kelly asked, hoping to change the subject to something more jovial.

Charlotte gave a little shrug. "The usual. Businessman, divorced, travels, children." She made a face. "I can deal with all of it but the kids."

Kelly said nothing.

Charlotte caught her mistake. "Not that there's anything wrong with having kids, but, I mean, you already *have* them. I don't. And the last thing I want is a man tied to every-other-weekend obligations."

"Ah." Kelly raised an eyebrow. "Maybe he'll be like Todd and rarely see his kids anyway."

Charlotte sighed. "Great. A crappy father. Forget it. Relationship over."

Kelly laughed.

"Seriously, Kelly, when're you going to take the plunge and get back into the game?"

How many times had they discussed this? Charlotte already knew the answer, but Kelly didn't mind reminding her. "No way, Char. I'm not stepping back into those shark-infested waters. I'll just live vicariously through your stories." And then, with a mischievous look in her eyes, Kelly whispered, "Besides, who says I don't have a hot date tonight?"

Charlotte's eyes widened. "You mean four teenage girls?"

Shaking her head, Kelly corrected her friend. "Nope. My mother's coming over later. You know, to keep me company for a bit."

"Wow, really?" Charlotte raised her eyebrows. "That's great."

"I had asked Jackie but—"

Charlotte interrupted her. "Please. You don't even have to say it."

Kelly gave her a small smile. "Some things never change, I guess."

"I'm glad your mother's coming. Maybe that will keep Zach in check for a bit tonight. You don't need any of his antics around the girls, I'm sure." Charlotte glanced at her phone and sighed. "I better run. I'm supposed to meet him at seven."

"It's ten after!"

Charlotte gave her an amused look. "Exactly. You know the expression. Good things come to those who wait."

Kelly laughed and walked over to embrace Charlotte. "Thank you," she said as she pulled back and looked at her friend.

After reaching down for her purse, Charlotte slung it over her shoulder. "For what?"

"For being a breath of fresh air, my friend," Kelly replied as she walked Charlotte to the front door. "A wonderful and welcome breath of fresh air."

CHAPTER 8

Kelly sat next to her mother on the sofa, watching a movie that she had seen a dozen times before, but preferring the familiar to something new. She didn't need to concentrate so much that way. And that helped to keep her focused, because she felt as if she was on heightened alert, waiting for something to happen. But, so far, everything had gone smoothly.

Oh, the girls had been noisy, running around and laughing as they took group selfies and then clamored around each other's phones with shouts of "Let me see!" And then there had been the hour of blaring music from Fiona's room and the sound of pounding feet. They were dancing or jumping around, something innocent—despite being loud—that had made Kelly smile.

Now they had ordered two pizzas, and the girls were upstairs, maybe a little too quiet, waiting for the delivery. Kelly glanced at the clock. They still had another forty minutes or so to wait. It was a Friday night, after all.

"Want another coffee?" Kelly asked her mother as she stood up.

Her mother shook her head. "It'll keep me up all night."

"It's decaf, Mom."

"No, but thanks anyway."

Kelly walked over to the Keurig and popped in a new coffee pod. They hadn't talked much, her mother and her. Not about anything deep or important. Just superficial things: the upcoming holidays, the impending winter, and the annual charity event that helped raise money for the American Heart Association. Ever since Kelly's father had died from heart disease, her mother had been very involved in helping that organization. It kept her busy.

Despite her mother's willingness to sit with her, Kelly felt empty, as if something were missing. She leaned against the counter, waiting for her coffee to finish, and stared at her mother.

She was aging. There was no denying that. She was short and petite, too active to get caught up in that vicious cycle of gaining a lot of weight as she grew older. She kept her hair dyed a dark chestnut brown, hiding her grays with hints of highlights. And while it fooled no one, Kelly did admit that it hid her true age.

And yet, in her mind, Kelly remembered the mother of her youth. She had stayed home to be with her children and always had supper ready at six o'clock on the dot. Whenever Kelly had needed her, her mother had been there with a hug or a tissue and always with a willing ear to listen to her daughter's woes.

There were moments when Kelly just wanted to return to being Fiona's age, to sit with her head on her mother's shoulder and feel her caressing the side of her face. She longed for the days when her mother would tell her that everything would be OK; that this, too, would pass.

Kelly knew that she was too old for that. But she just wished that she could talk to her mother. Like she used to be able to do. It had been ages since her mother had really looked her in the eye and asked how she was doing. Somewhere along the way, her mother had closed herself off from any kind of real conversation, like she could protect herself from life's difficulties by pretending they didn't exist. *Where had that maternal woman gone?* Kelly wondered. And then, on a whim, she decided to try to get her back.

"What do you think I should do about Zach, Mom?" she asked as she walked back to the sofa.

Her mother looked at her, her dark eyes wide as if she didn't understand the question. "What do you mean, dear? Is something wrong with Zach?"

Kelly gave her an incredulous look. "The way he's behaving."

Her mother gave a small laugh and waved her hand in a dismissive manner. "Oh please, Kelly. Boys will be boys. Why, Eddie misbehaved when he was a teenager, too."

Kelly frowned. "No he didn't."

Her mother shook her head, still smiling. "You girls! You both think you knew everything that was going on, don't you?" She wagged her finger at Kelly. "Your brother was quite the scoundrel."

She almost laughed. Eddie? Boring, uptight Eddie? "No, Mom. No he wasn't."

"I'll have you know that he was almost suspended for smoking under the football bleachers when he was supposed to be at band practice."

Inwardly, Kelly groaned. "That's not the same thing."

Her mother appeared affronted by Kelly's comment. "I beg to differ. It was quite the scandal. People didn't *do* that twenty years ago."

This time, Kelly laughed. "Yes they did. And much worse."

"Well, not my son." She pursed her lips and gave Kelly a stern stare. "And not my daughters, either."

Pulling her legs up underneath herself, Kelly leaned her arm against the back of the sofa. "Mom, I asked you about Zach. He really has me worried. Can we focus on that?"

"I was focused on that."

"No, no you weren't." Kelly hated how she sounded as though she were arguing with her mother. Now she remembered why she had avoided sharing her problems and concerns with her mom for so long. Every conversation seemed to wind up this way. "You were talking about Eddie smoking a cigarette, but I'm talking about Zach doing drugs and hanging out with that terrible kid Michael."

"I was worried about Eddie back then, too," her mother added defensively. "That's what mothers do. Worry."

"Oh Mom." She couldn't help it. This time, she groaned out loud. "In a heartbeat, I'd trade Zach smoking one cigarette for what he's actually doing. Heck, he could smoke a pack a day and it would be better."

Her mother shook her head and made a clicking noise of disapproval with her tongue. And then she glanced at the clock and sighed. "I didn't realize how late it is. I think it's time for me to leave."

"It's only nine o'clock."

"I need to feed the cats."

"Well, I guess if you really must leave," Kelly finally said, trying to mask her disappointment. "I thought we were watching the movie, though."

Her mother stood up and glanced at the television. "I've already watched that movie anyway."

I thought you were here giving me moral support. "OK then." Hurt, Kelly began to walk her mother toward the door. "Be careful driving home. It's a Friday night. Crazies are out."

Before they reached the foyer, the front door opened and Zach sauntered into the house. Behind him stood a tall, willowy teenager who looked more like a man than a child. His shiny blond hair hung over his eyes, casting a shadow across his face. He wore a loose-fitting garment, far too heavy for that time of year, which resembled something from Woodstock in the '70s, not Morristown when 2020 was just around the corner.

"Hey, Ms. Martin."

For a long moment, Kelly stood there and stared at him. *Do I know you?* she wanted to ask. But as soon as the question entered her mind, she knew the answer: Michael Stevens.

She had only met him once, while picking up Zach from a freshman football practice a few years back. But that had been enough. Kelly

54

had pulled up to the practice house and, when she didn't see Zach anywhere, rolled down the window to ask someone to fetch him.

"You mean gay boy?" the young man with short dirty-blond hair had quipped teasingly. But he hadn't waited for her response before walking over to the practice house, opening the door, and shouting for Zach.

Kelly had asked Zach about the boy. Zach had laughed, unconcerned about the derogatory name that he'd been called.

"That's Michael," Zach had told her, a secretive smile playing on his lips. "He's my friend."

Friend. Zach had said the word with so much pride. Growing up, he never had many friends. So Kelly had overlooked Michael's disparaging remark, chalking it up to teenage boys teasing each other. Over the next few weeks, she heard Zach talk about his new friend on multiple occasions, but she never met him again. Several times, she had inquired about this mysterious Michael Stevens, suggesting that Zach invite him over—a suggestion that was met with eye rolling and "that's gay!"

So she had given up.

And once Michael had entrenched himself into Zach's life, things began changing. Not slowly. No, it wasn't a slow metamorphosis like a caterpillar into a butterfly. It was more like a meteor destroying a planet, a one-shot deal that covered the earth with a layer of ash, wiping out life as she had known it. Gone were the family dinners and movie nights. Instead, Zach disappeared more and more frequently, often claiming he was at his father's, which, with a little prying, Kelly discovered to be a lie. When Zach was home, he was impossible to deal with. His mood swings made her feel as if she were walking on eggshells.

Kelly felt certain she knew the root cause of all of these unpleasant changes: Michael Stevens.

Some friend.

Kelly stood there, staring at Michael Stevens in her foyer. She felt a tightening in her chest and fought the urge to reach out to touch the foyer table and steady herself. What was he doing in her house? Hadn't he caused enough trouble?

But Michael seemed unfazed. He walked past her, bent down to tie his sneaker, and then stood up, putting his hands in his pockets and following Zach up the staircase.

"Who was that boy?" her mother asked.

"That's Michael, Mom." Kelly stared after the two figures who had disappeared into Zach's room and shut the door. "You know. *Michael.*" She hoped that, by enunciating the boy's name, her mother would realize what she wasn't saying. That Michael was the person who had started all of this, had introduced Zach to drugs, had encouraged him to experiment more and obey less. That Michael was the source of all their problems.

But her mother realized none of that.

"Well, if you want to worry about something, maybe it's Zach's poor manners. He always did suffer in that department." Her mother reached for her purse and hung it over her arm. "He didn't even say hello to me."

Yes, Kelly thought wearily as she opened the front door for her mother, *it's time for you to leave.*

CHAPTER 9

Seated at the kitchen counter, reading the Saturday paper while nursing her third coffee of the day, Kelly heard a car pull into the driveway. She braced herself, knowing that it was, undoubtedly, Debbie Weaver. The last of the mothers to pick up their daughters.

"Hello?" the too-familiar singsong voice called out from the front door, which immediately set the dogs into a loud frenzy of frantic barking.

Kelly called out for them to quiet down.

"There you are!" Debbie walked down the hallway, nonchalant about having let herself into the house, and gave Kelly a light embrace with an air kiss on the cheek.

Kelly hated air kisses but plastered a smile on her face anyway. "Did you enjoy your evening?"

"Absolutely!" Debbie gave a little laugh as if there was an unspoken secret in her response, but Kelly didn't get it. "And how were the girls?"

What was there to say? Four girls meant a lot of noise, a lot of half-finished cans of Coke, and a lot of empty pizza boxes, especially when Zach apparently made a late-night appearance in the kitchen and scarfed down the better portion of one remaining box. That was probably why most parents didn't host sleepover parties.

And then there had been the Michael situation.

Kelly hadn't made a fuss about Michael being in the house. She hadn't wanted to make a scene and ruin Fiona's night. Inside, however, she had seethed. For over two hours, she sat downstairs, alone in the television room, waiting for Michael Stevens to leave.

When he finally did, he paused long enough to shout up the stairwell to Zach, calling him, once again, by that terrible nickname. Despite it being late, the four girls had run downstairs to help themselves to ice cream and popcorn, a strange combination. Kelly had excused herself and, on her way upstairs, paused to lock the front door. That had been when she heard one of the girls, possibly Molly, comment on how cute she thought Michael was.

Kelly had shuddered and hurried upstairs, stopping only to make certain Zach hadn't snuck out with his "friend" before she retired to her room for what became a long, sleepless night.

"How were the girls?" She repeated Debbie's question. "Perfect little angels," Kelly replied, figuring it was the simplest answer to a question that she knew Debbie didn't care about.

"You know, it's been a while. We should do lunch sometime."

For a moment, Kelly thought she had misheard Debbie. Only Morristown's A-listers were ever invited to "do" lunch and, ever since the divorce, Kelly had fallen rather far from the A-list. She wasn't even certain if she was *on* any lists besides the Do Not Invite or Call list. "That sounds great," she heard herself say.

"You're on Facebook, right?"

"I don't check it too often, but yes." She glanced at the clock. "Let me get Molly for you. I'm sure you're in a hurry." She didn't give Debbie a chance to continue the conversation. Instead, she got up and hurried to the bottom of the stairs. "Molly? Your mom's here."

"Coming!"

Kelly waited a few drawn-out seconds, hoping that Molly would come charging down the stairs. When Molly finally walked down the stairs, slowly, she looked unhappy.

"Everything OK?" Kelly asked.

"Yeah, but I'm missing something." She scanned the floor with her eyes, a concerned look on her face. "I think it fell out of my backpack."

"Well, whatever it is, if we find it, Fiona will bring it to school on Monday, OK?" Kelly didn't want to sound in a hurry, but, selfishly, she wanted the house back to herself.

"I, uh, I guess." She flung the backpack over her shoulder and glanced around one more time before thanking Kelly and hurrying out the front door.

Relieved, Kelly leaned against the shut door and closed her eyes. For a few minutes, she just listened to the quiet in her house. Zach hadn't awoken yet and, frankly, that was fine by her. After the previous night, Kelly needed a break. She was exhausted from not sleeping and wanted to catch up on some work that she hadn't completed during the week.

Two hours later, as Kelly made her second pot of coffee, she heard the shuffle of footsteps on the stairs. She glanced over her shoulder, waiting to greet Fiona. However, to her surprise, it wasn't Fiona who walked around the corner. It was Zach.

"Hey."

Not hello. Not good morning. Just "hey." But it was a start.

"I'm surprised to see you down here," she said, trying to mask the depth of her disbelief. "You usually sleep in later."

He shuffled by her and reached for the refrigerator door. She watched as he opened it, grabbed the plastic milk jug, and popped off the top. With four large gulps, he finished it and put the empty container on the counter. "Yeah, whatever."

"You could throw that out," Kelly said, pointing to the corner near the basement door. "The recycle bin is over there."

He ignored her and returned to the refrigerator, where he stood in front of the open door again, this time scouring it for food, no doubt.

She wanted nothing more than to walk over, reach out her hand, and slap the door shut. She could feel the cold air blowing past him, wasting her money. The electric bill was always too high, and Kelly was tired of walking around shutting off lights behind both Zach and Fiona.

He finally took out a package of lunch meat, cheese, and the mayonnaise. Without saying a word, he began to roll up the sliced turkey and dip it into the opened mayonnaise jar.

Kelly cringed. "There *is* bread, you know."

Silence.

One piece after the other, Zach gobbled down an entire package of turkey and all of the sliced cheese. Kelly shut her eyes. She just couldn't watch the disgusting display of gluttony before her.

When she finally heard Zach screw on the mayonnaise jar lid, she forced herself to look at him. She didn't like what she saw.

"I was, uh, surprised that you brought Michael here last night," Kelly said at last, hoping that she sounded pleasant.

Zach smiled to himself.

"He's driving now?" she asked cautiously.

Zach shook his head.

"Then how does he get around?"

"Walks, I guess," Zach said. "Or he has friends that drive."

That was the most that Zach had spoken to her, outside of arguments, in months. As much as Kelly hated Michael, she realized that Zach felt otherwise. "I see. Friends?"

Zach's eyes flickered in her direction. "He's not gay."

She hadn't thought that. However, now that Zach mentioned it, she couldn't help but say, "He calls you that awful name. Gay boy."

"He calls everyone that."

"It's derogatory."

"It's a joke," Zach said, his gray eyes narrowing.

"People get offended by jokes like that."

Zach shook his head and exhaled loudly. "Get over yourself," he mumbled and shuffled out of the kitchen. Within seconds, Kelly heard the sound of his bedroom door shut, and she suspected that, because his munchies had been satisfied, he wouldn't reemerge for the rest of the day.

Despite wanting her son back—the real Zach and not this hollowed-out shell of a human—she didn't care if he stayed up there for the next week. She couldn't take much more. Living like this was not living; it was just barely functioning, and even that was beginning to take its toll.

CHAPTER 10

The next morning, Kelly stood in the hallway, banging on Zach's bedroom door. The sound of her fist reverberated against the wood, loud in the otherwise quiet of her Sunday morning. "Come on, Zach! We have to go!" One glance at her cell phone and she knew that they'd be late for church. Again.

"Stop!" he half moaned and half cried, the sound of his voice muffled from what Kelly suspected was the pillow covering his face.

Fiona stood at the bottom of the stairs, one hand on her hip and the other on the banister. She wore a plain blue floral dress with half boots, her hair in a messy bun at the nape of her neck. And she was not happy. With a deep scowl on her face, she stared at her mother. "Mom! If he's not going, why do I have to?"

Kelly shut her eyes and counted to ten. Twice. She didn't need this today. It wasn't often that she made the kids go to church, but this day was important. Earlier that week, she had called Pastor Russell and requested a meeting after the eleven o'clock service. A *family* meeting, and that meant with Zach and Fiona, too.

"He's going," she snapped back before banging on the door one more time. "Get. Up."

From behind the door came a noise that, to her relief, sounded as if Zach was actually listening to her. The bed frame creaked, and she heard him shuffling across the hardwood floor. For a split second, Kelly relished the moment, shocked that he *had* gotten up and hopeful that it meant he might be outgrowing this awful, terrible stage.

But her hopes were quickly dashed.

The door suddenly opened, and she found herself staring at the angry, twisted face of her son.

"Shut! Up!"

He didn't just yell it; he screamed it. In her face.

"Can't you get the picture? I'm *not* going!"

Kelly took a step backward, her heart suddenly racing. It wasn't just that he had invaded her personal space but *how* he had invaded it. His face looked blotchy and marked by angry red pimples. And his gray eyes were bloodshot. The worst, however, was the way his mouth had twisted into a furious grimace, which only enhanced his expression of pure, unadulterated rage.

For the first time, she felt frightened. Only this time, she wasn't afraid *for* her son but *of* her son.

"Zach, please." Her voice sounded calmer than she felt, which surprised her. Inside her chest, her heart pounded, and she felt her palms grow sweaty. She hated that Fiona was at the bottom of the stairs, witnessing this scene. "We have that meeting after—"

"I'm not meeting with any stupid pastor!"

"Zach!" This time, her voice lacked the patience she had conveyed just seconds earlier. "Don't talk like that about Pastor Russell."

He narrowed his eyes. Something fierce flashed there. A darkness that spoke of deep-rooted inner demons that, with all likelihood, even a pastor couldn't handle. *When had Satan gotten his hands on her son?* she wondered. Surely somewhere in his past there had been a point of no return. A moment in time when, had she seen it coming, she could have protected Zach. Shielded him from taking that final step to the dark side.

"Don't tell me what to do." He enunciated each word in a short, clipped manner, and Kelly felt her own anger increase.

How dare he? she thought. How dare he talk to her with such contempt?

"Clean up your toys, Zach," Kelly said as she stood in the doorway of the television room.

He was sitting on the floor, playing with his trucks and blocks. It was one of his favorite pastimes: building roads and bridges so that he could push his little Matchbox cars around, pretending to have races or even accidents. Normally Kelly didn't mind. The more he played with his cars, the less television he watched. But he always tended to leave behind the toys when he wandered on to something else.

"No."

Kelly's eyes widened. "Excuse me, young man? What did you say?"

He continued pushing the red Ford Mustang around a pileup of crashed cars. "I said no."

She turned to Todd, who sat at the kitchen table, reading the day-old newspaper. "Did you hear that?"

He barely glanced at her. "What?"

"I just told Zach to clean up and he said no to me."

Todd sighed and set down the paper. He glanced at the toys in front of his son and then made a face. "Come on, Kelly. He's only three." And then, to Zach, he said, "Hey sport, want to go outside and toss the football?"

"Yeah!" Immediately, Zach stood up, knocking over the bridge and kicking some of the cars across the carpet. He ran to his father and jumped up and down as he grabbed for Todd's hands.

"Zach!"

Zach froze at the sound of Kelly's voice.

"I told you to pick up those toys. You listen to me."

But Todd glanced down at his son and gave him a little smile. A conspiracy. "Don't listen to Mommy. She'll clean it up. Let's go, kiddo."

Kelly stood there, her mouth hanging open as she watched her husband and son run out the door, leaving her behind to clean up Zach's mess.

"Don't you talk to me that way," Kelly snapped.

"Why not?" Was that a hint of a smirk on his lips? "Dad always did."

And there it was: the truth. Kelly grimaced before narrowing her eyes and squaring her shoulders. "Listen to me, Zachary Martin. You live under my roof, you live by my rules! And you will speak to me with respect. Now go get dressed. You *are* coming to church with us."

He muttered a vile profanity, and Kelly caught her breath.

"Guys!" Fiona called out. "Come on! Knock it off!"

And that was when Zach flew forward, shoving his shoulder against his mother as he burst past her. Just his large size would have been enough, but the speed of the movement caused Kelly to stumble. She fell against the wall, knocking into the table and the mirror that hung over it. As Zach disappeared into the bathroom, gratuitously slamming the door shut behind him, the mirror slammed down onto the hardwood floor and shattered into thousands of little pieces.

Kelly stood there, staring at the mess, and knew that the light reflected in the shards was a replica of her life: fractured and broken. In each piece, she saw a sliver of herself, a small splinter of her blue eyes, her drained face, and her hunched shoulders. For a moment, she felt nothing but defeat. She squinted and tilted her head, staring at the mess on the floor. There was no way to fix it. Even if she could put the pieces back together again, she'd still see the cracks and chips. It was damaged. Garbage. Impossible to salvage.

She lowered her head, her shoulders falling and slumping forward. After so many years of stress and anguish, battles that she fought alone, she felt overwhelmed. She didn't want to feel the pain anymore. It couldn't go on like this; if it did, she would become numb to her emotions, and that wouldn't help anyone. But for now, she felt all of the angst, the worry, the fury, and the dread of what the future might bring.

She shut her eyes and swallowed, as if that might contain her grief. But it didn't.

Before Kelly knew it, tears streamed down her cheeks. She opened her eyes and looked into one of the larger pieces of the shattered mirror and saw a tear gently roll down her cheek. Absentmindedly, she wiped at it. *No,* she thought, *I will not cry.* And yet, once the tears started, she couldn't stop them from falling.

The more she tried to will them to stop, the quicker she felt the dampness on her cheeks. And then, from deep within her core, the sobs came.

Giving in to her despondence, Kelly lifted her hands and covered her face, releasing all of the anguish and sorrow that she had somehow managed to hide for the past months . . . no, years. She cried for everything that had gone wrong: her miserable marriage, the painful divorce, Zach's horrendous addiction, her daughter's valiant resilience.

"Mom?"

The soft voice, so full of concern and compassion, only made Kelly cry harder. How much more did Fiona need to see? Kelly turned around and embraced Fiona, clinging to her daughter's petite body and crying into her loose hair. "I'm so sorry, Fiona," Kelly whispered.

"For what, Mom?"

Kelly hugged her closer and kissed the top of Fiona's head before whispering, "Everything."

CHAPTER 11

"So he didn't want to go to church," Todd said from the other end of the phone. "Big deal."

Nothing was a big deal to Todd. Ever.

Taking a deep breath, Kelly shut her eyes. Why did he have to make everything so difficult? She hated talking to him on the phone. For starters, she never knew whether or not he had been drinking. And he always had a false sense of superiority when he talked to her. The only thing worse was email communication. His harsh barbs and jabs could send Kelly into a tailspin of depression. She avoided *that* at all costs.

"That's not the point, Todd."

"Then what *is* the point, Kelly?"

She hated the way he enunciated her name: *Kell-lee.* He always sounded so condescending when he said it that way, like she was an idiot or making a big deal out of nothing. While it shouldn't have surprised her—for a tiger's stripes never truly changed, even if they faded a little—she continually hoped that he might realize that something was wrong with their son.

Seriously wrong.

"The point, *Todd,*" she said, using the same tone when she spoke his name, "is that *our* son was physical against me and did it in front of *our* daughter."

Remember her? she wanted to say, but she knew that doing so would be counterproductive. Plus she didn't want to give him any reason to *not* focus on Zach. Reminding Todd that he never asked about Fiona or inquired as to how she was doing, that he had, in fact, forgotten about her from the moment she was born, would just invite another argument that would end with nothing getting settled about Zach.

"Living like this . . . it's going from bad to worse," Kelly added, "and it's not fair to Fiona." *Or me,* she wanted to add. But she knew that he didn't care what was fair to her.

Todd gave a short laugh. "You're so overdramatic, Kelly. He bumped into you on the way to the bathroom. You make it sound like he was beating you."

"He's seventeen, Todd. He shouldn't be 'bumping into' his mother or pushing her aside or anything else." She tilted her head, pressing the cell phone in between her cheek and shoulder, so that she could stir the spaghetti. Fiona's favorite. Kelly felt the need to do something special for her daughter. With all of the crises surrounding her brother, Fiona's needs were often overlooked. "He sleeps all day. Refuses to go to school. Stays up all night playing those video games. And I know he's stealing money from me for drugs."

"He's a teenage boy."

Kelly clenched her teeth. "He needs help, Todd. I don't understand why you don't get that."

There was a momentary pause and, for a second, Kelly thought he had hung up on her. If there was one thing she had learned over the years, it was that Todd did not like being told what to do. Especially by a woman. He also didn't like being made to feel stupid. She braced herself for the aftermath.

"Well, Kelly," he started, enunciating each syllable. "Zach is just fine when he's over here with me. I haven't experienced any of these behavior issues in my house. Maybe the problem isn't Zach, but you."

She clenched her teeth, her heart beginning to palpitate at the familiar way Todd liked to turn things around. He was the master of deflection and, when she heard his words, she fought the urge to throw the phone across the room.

"You always were an inconsistent parent," he continued, that cutting edge in his voice sending knives through her spine. She froze, unable to think as her pulse raced.

Her chest tightened and she knew, just knew, that the light in the room was dimming. She couldn't see anything but darkness out of the corners of her eyes. It was as if she had fallen, in slow motion, down a deep well, and the light above her was slowly narrowing as she sank further into the depths of darkness.

"You're crazy, you know that?"

She sat at the kitchen table, her shoulders hunched over and her hands covering her face. Upstairs, the baby was crying and, from the other room, she could hear Zach playing his Nintendo game. All she had needed was a break. Just a few hours to take a nap and not have to deal with dinner or cleaning or laundry. Fiona was cutting new teeth, and Zach had been a handful all day. He hadn't wanted to go to preschool. As usual, Todd had acquiesced. And why not? Kelly's career had been put on hold until Fiona was older. Kelly needed to be home with the baby, after all. At least that was what he always said, as if staying home with the baby wasn't work.

So, when Todd had gone to the office earlier that morning, he left Kelly with both children without even asking if she minded.

And she did mind.

Very much.

Now that he had returned—late, as usual—Todd had been greeted by a train wreck sobbing at the table. His compassion remained unprovoked as he drained his glass of gin. Without skipping a beat, he poured himself a second. Three-fourths gin, one-fourth tonic. In a tall glass.

"You just don't understand," Kelly cried softly.

"Look." He took a swig of the gin. "I worked all day. I'm not coming home to do your job. Order food if you want, but you need to take care of the baby and Zach."

The baby. Just once Kelly wanted to hear him say her name.

"I'm going outside. I need to cut the grass. Unless, of course, you want to do that for me."

He didn't give her a chance to say yes or no. Instead, he stormed to the garage door and disappeared outside, leaving Kelly with the chaos that was increasingly becoming her life.

"Kelly? Are you still there?"

She shook her head as if that would give her the strength to forget the past. She didn't have to take that verbal abuse from him anymore. She was free of him now, right? Except she wasn't. The court system had made certain of that. After all, *both* parents had the legal right to be involved in their children's welfare. But only if and when they wanted to be. Todd could deny treatment for Zach, and the only recourse Kelly would have was to go to court, which could take months and, by then, Zach would be eighteen and free to make his own decisions.

No, Kelly wasn't free of Todd, and she doubted that she ever would be. And, to make matters worse, he knew it.

"This is about Zach, Todd," she managed to say through clenched teeth. "He needs to go to another rehab—a real one. A reputable inpatient facility this time."

"We tried that. It didn't work."

His voice sounded so flat and emotionless.

"A different inpatient rehab, Todd." Why did she have to explain this to him? "A *better* inpatient rehab. And not just for thirty days."

There was a slight pause on the other end of the phone. Kelly could imagine him standing in his kitchen, staring out the window, his glass of gin sweating on the counter. Had he reached for it? Taken a healthy swig for a little extra bump to his audacity?

"Insurance doesn't cover those rehabs. You know that," he said slowly. "Do you have that kind of money, Kelly? I sure don't, not with all of the child support I give you."

No, she thought, *I don't have that kind of money.* But she would never let him know that. She had paid her share of the last rehab on a credit card and was still paying it off. "I don't care what it costs. He needs help, Todd. That's more important than money."

"Well then."

That was it. Two words that could mean anything. Was he commenting his surprise that she would find the money? Or was he commenting his support for Zach's return to rehab? His response was noncommittal, a typical Todd maneuver.

"What's that supposed to mean?"

He paused, and Kelly was certain she heard ice tinkling against a glass. Yes, he was definitely drinking. "I'll think about it."

What on earth was there to think about? If Zach didn't get help, he'd be dead within a year. She knew enough about drug abuse, even with something as seemingly benign as a teenager smoking pot, that addiction to one substance often led to addictions to others. It might be pot today and LSD tomorrow and then, God forbid, something even worse, like heroin or meth. The way Zach had been behaving recently made Kelly wonder if he might be experimenting with other drugs already. It wasn't as if he would open up and confide in her. In Kelly's opinion, Zach definitely needed to go to another rehab center, preferably an inpatient. And yet, Todd just wanted to "think" about Zach getting professional help again? As if the drug problem might just disappear on its own?

Her temper flared so fast that she couldn't even respond to his terse reply. Instead, she simply hung up the phone.

She knew what he wanted. An argument. But she didn't have the strength to engage in verbal warfare. She was too exhausted for his games. And the fact that he felt as if he, not she, had the final say in the matter was infuriating. A control freak. That was Todd. Only he didn't realize that he had no control. Not over her or the children and certainly not over himself. Gin controlled him, robbing him of any sense of self-authority. Still, he loved to pretend that he could manipulate her, and Kelly wasn't going to fall back on her knees again, crumbling like a broken doll under the weight of his manipulation. No, not this time.

This time, she had to take charge in order to save her son.

CHAPTER 12

On Tuesday morning, Kelly stood outside of the high school and took a deep breath. *You can do this*, she told herself for the tenth time before she finally reached out and pressed the buzzer outside the front doors. She waited for what felt like an eternity.

Something crackled from the intercom. "Yes?"

"Kelly Martin. I have a meeting scheduled with the principal."

No acknowledgment, just a loud humming noise and a click.

Kelly pulled the heavy door and opened it enough so that she could pass through. A security booth greeted her, the woman who sat there barely glancing up as she gestured to the sign-in book. "Identification, please."

Setting her purse on the ledge, Kelly dug through it, looking for her wallet. As usual, it lay at the bottom. She opened it and withdrew her license. The security guard looked at it and nodded, not once raising her eyes to verify that Kelly was, indeed, the holder.

Great security.

"Here's your badge."

Kelly took the plastic ID card and held it in her hand. Was she supposed to wear it or just carry it? She waited for the security guard to tell her, but the woman was already engrossed in something on her cell phone. With no further instructions, Kelly simply walked away from the security booth and headed down the hallway in the direction of the main office.

Just the previous day, she had called, demanding a meeting with the principal. She wasn't even sure if that was the person she needed to speak with, but she figured she'd start at the top and, if needed, work her way down. Sheer desperation had led her to contact the school. Surely they had more experience than she did when it came to dealing with teenagers and drugs.

"Ms. Martin?"

She looked up and saw a blond-haired man wearing a burgundy school jacket approach her. He was about her age, maybe a year or two older, but that was only apparent from the wrinkles around his eyes and forehead. Otherwise, she might have mistaken him for a senior at the school, for he was more fit than most men half his age.

Over the left breast of his jacket, in white lettering, was written "Thomas Keates, Coach." She didn't immediately recognize the name, and it took her a moment to place his face. *Ah,* she thought, suddenly remembering that he was the football coach. That explained his physique.

"Coach Keates, yes?" She didn't know why she said that since his jacket already confirmed his name. "I'm sorry. I'm a bit—"

"Frazzled. I get it."

She stopped walking and stared at him. "Is it that apparent?"

He laughed, his dark eyes crinkling into half-moons. "No, not at all." He gestured toward the main office. When she started walking, he accompanied her. "The principal asked me to sit in on your meeting. He gave me a little background information, that's all."

Realizing that he knew about Zach, Kelly felt the heat rise to her cheeks. "Oh. I, uh, I hadn't realized anyone else would be in the meeting."

Thomas held up his hand as if to tell her that it was OK. "He invited a few other people, too. We take this stuff seriously, you know."

At the door, he paused before opening it and stepping aside, waiting for her to walk through the opening. "I can only imagine what you're going through."

No, she thought. *No you can't.* But she didn't know this man and didn't want to point out the obvious. So, instead, she heard herself say, "You may not know that he's been to multiple rehabs, Coach—"

"Thomas. Just Thomas."

"All right then. Thomas." She felt awkward calling him by his first name. "No one has reached out to me about Zach. Not once. In fact, his guidance counselor—"

"No longer works here," he said, finishing her sentence. "I agree. Ms. Longfield didn't have the best interest of at-risk students as a priority."

Kelly cringed at the words "at risk." She knew what that meant: troubled kids from broken homes, at a higher risk of succumbing to the evils of substance abuse. In other words, Zach.

Thomas was still standing there, waiting for her to walk through the opened door. "But we can talk about that inside, OK? Just know that we're here to help."

Somehow Kelly didn't believe him.

He guided her through the main office, leading her around several cubicles and into the back. When they came to a large wood door, he rapped his knuckles against it twice. From inside, someone called out "Come in."

Once again, Thomas opened the door for her.

Inside was a large conference room. The table could seat at least fourteen people, but half of the chairs were empty. Still, Kelly was shocked to see so many people waiting for her. She had thought she was only meeting with the principal. Now, she felt as if she were walking into an ambush.

Principal Smith gestured toward a chair. "Please, Mrs. Martin, have a seat."

She hesitated before doing as requested.

"Allow me to introduce everyone. You know Coach Keates, I see. I've invited the nurse, Mrs. Risk; Zach's guidance counselor, Mr. Adler; his English teacher, Mr. Poole; and two of our security guards, Jake and Bobby." He gestured toward each person as he introduced them. "And, of course, our dean of students, Mrs. Edwards."

Kelly felt her head start to swim. There were too many people in the room. It was her against them. Her palms grew warm and she wiped them on her pants. "I . . . I didn't realize that so many people . . ." Her words faded. She couldn't complete the sentence. The vision of a deer wandering into a pack of wolves flashed through her mind, but she immediately pushed it away. They were on the same page, after all, right? That was what Thomas had indicated when they entered the room.

"Now, Mrs. Martin—"

"Ms. Martin," she corrected, not quite recognizing her own voice.

The principal inclined his head toward her, a silent apology for the oversight. "I asked everyone to join us so that we could discuss the situation with Zach."

"The situation." Smith's words struck Kelly as odd. Zach was not a "situation" but her son.

"Perhaps you'd like to bring everyone up to date on where things stand?"

"Where things stand"? The vision of the wolves returned.

Kelly leaned forward, resting her arm against the edge of the table. "I . . . well, as you may know . . ." She glanced at the coach, who nodded his head once as if encouraging her to speak freely. She cleared her throat and plunged into the pack. "I'm losing my son." Her eyes scanned the room. "Drugs have him. Drugs from this school."

Mrs. Edwards shifted her weight and sat up straighter.

Kelly stared at her before turning to look at the principal. "Look. I'm scared. I don't know who my son is anymore. I don't even know what drugs he's on. I need your help." She paused, hesitating for the briefest of moments before she added, "The school has played a role in this, and I want to know what you are going to do about it?"

Principal Smith tapped his fingers against the arm of his chair. The movement made a dull thumping sound that Kelly found condescending. "What we are going to do about it?" he repeated.

Kelly pressed her lips together, partially grimacing at his tone. "The drug deals are happening in your hallways, Mr. Smith. So yes, what are you going to do about it?"

"That's a bold claim," Mrs. Edwards said. "And you know that how, exactly?"

Immediately, she felt cornered. Had she just blown it? For the first time, she regretted not insisting that Todd come with her. Despite all of his flaws, at least he knew how to engage in verbal warfare. In fact, it was probably Todd's best characteristic. "Besides school, the only kid he hangs with is that Michael Stevens—"

Thomas made a noise, and both of the security guards mumbled under their breath.

Kelly stared at them. "You're familiar with Michael, I take it."

Thomas raised his eyebrows and gave a slight roll of his eyes. "He was on the football team freshman year. Briefly," he added far too quickly, and Kelly caught the hidden meaning in his words.

She wondered if Michael had been caught using drugs and been thrown off the team. Thomas avoided looking at her, shifting his eyes toward the security guards as if passing the baton to them.

One of them, the larger of the two, spoke up, his deep voice filling the room. "Yes, we are familiar with Stevens. He's been a source of"—he paused and glanced at the principal—"concern for a while."

"Concern?" Kelly frowned. A teenage kid dealing drugs in the hallways was much more than a concern. It was a problem. A big problem. "If you know about Michael, why is he still here?"

Mrs. Edwards folded her hands and placed them on the conference table before she began speaking. "Mrs. Martin—"

"Ms. Martin," Kelly snapped.

"Ms. Martin." The woman pursed her lips, clearly not appreciating Kelly's correction. "Morristown High is a public school."

"I'm well aware of that." Kelly didn't care if she sounded abrupt.

"There is only so much we can do with some of our more"—she hesitated as if searching for the appropriate word—"troubled students."

Principal Smith nodded. "Public school administrators have their hands tied, Ms. Martin. We serve a very diverse population."

"Diverse?" Kelly almost laughed. "I wasn't aware that drug dealers were considered part of diversity."

"You know what I mean."

"No, frankly, I don't." She pushed her chair back from the table, about to stand up, but then thought twice about it. She wanted to storm out of the room and head to the nearest law office. "You have a student dealing drugs in the hallways and you haven't expelled him? Have you at least contacted his parents?"

An uncomfortable silence fell over the room.

Mrs. Risk spoke up at last. "Suspension and expulsion are two tools we have to manage some of the more troubled students, yes." She glanced at Principal Smith and then Mrs. Edwards before she continued. "The problem is that, when enacted, parents often complain about their children's rights to attend school."

Stunned, Kelly took a moment to compose herself before responding. Had she just heard the nurse correctly? "Wait a minute. Students who deal drugs prey on other kids. My kid. And you're telling me about *his* rights?" She gave a short laugh and shook her head. Clearly, the rights of the one usurped the rights of the many. "Unbelievable."

"Look, Ms. Martin," the principal said, his voice suddenly sounding more authoritative. "There are things that we can do and things that we cannot. Let's focus on what we can do, and that's getting Zach to graduation."

Of course, Kelly thought. Graduation. Zach was nothing more than a number to these people, a number that did one and only one thing: impacted their state funding. Rather than protect the students, the administrators merely wanted to pass them through the funnel and out the front doors, a rolled-up diploma in one hand and a murky future in the other. As long as they became someone else's problem, the school didn't care. It was a well-oiled machine that had few allowances for breakdowns.

The reality struck her. They didn't know *how* to help her with Zach's problem. They didn't care that he was her son. To them, Zach was, indeed, a situation, a situation that needed to be swept under the rug in order to move him along as quickly as possible.

CHAPTER 13

"Ms. Martin!"

Despite hearing her name, Kelly didn't stop walking. She couldn't. Her mind was focused on one and only one thing: making it to her car so she could get away from the school. She felt dirty, as if she had been violated at a fraternity party. Her skin crawled, and she needed to retreat to the safety and security of her home. Behind those four walls, she could control her world, or, at least, her world without Zach. But that was better than what she had just experienced.

"Ms. Martin, please!"

She heard the sound of feet hitting the pavement behind her. Disgusted, she stopped walking and let Thomas catch up to her.

"What do you want?" She enunciated each word, her irritation clear and evident both from the tone of her voice and the scowl on her face.

"I wanted to tell you that not all of us feel that way."

Kelly narrowed her eyes and gestured toward the building. "I didn't hear you saying that during the meeting, Thomas."

"Look, I care about Zach. He was a tremendous addition to the team during those three seasons he played for me. He's a good kid."

"*Was* a good kid," she corrected. "Now, he's just a shell of who he used to be." She met Thomas's eyes; he was staring at her with what looked like genuine concern. But that angered Kelly. Where had his concern been just ten minutes earlier? "My son is gone. I don't know who occupies his body now."

Thomas lowered his gaze. "I'm sorry."

"You should be." She waved her hand once again toward the school. "All of you should be. These students are people's children. They are our hopes. Our dreams." She leaned forward, pausing until Thomas looked at her. "Our futures. But you're letting a few very rotten apples destroy the entire lot of them!" She raised her hand to her forehead and shut her eyes. At that moment, she silently vowed that her daughter would never step one foot into that school. "What's worse is that you know how to get rid of the bad apples to save the rest but you don't. Instead, you merely look to sell the whole lot of them!"

"That's not fair!" Thomas reached out and touched her arm. It was a gentle gesture that surprised her. "I care, Ms. Martin," he said in a soft voice. "And I want to help."

Kelly, however, didn't trust him. Trust too easily given was often too easily lost, and its loss came at a great price. She had learned that costly lesson long ago. "You all just admitted that you can't."

He glanced over his shoulder as if to make certain no one might overhear their conversation. Then he lowered his voice. "Look, I'm going to tell you something that, if you repeat it, I'll deny I ever said."

She put her hand on her hip and waited.

"That Stevens kid."

Suddenly, Thomas held her undivided attention.

"We've tried to expel him. The best I was able to do was throw him off the football team for having a bad attitude. But when it comes to expulsion? Word is that the mother raised a fuss and threatened to lawyer up. Education is a right, Ms. Martin, not a privilege. Mrs. Risk and Principal Smith weren't kidding about their hands being tied. Besides, what a student does off premises is not something we can control."

"But he's doing it *on* premises," she countered.

"And he's exceptional at not getting caught."

Kelly exhaled, the wind being knocked out of her lungs at the realization that maybe the school administrators *were* on her side, at least insofar as they couldn't do anything to save Zach. But they could help get him through his last year. Maybe. "It's just so . . ." She didn't know how to finish the sentence. How could she care so much while other people cared so little? "Distressing," she finally said.

"I can't even imagine."

"You have no children?"

He gave her a half-hearted smile. "I have dozens of children, Ms. Martin. Every year, some move on when new ones move in. Trying to keep track of these boys is a full-time job, believe me."

She raised an eyebrow at his comment. It wasn't the same thing as having given birth to a new life, but she didn't want to tell him that.

Thomas, however, must have read her mind. "I know, I know. It's different. I get to go home at the end of the day and relax without worrying, right? The problem is, Ms. Martin, I *do* worry. I have seen more Michael Stevenses than you'd think possible. I mean, Morristown isn't *that* big. But every year, it's the same game, just different faces. And I see Zach Martins, too. Good kids with exceptional potential. They either make it or they don't." He paused and glanced up at the sky, squinting at the sun. "I thought Zach might have been one of the lucky ones. But the Stevenses of the world have a way of targeting the weaker ones, getting their hooks into them, and pulling them into the dark side with them."

"My son is not weak," Kelly said tersely. As soon as the words left her mouth, however, she knew that it was a lie.

Immediately, her throat began to ache and she swallowed, as if she could suppress the raw emotions that threatened to burst forth. *Don't cry*, she told herself, despite knowing that she couldn't hold back the tears. Quickly, she turned around so that Thomas couldn't see her, even though he surely suspected that she was crying.

"Hey."

She felt his hand on her shoulder, a hesitant but compassionate gesture. For a moment, she wanted to shrug off his touch, but it had been so long since anyone other than Fiona and Charlotte had actually touched her.

"Ms. Martin," he said in a soft, soothing voice. "I didn't mean—"

"Stop calling me that!" She sniffled and turned around, facing him as she wiped at her eyes. "I hate that name."

He stood there, silent.

Kelly sighed, her shoulders drooping. "I'm sorry. I shouldn't take my frustration out on you."

"No, no." He gestured with his hands. "It's fine. I totally understand. What you're going through . . ." He paused as if searching for the right words to comfort her. "Well, I haven't gone through anything like this, but I see the end result time and time again. The pain. The suffering. The loss. You have the right to be upset, Ms. Martin—"

"Kelly."

He gave a single nod. "OK, fine. Kelly then. The thing that I admire, Kelly, is that you are doing something about it."

She appreciated his kindness. It wasn't something she was used to experiencing. "I'm not doing anything. If I was, he'd be clean and we wouldn't be having this conversation."

Thomas gave a slight laugh. "I see your point. However, see mine. So many kids are going through this, and the parents just bury their heads in the sand. They don't want to face the issues, so they ignore them. Very few parents fight for their children and, despite not knowing you, I can tell that you are a fighter."

His compliment stunned her. When was the last time someone had commended her for anything?

Before she could say another word, her cell phone buzzed. Thankful for the distraction, she fished it out of her purse. Charlotte. "I'm sorry, Thomas. I have to take this."

He nodded as he reached into his back pocket. He pulled out a little white card, then handed it to her. "Look, if you need anything, please don't hesitate to call or even text. I really care about your son, Kelly. He has amazing potential."

Taking the card, she glanced at it. "Thank you."

He started to walk away, and Kelly pressed the button on her phone to accept Charlotte's call.

"Hey girl, where have you been?" Charlotte gushed. "Do you have time to meet up for a coffee at Starbucks?"

Kelly glanced at the phone to check the time. Fiona wouldn't be home for another two hours. "That sounds great."

"I'll meet you there in fifteen, OK?"

As Kelly hung up the phone, her eyes drifted back to the figure of Thomas, her son's former football coach, as he walked through the parking lot toward the back door. After such a disheartening meeting with the school administration, Kelly suddenly found herself feeling a little bit lighter. Thomas's supportive words and Charlotte's unexpected invitation were like little gifts, small packages that held bright rays of sunlight on an otherwise gray and cloudy day. *God works in strange ways,* she thought as she turned around and headed toward her car. Just when she felt like she was at her weakest, he had sent her two angels to bring her back to her feet.

CHAPTER 14

On Wednesday morning, Kelly braced herself for another fight with Zach. If she had to call the police again to help get him up and to school, she would. If nothing else, she needed a break. Just a few hours without Zach in the house, his heavy presence casting shade on her day.

She didn't care if he went to school and did nothing. Let him be the school's problem for a while. After all, it was their lax policies in dealing with the troublemakers and drug dealers that had gotten her and her family into this mess to begin with. Michael Stevens. The known drug dealer who still roamed the hallways of Morristown High School, lurking among the students as he scoped out his next victims.

That was how Kelly saw Michael: a predator living among his helpless prey.

Only she knew that Zach wasn't truly helpless. And she realized that it wasn't 100 percent Michael's fault. Despite his star-caliber place on the football team, Zach had always suffered from bouts of low self-esteem. In hindsight, it was clear that the pressure to perform well for the team had only exacerbated his insecurities. Like a true hunter, Michael had identified his prey, sniffing out that weakness and using it to his advantage, first offering friendship and then offering drugs.

"Zach?" She knocked on the door. "You getting ready for school?"

No answer.

She began to feel irritated. She didn't have time for this. Her children tended to forget that she had to work. Even though she worked from home, she needed to get on to her computer, grade papers, and communicate with her department chair. She might only be an online professor, but she still had a responsibility to her students.

Regardless, she couldn't play games with Zach today. He had taken up too much of her time as of late. And it was beginning to add unnecessary extra pressure to her otherwise already-full plate.

"Zach, come on!" Two more short, quick raps. When she didn't even hear him shuffle or shift in the bed, she knew that she had to go in. Taking a deep breath, Kelly waited a few seconds before knocking harder on the door. "Zach. You need to get up."

Kelly reached for the door handle, but when she went to turn it, she discovered it was locked.

She clenched her teeth. She had warned him about locking the door. Irritated, she jiggled the handle a few more times, hoping he'd wake up and open the door. She didn't need this today. She wanted nothing more than to get him to school so that she could spend a few hours working in peace and quiet. But first, she'd have to change out the doorknob with one that didn't lock. That was what she had said she'd do if he locked the door again. Now that he had, she had no choice but to follow through. Otherwise, it was just one more empty threat that removed any hint of consequence from the boy's life.

This time, she banged on the door. "Zach!"

Fiona's door opened, and she stumbled out of her room. "Jeez, Mom. I had another thirty minutes to sleep, you know."

Kelly snapped, "Get me a credit card or something."

"Huh?"

"One of those little plastic card things."

"Why? Did he lock the door again?"

But Kelly was beyond the point of giving a reasonable explanation. "Just do it!"

"All right, all right. Where's your purse?"

Kelly glanced toward her bedroom. It was padlocked already. She had installed that on her door when she had learned that Zach was stealing money from her purse. When she wasn't in the room, she locked it from the outside. And at night, she locked it from the inside. It was like living in a prison within her own house.

She stepped over to the door and pressed the padlock's buttons in the right sequence. "On my bed. Go."

Fiona scurried into her mother's room, and Kelly returned her attention to attempting to rouse Zach. This was no longer a weekly occurrence but, rather, a daily one. And she was tired of it.

She banged on the door again. "Zach, I'm not fooling around. This has gone on far too long. You can't ignore me and you *are* going to school!"

Fiona returned and pressed a plastic card into her mother's hand.

Kelly took it and slipped the card into the narrow slot between the door and the frame, wiggling the card until she heard a click, and the door slowly opened.

"That's how you do it?" Fiona exclaimed. "Sweet!"

The room was almost completely dark, the blinds having been pulled down. However, Zach had cut a hole in one of the blinds, so a sliver of light illuminated the form lying in the bed. Kelly reached for the wall to turn on the lights but saw that the switch had been broken, probably from Zach hitting it during one of his rampages in the past.

And there was garbage strewn across the floor. Empty Coca-Cola bottles and food wrappers. His dirty clothes were tossed on his desk and chair, his hamper overflowing. *Great,* she thought. *Something else I need to do.*

"How many times have I told you to put the hamper outside in the hall when you need clothes washed?" she grumbled as she walked across the room and tugged at the window shade. Instead of rolling up, it fell down, flooding the room with light. "Great." *Just add that to the list of things to fix,* she thought.

She turned around, ignoring the mess on the floor. But her eyes fell onto the numerous holes punched in the walls and the expletives scratched into the side of the dresser. Zach had used his Swiss army knife to carve that beauty into the otherwise perfect mahogany piece of furniture during one of his last fits over the summer. What had once been a well-appointed room, decorated with her grandmother's old bedroom set that Kelly had fought Todd to keep during their divorce, now reflected the turmoil of Zach's addiction.

Maybe it's time for Zach to spend more time at Todd's house, Kelly thought bitterly. *Ruin his father's things for a change.* She had calculated that Zach had destroyed over ten thousand dollars' worth of items: a kitchen chair, the oven, two laptops, a smartphone, a window, his bed, the walls, and even a door onto which he had spit spaghetti sauce, which dribbled into the crevices and needed to be repainted.

Yes. It was definitely time for Todd to step up and take over. She needed a break and just then, she wasn't even certain if she cared that Todd drank. The two of them could console each other, drown in their misery together with beer and gin for all she cared. Her patience had ended with living like this.

"Zach, you need to get up. Now!"

Kelly moved over to the side of the bed and crossed her arms over her chest, glaring down at him. When had it gotten to this point? And how could he possibly think that this was any type of life? Where could he possibly go from here? It broke her heart to see him like that, a complete blob with zero purpose in the world. So many people struggled with poverty and illness, wanting nothing more than to have a roof over their heads, food on the table, and the chance to make something of their lives. Zach was merely wasting his opportunities, flushing the good ones down the toilet with the bad.

As Kelly reached to grab the sheet and pull it away from her son's body, she was nervous that he might freak out at her again. Mentally she wasn't prepared for a fight. She was tired, plain exhausted, from the emotional turmoil that Zach wrought in her household.

But he didn't move.

"Zach?" she whispered.

From behind her, she heard her daughter's voice. "Mom?" Fiona sounded the concern that Kelly began to feel. "Is . . . is he OK?"

Silently, Kelly stood there, staring at Zach. She felt a disconnect between what she saw and what her mind was telling her. For the briefest of moments, she couldn't put the pieces together. He lay there so still.

"Why isn't he moving?" Fiona asked, her voice starting to rise so that she sounded shrill.

Kelly reached over and, ever so gently, touched Zach's shoulder. She pushed him a little, waiting for a reaction. When there was none, she shook him once and then tugged at him so that he fell onto his back, his long and dirty-blond hair covering part of his face. Something white and foamy clung to the corners of his mouth.

"Mom . . . is he OK?"

Moving her hand to his arm, Kelly touched Zach's skin. It felt cold. She tilted her head, still not quite understanding that no, her son was not OK. She studied his face, the pale color, and then noticed the vomit on the sheet. Beside him lay an open square of tinfoil with a hint of white flakes along the edge. Squeezed between the mattress and the wall was an empty bottle of gin. Beefeater. The brand that Todd drank.

"Call 9-1-1, Fiona," Kelly cried out as she sank onto the bed and lifted Zach, holding him in her arms with his head on her lap. "Now!"

CHAPTER 15

"Overdosed?"

Kelly stared at the doctor in the blue scrubs, a stethoscope hanging around his neck. The word resonated in her ears, and she tried to match it with the image of her son, lying in bed with his arm twisted at a weird angle and his head hanging over his shoulder. Two conflicting thoughts ran through her mind: it made sense, while, at the same time, it didn't.

"I don't think I understand," she whispered.

The doctor didn't respond immediately, as if waiting for her to say something else, but she could think of nothing else to say.

"I presume you aren't asking what that means," the doctor said at last.

"No, of course not." Kelly blinked. "But how? Or maybe the better question is, What?"

The doctor pressed his lips together as he took a deep breath. In that brief moment, Kelly found herself wondering how often the doctor had to deliver such news. Was there a standard script that they used? Did all parents react the same way? Did they ask the same questions?

"It appears there was a heavy mix of alcohol and prescription medication."

That answered her first question. Clearly, each overdose had a different combination of variables that contributed to it.

"But Zach doesn't take any medicines," she heard herself say, and, as soon as the words left her lips, she faltered. Of course he didn't take medicine. At least not prescribed to him. But that was what illegal drug abuse was all about: taking drugs that someone shouldn't be ingesting. The color drained from her face. Why had she thought Zach's problems stemmed from *just* marijuana? Had she been so blind to the truth? Were her suspicions correct that he might have tried other drugs as more than an experiment? "That was stupid. I'm sorry."

"I'm sure this is a lot to digest," Dr. Kemp said.

"What I meant is that we don't have any medicines in our house." She looked at him, a blank expression on his face. "Where would he have gotten them?"

The doctor shrugged. "Friends. The world's greatest drug dealer is someone's medicine cabinet. Kids steal their parents' prescriptions and sell them on the streets or at school."

Once again, Kelly felt ignorant. Of course she should have guessed that. In fact, deep down, she may have known it. That was one of the reasons she didn't keep any medicine in her house. She kept her own antidepressants in her purse, zipped in an inside pocket that she never accessed near the children.

And she suddenly realized that, once again, she had probably responded exactly as any other parent in the same situation: not comprehending the extent of the true problem. "None of this makes sense," she whispered. "I mean, I knew he was using drugs, but I thought it was just pot, you know?" She looked at the doctor. "And I've been trying to get him into counseling, even another rehab, but his father . . ." She couldn't finish the sentence, suddenly overwhelmed by a heavy sense of failure. Why hadn't she fought harder against Todd? Why had she let him bully her into inaction? All of this could have been prevented, if only Todd hadn't been such a passive-aggressive dissenter.

"I understand, Ms. Martin," Dr. Kemp said softly. Just the way he said it comforted her, and yet, she knew that he had years of experience saying those same words to other parents. "I've called for a social worker to come speak with you. To discuss your options."

"Options?"

Dr. Kemp didn't have time to respond as the waiting room was suddenly filled with a new energy.

Todd ran into the room, his tie halfway undone and the jacket of his business suit unbuttoned. He had a frantic expression on his face as he hurried over to where Kelly stood with the doctor. If she had expected Todd to embrace her or provide an inkling of support, she was clearly mistaken.

"What happened with Zach?" He practically breathed each word. Clearly, he had run from his car to the emergency room, his anxiety fueling his panic. "Is he OK?"

"Mr. Martin, I presume," Dr. Kemp said. "I'm afraid that Zach is in an induced coma right now."

"A coma?" The color faded from his face as Todd turned and looked at Kelly. "What happened? He was fine yesterday when he stopped by my house."

Kelly frowned. She hadn't known that Zach went over to see his father. In fact, she hadn't known that he left the house at all. She wanted to ask Todd about that, but for the moment, there were more pressing issues.

"Your son overdosed."

"Overdosed?" The way Todd repeated the word, it sounded not just as if he didn't believe the doctor, but as if the possibility of such a thing occurring was completely nonexistent. Kelly shut her eyes and fought the urge to reach out, put her hands on Todd's shoulders, and shake him, back and forth, as hard as she could.

Hadn't he listened to *anything* she had been telling him? Was he truly so blind to the fact that Zach was, indeed, a drug addict? Kelly took a deep breath, opened her eyes, and stared at her ex-husband as if he were a complete stranger—which, in many ways, he was.

"On what?" Todd asked incredulously.

"Drugs, Todd."

He scoffed at her. "I *know* that, Kelly." *Kell-lee.*

"It looks like alcohol—gin to be specific—mixed with prescription drugs."

"Where would he get prescription drugs?" He glared at Kelly. She wasn't surprised that he hadn't asked where Zach had gotten the booze. "Is he taking something you didn't tell me about?"

"No."

But Todd wasn't listening. "The PSA specifically states that you're supposed to notify me of everything, Kelly." *Kell-lee.* He smacked one of his hands against the other as he repeated, "Everything!"

"He wasn't taking anything!" she said, her voice rising just enough to be heard over him. "Can you stop, just once, trying to blame me for everything? Zach's in a coma, and you're more concerned with pointing the finger? Get your priorities straight, for crying out loud!"

The doctor cleared his throat. "Look, the bottom line is that Zach could have suffered brain damage." He paused to let his words sink in. "We won't know until he wakes."

Immediately, Kelly felt as if her heart skipped a beat. Brain damage? *Oh Zach,* she cried to herself. Why would anyone take such risks? "But he *will* wake, right?" Kelly asked, her expectant hope obvious in her voice.

Todd made a noise deep in his throat and shook his head slightly.

The doctor ignored him. "In my experience, I feel that's a safe bet, Ms. Martin. It doesn't appear he was unconscious for too long. You found him in time."

"Can you tell what drug he took?"

"Drugs, you mean. There were multiple."

Kelly shut her eyes and rubbed her temples with her fingers.

The doctor continued. "The blood tests indicate that it was Xanax and Adderall."

Todd frowned. "Adderall?"

"It's a medicine for ADHD. A stimulant." The doctor took a deep breath. "A lot of young people take it, either by mouth or by crushing it and snorting it. Gives them a high. But mixing it with alcohol can be deadly." He reached out and pressed his hand against Kelly's arm. "You were fortunate to find him when you did, Ms. Martin."

Todd looked at Kelly. "Where would he get Adderall or Xanax from?"

Before she could answer, the doctor spoke up. "Anywhere, Mr. Martin. You'd be surprised how accessible these drugs are. Just look in any medicine cabinet and there's a whole arsenal of drugs. The kids raid their parents' cabinets and sell it to other kids. And not just the orange bottle drugs, either. There've been issues with simple cold and flu medicine. It's a very concerning problem." He paused and leveled his gaze to meet Todd's. "We see far too many pharmaceutical overdoses each month. You'd be surprised how common it is."

"Adderall," Todd muttered.

"Thank you, Doctor."

Dr. Kemp nodded and, with a quick glance at Todd, he excused himself, leaving Kelly standing there with her ex-husband.

For a long moment, neither of them spoke. Todd looked deflated, his previous burst of bravado replaced with a subdued expression of shock. Part of Kelly wanted to console him, to cry on his shoulder in a rare moment of solidarity. But she remembered seeing that Beefeater bottle wedged against the wall and knew that, despite a court order prohibiting Todd from keeping alcohol in the house if the children were going to be there, he had contributed to this tragedy. And yet, he continually blamed her for all of Zach's problems.

So instead of saying anything to him, Kelly wrapped her arms around herself and walked to the far end of the waiting room. She'd rather sit in isolation than in the company of her ex-husband.

CHAPTER 16

As soon as she was alone, Kelly called her mother.

Her mother answered with a cheerful greeting followed by "What a pleasant surprise, honey!"

What a way to start the call, Kelly thought as she leaned against the wall in the waiting room. Somehow she had managed to calm herself enough to enter into what she referred to as her autopilot mode. It was the only way that she could deal with crises. Setting her emotions aside, even if temporarily, helped her get through even the worst disasters. Her divorce had been the last time she had to use it. This, however, was definitely worse.

She kept her back to the door in case anyone entered the room. She was alone, Todd having disappeared to the cafeteria to fetch them both a coffee. At least he was being civil for now.

"Mom, I . . . " she began slowly, trying to find the right words to break the news to her mother.

"How *are* you?" her mother gushed as if Kelly never called home.

"Frankly, I'm not doing so hot, Mom. I have to tell you something."

There was a moment's pause, the slightest hesitation on the other end of the line. "What's going on, Kelly?"

"I'm at the hospital."

Her mother gasped. "Are you all right? What happened? Please tell me it wasn't a car accident."

"No, it's not me, Mom. It's . . . it's Zach. He's in the ICU." Kelly took a deep breath. She had to say it, but the word felt as if it was too difficult to enunciate. *Overdose.* She raised her hand to her head and rubbed the bridge of her nose. "He overdosed."

"Oh sweet Jesus!" It sounded as if her mother collapsed into a chair. "Is he . . . ?"

"He's going to be fine. At least they think so."

"Was it that heroin?"

"What?" Kelly winced and made a face. Is that what people would think? That Zach was using heroin? "No, Mom."

"Well, what do I know, Kelly? I mean, I never heard of people overdosing on marijuana." *Mary*-juana. That was how her mother pronounced it. "And I suspect that cocaine is too expensive for a teenager. I wouldn't know, of course. I never did any of those things."

"Jeez, Mom, can you give me a chance here?" Under different circumstances, Kelly might have laughed. But not today. "He mixed alcohol with prescription drugs."

A pause. But just for a brief moment. "So it was an accident?"

Her mother's question caught her off guard. Kelly hadn't considered the alternative. "I presume most overdoses are, yes."

"Where's Zach now?"

Kelly stretched her back so that she was fully leaning against the wall. "I told you. He's in the ICU at Morristown Memorial."

"You mean Atlantic Health System? I think they changed the name a few years back."

"Whatever." This time, Kelly rolled her eyes. Why was any of this important? She had just told her mother that Zach overdosed, and she was more concerned about the proper name of the hospital? "Yes, that place."

"Shall I come to you?"

That was the last thing Kelly needed. Not with Todd lingering around the hospital. "No, but thanks, Mom. I could, however, use your help with Fiona. She's at home. Charlotte is with her right now."

"She didn't go to school?"

Kelly caught her breath. "No, Mom. She was a little upset, you know?"

"Oh yes. Of course." Kelly heard the sound of some papers shuffling in the background. "I'll gather my things and head right over to your house. Make you supper, too."

"Food is the last thing I'm thinking about."

Her mother made a clucking noise with her tongue. "You need to keep up your strength, Kelly. You can't starve yourself and get sick."

There was merit to her mother's words, and Kelly quickly thanked her before she hung up the phone. That was one thing that Kelly could always count on. Her mother would drop everything to help out one of her children. Even if, sometimes, she seemed a bit disconnected with reality, she always put her children and grandchildren ahead of everything else.

One down, two to go, Kelly thought.

Her next call was to Charlotte, who answered the phone on the first ring with an abrupt: "How is he?"

"Fine. At least they think he's going to be fine. He's in a coma right now."

"Dear Lord."

Kelly quickly added, "But that's typical, or so the doctor indicated. How's Fiona doing?"

She could hear Charlotte walking across the floor as if moving away from someone in order to find privacy. In a lowered voice, Charlotte answered at last. "She's doing all right. Not great, but all right. She's had a few tears, which, you know, for Fiona isn't too typical. She's worried."

"I'm sure." Kelly felt as if her heart might break. How could Zach have done this? Not just to himself but to the people who loved him?

And while she knew that the boy lying in the bed in the hospital room down the hallway was her child, she also knew that he wasn't her son. Not the son that she had loved and coddled, hugged and kissed during his younger years. "Let her know that Zach's going to be fine."

"I will."

"And my mother's on her way over to relieve you."

After she hung up with Charlotte, Kelly turned off the ringer and shoved her cell phone into her purse. She didn't want to talk to anyone who might call. Surely the word would spread, especially after Jackie found out. And Fiona probably had hit the social media trail with the story. That was, after all, what teenagers did—air their drama on the Internet for everyone to discover. No, for now, she needed to think and consider her options without interruption.

She paced the room, her shoes making a soft shuffling sound on the blue industrial carpet. Wrapping her arms around her body, she tried to imagine what would happen when Zach finally awoke from the coma. Presuming he didn't have brain damage, would he be contrite? Remorseful? Or would he be filled with bitterness and anger like always? How would he react to attending another rehab? Would the courts get involved, or would it strictly be a decision between her and Todd?

That thought gave her a moment of panic.

God, she prayed, *please let the court get involved. Please let someone intervene so that I don't have to fight for Zach's recovery on my own.*

"Hey."

She turned and saw Todd standing in the doorway. With his graying hair and increasing girth, he barely resembled the man she had married almost twenty years ago.

Todd approached her, extending one of his hands to give her the coffee.

"Thanks."

"Any word yet?" he asked, glancing over his shoulder toward the hallway.

She shook her head.

Todd sighed and plopped down into a chair. "What a mess."

"You know he needs to go away—to a real inpatient rehab facility this time," she said, standing near him but refusing to sit down. That would feel too much as if they were a couple. Better to keep her distance, she thought. Accepting a coffee was as familiar as she wanted to be with him.

"Let's survive the next few days, Kelly," he said, his tone kinder than usual. "Get him better physically before we address the other issues."

"Issues." That was what Todd called it. "Addiction" was the word Kelly used. For a moment, she wanted to correct him. That, however, would have started an argument. So, for the time being, she kept the peace, voluntarily, choosing to lose *that* battle in order to save her energy for the inevitable war.

CHAPTER 17

When Kelly finally returned home from the hospital on Wednesday, it was almost midnight. Todd had left earlier that evening, but Kelly insisted on staying by Zach's side, rubbing his hand and remembering the days when she had held him in her arms, staring down at his cherubic face. When had her little boy changed? When had he become a miniature version of his father?

She hadn't wanted to leave Zach, but the nurses insisted, claiming that there was nothing else she could do, plus visiting hours were over. Kelly almost argued that other patients in the ICU still had visitors lingering in their rooms but decided against it. She was exhausted, and she had Fiona to think about and her mother to relieve.

To her surprise, she was greeted by Charlotte, not her mother.

Charlotte stood in the kitchen, waiting for Kelly, a glass of white wine in her hand and an empty glass waiting expectantly on the counter.

"Hey, you."

Kelly dropped her purse on the floor and barely made her way into the kitchen before breaking down into tears and collapsing in Charlotte's arms. She sobbed against her friend's shoulder, clinging to her as if Charlotte were the only life support she had left in the world. Maybe she was.

After such a long and horrible day, Kelly was glad that it was almost over. And yet, she knew that she'd never be able to sleep. Instead, the long, empty night would be a continuation of the awfulness that was rapidly becoming her life.

After a few minutes, when Kelly's sobs began to slow to mere whimpers, Charlotte pulled back. "Come on, now. He's going to be OK."

"I know." She took a paper napkin offered by Charlotte and blotted her cheeks. "It's just so . . ." What was the word? All day long she had felt a void, as if she were facing a dark chasm. In a way, she stood on the edge of a cliff, staring into the plummeting darkness before her. But, in another way, she knew that she had actually taken that step. Was she falling? Or was she merely floating to the other side? "Final, I guess."

"Final?" Charlotte made a face. "I don't understand."

Kelly moved to the other side of the kitchen. "I guess it's like when you had that falling out with your sister. Remember?"

Charlotte gave a single laugh. "Remember? How could I forget?"

"After all of those years of her abusing you—right?—you had that one moment when there was simply no turning back." Kelly stared out the window over the kitchen sink, her imagination seeing light in the darkness outside. "You decided to finally stand up to her and not take it anymore. And there was no going back. You could no longer deny it, and it was time to fix yourself, even if you couldn't fix the situation." She glanced over her shoulder at Charlotte. "That's how I feel right now."

"Kell." Charlotte leaned against the counter, crossing her arms over her chest. "You never denied that he had a drug problem. *You* weren't the one fighting the obvious. If Todd could've gotten his head out of the bottle and seen what was happening—"

"He saw it all right."

Charlotte took a deep breath. "OK, he saw it, but he denied it. If he had admitted it, Zach could've gotten help long ago. I mean, this has been going on for—what? Three years?"

"He's gotten help," Kelly pointed out.

But Charlotte would hear none of it. "You mean those outpatient rehabs with their 'family' therapy nights." The way that Charlotte said the word "family," using her fingers to make air quotes, made it clear what she thought about it. "What a joke."

Kelly couldn't argue with her friend. They *were* a joke. "I could've gone to court. Insisted on another inpatient facility or, maybe, gotten custody taken away from Todd."

At this, Charlotte scoffed. "Oh please! The court system's just as much of a joke as those outpatient rehabs."

Kelly sniffled and dabbed at her eyes to dry her tears. "Well, that *is* true." Sighing, Kelly crumpled up the napkin and tossed it into the sink. She'd throw it out later. "How's Fiona?"

With a gentle shrug, Charlotte made a face. "Angry. Hurt. Scared. And admitting none of those things."

Typical. What teenager would admit to any of those emotions?

And then Kelly remembered that she had called her mother earlier, that morning. Had it really been *that* morning? The day felt like it had been a year. "What're you doing here anyway? My mom was supposed to relieve you."

"And she did," Charlotte said. "But I couldn't just go home, Kelly. Not without knowing what was going on. So I ran a few quick errands, let out my cat, and came back. I figured you'd be home late anyway. And, of course, that you might want a glass of wine and a shoulder to cry on."

Leave it to Charlotte to know how to comfort her. Kelly let her pour a healthy-sized glass of wine, even though she didn't feel like having any. But, just to be polite, she sipped at it before thanking her friend.

"I trust Todd was there?"

Kelly rolled her eyes.

"Oh gee, I can hardly wait to hear what crap he pulled this time."

Kelly took another sip of the wine and then set down the glass. "The typical. Blamed me when he heard."

"Of course," Charlotte said with a perfectly serious expression, but her voice dripped with sarcasm. "Everything's always *your* fault."

"Exactly."

"He contributed nothing to the problem, right?"

"Right." Whether it was the wine or Charlotte's realistic take on the situation, Kelly found herself feeling a little more relaxed.

"I mean, it had nothing to do with how he treated you in front of the kids or the fact that he got drunk every night."

Kelly shook her head. "Nope."

Charlotte made a disgusted face. "Such a narcissistic little man."

This time, Kelly managed a small laugh. Charlotte had always claimed that Todd, like her own ex-husband, was abusive toward her because he was too full of himself. She pointed out that every flaw Todd found in Kelly was actually a projection of his own character weaknesses. She even went so far as to call it "Little Man Syndrome," and, for some odd reason, Kelly always found that image humorous.

"That's my girl," Charlotte said, giving her a warm, empathetic smile. "Look, you and I are a lot alike, Kelly. We're survivors. And I know that you will get through this. You will fight for Zach, even if it means having to battle Napoleon and his issues. But I want you to know that I'm here for you every step of the way, OK?"

Swallowing back more tears, Kelly nodded. She couldn't speak because surely then she would cry. As usual, Charlotte seemed to sense this. So, rather than push Kelly to the brink, she merely set down her wineglass and reached for her purse.

"You know where to reach me, Kelly," Charlotte said. "If you need anything with Fiona, just ask."

Her offer almost made Kelly cry again. "Thanks, Char."

Her friend gave her an encouraging smile. "Now, I want you to try to sleep. It'll be hard, but if you can grab even a few winks, you'll be in better shape for tomorrow and whatever new battles face you."

After a quick embrace, Charlotte quietly left the house.

For a long moment, Kelly stood in the kitchen, surrounded by silence. She shut her eyes and thought back just twenty-four hours earlier. Back to when life was normal—or, at least, normal for her. There had been no hospital, no ambulance, no drug overdose. She didn't have to worry about explaining what had happened to her son to her employer or her church or her family. And then Zach had changed all of that. To the rest of the world, he had become just one more statistic in the war on drugs.

Sighing, Kelly poured out the rest of her wine. She set the empty glass in the sink and started to walk away when her eyes fell on the bottle. Alcohol. Just another drug, no different than marijuana, cocaine, heroin, or doctor-prescribed medicine. It was a drug, and Kelly didn't want any more drugs—legal or illegal—in her home. Hadn't both kinds stolen enough from her?

Disgusted, she grabbed the bottle and poured it out. The liquid rushed down the drain in a golden clockwise wave. She watched, a feeling of power and control slowly washing over her. She would no longer let anything like alcohol or drugs ruin her life. Never again.

Once the wine disappeared down the drain, Kelly set the empty bottle in the sink next to her glass. Only then did Kelly turn out the kitchen light and slowly make her way up the stairs.

CHAPTER 18

At ten thirty on Thursday morning, Kelly sat by Zach's bedside, her hand caressing his arm. For two hours, she hadn't been able to stop staring into his face, her eyes searching for answers. *Why, Zach?* she wanted to say out loud. *Why would you do this to yourself?*

She never could understand drug addiction. Oh sure, she hadn't been completely innocent in high school. She had drunk her share of beer and smoked a little marijuana. Didn't everyone in Morristown? But, upon graduation from college, she had straightened up and focused on her graduate studies. There was a time for everything, she told herself, a time to play and a time to work. Her time to play was over.

Addiction was something different. It was something of the devil, a monster that took control of certain people and ruined lives. Kelly had often wondered why the government didn't do more to stop it. Simply arresting dealers and rehabilitating users was not enough. Dealers returned to dealing, and most users returned to using when they were released. The system was not working, her son being a perfect example of the law's failure to fundamentally solve the problem.

But Kelly voiced none of her thoughts aloud. She knew that some patients awoke from comas and said that they could understand the voices that had been in the room while they were unconscious. Kelly certainly didn't want Zach to hear what she was thinking.

When she did speak, she offered only positive thoughts and nothing that might chase him further into the dark hole where he currently resided.

The past twenty-four hours had both flown by and dragged on forever, a simultaneous conflict in time. She hadn't been able to sleep, tossing and turning all night. She had gotten out of bed twice and called the nurses' station each time to inquire how Zach was doing and whether or not he had awoken. Both times she had been told that everything was the same.

After getting Fiona to school, Kelly had driven straight to the hospital. She needed to be near him, hoping that her voice or even just her presence might help him awaken.

The only reason that she knew it was almost noon was because someone brought her a tray of food. Kelly barely gave it a glance. Her appetite had disappeared with her son.

"Kelly?"

She looked up, surprised to see Thomas standing in the doorway. He wore a pair of freshly ironed khaki pants, a burgundy Morristown High polo, and a stylish jacket, unzipped in a casual sort of way. With his blond hair hanging just slightly over his forehead, he could have passed for a player on his own football team. But Kelly suspected that he was in his early forties, for she remembered hearing that he'd been the football coach at the high school for at least ten years.

"May I?" Thomas gestured toward Zach as if asking for permission to enter the room.

"Of course." Kelly straightened and slowly withdrew her hand from Zach's arm. She wondered how long the coach had been standing there.

"I hope you don't mind that I came," Thomas said as he entered the room. "I heard about the . . ." He trailed off, clearly uncertain how to broach the subject of Zach's condition.

"Overdose." Kelly saved him the pain of saying it. "It's all right, Coach."

"Thomas, please."

She nodded her head. "I'm OK with you saying the word 'overdose,' Thomas. It doesn't make me uncomfortable to hear it. I mean, it's the truth, right? That's what happened. No sense trying to hide it."

"What are the doctors saying, if I may ask?"

"Alcohol and prescription drugs."

Thomas shook his head, just a little, as he glanced down at Zach. "And the prognosis?"

"He aspirated on his vomit." Just saying those words sent a shiver up her spine. "They don't think he was unconscious for too long, thank God. But they won't know if there was any brain damage until he wakes from the coma."

She wondered how Thomas had managed to make his way into the ICU. She had been told that only family members could visit and, unlike the rest of the hospital, they were very strict about visiting hours.

"I'm terribly sorry, Kelly." And he sounded genuine. She appreciated his sincerity. "I wanted to stop by to let you know that, if you need anything, just ask, OK?"

She couldn't imagine needing anything from him, a complete stranger to her, but maybe there was something he could do for Zach.

"Talk to him, Thomas," she said, her eyes wide and suddenly hopeful. "They say that comatose patients can hear people talking to them. Maybe you could talk to him."

Thomas looked taken aback, but he stepped closer to the bed.

"He respected you, right? You said so yourself." What she didn't say was that Zach hadn't respected her. She wondered if Thomas picked up on that.

"Well, he respected me as a coach, I suppose," Thomas said, his voice wary. "But not enough to quit the drugs."

"It wasn't drugs that kept him off the team," she reminded him. "It was the concussion."

"Mmm." Thomas gave a single nod as if remembering that fact. He leaned down so that his mouth was near Zach's ear. Gently, he touched Zach's shoulder as he spoke. "Hey, champ." Thomas glanced at Kelly, clearly uncomfortable speaking to the still, unresponsive boy, but nonetheless willing to do it. "You got everyone worried here, Zach. Your mother especially. We need you to pull out of this, OK?"

Kelly pressed her lips together, eagerly watching Zach to see if he moved a finger or fluttered an eyelid. "Keep going," she whispered.

"OK, uh . . ." He hesitated. "The team's playing Delbarton this weekend. On Sunday, you know? We could really use you on the sidelines, cheering us on. You know how that rivalry goes, right?"

Kelly smiled to herself and nodded.

"Those boys always listened to you, Zach. What did they call you?"

Gay boy. Kelly cringed at the memory of Michael's nickname for Zach.

"The Big M, right?" Thomas chuckled. "Well, we could use the Big M helping to rile up our defense. I think you should help me with the defensive team, Zach. Get better and I'll put you to work, OK?"

To Kelly's disappointment, nothing happened.

Thomas took a deep breath, gently squeezed Zach's shoulder, and stepped away from the bed. He gave Kelly a quick glance. "I tried," he said softly.

"You did."

"Well, I best get going. I have my next class at one o'clock."

She had forgotten that he was also the physical education teacher. "Thank you so much for stopping to see Zach." She stood up and walked with Thomas toward the door. "By the way, how *did* you get in?" she asked, curiosity getting the best of her. "I thought only immediate family could visit the ICU patients."

Thomas raised an eyebrow, and a hint of a smile crossed his lips. "That's true." Then, with a mischievous grin, he leaned over and, with a low voice, whispered into her ear, "Unless, of course, you're the football coach and one of the nurses has a son on the freshman team." Standing up straight, he winked at her, and Kelly gave a soft laugh.

"Of course."

Thomas took a deep breath and plunged his hands into the pockets of his open coat. "Parents will do anything to help their kid get more play time during a game."

For a second, Kelly said nothing. She stared at Thomas, amazed that someone who was, basically, a complete stranger would take time out of his already-busy day to stop at the hospital.

What a kind man, she thought, noticing for the first time how dark his eyes were. "Thank you, Thomas," she said at last. "It really means a lot to me." Quickly, she added, "For Zach, I mean."

He pursed his lips as if trying to not smile. "For Zach." But he lingered for just another second or two before he stepped outside the door and backed away, his hands still in his pockets and his eyes on hers. "Remember, if you need anything, just call. And, if you think of it, keep me updated? A simple text works, too."

She nodded. "Promise."

And with that, he turned around and sauntered down the hallway toward the exit.

Kelly watched him until he disappeared through the double doors. There was something about Thomas that intrigued her. At first, it had been his candor in the parking lot. Now it was his kindness toward her son. But she couldn't suppress that niggling feeling that, perhaps, there was something more. Something that she didn't have time to really think about at the present moment, but, under different circumstances, she might have been happy to do so.

CHAPTER 19

Fiona slammed the front door and stormed upstairs, not even pausing to greet her mother.

Seated at the kitchen table, her laptop open and her cell phone nearby, Kelly looked up when she heard the sound of Fiona's bedroom door banging shut. After sitting next to Zach all morning, Kelly had spent most of the afternoon researching different inpatient rehabilitation centers and trying to find out which, if any, were covered by insurance. Unfortunately, because her name wasn't on the policy, she got little to no cooperation from the insurance company. And she knew that Todd would be no help.

He never was.

Now Kelly had to deal with Fiona?

Pushing back her chair, Kelly stood up, pausing to shut her laptop before heading toward the staircase. One of the dogs scurried out of her way, and Kelly had to maneuver around two others who lay sprawled out in the foyer. The fourth one was barking outside, probably at a squirrel.

At the bottom of the stairs, Kelly called out Fiona's name.

There was no response.

Sighing, Kelly began to climb the staircase. She had so much to do before she needed to return to the hospital. Todd would be there after his workday ended, and she didn't want to bump into him. After the accusatory way he had spoken to her at the hospital yesterday, Kelly knew it was best to avoid him if possible. She had enough stress and pressure without Todd infiltrating her emotional shield.

At the top of the stairs, Kelly stepped over Fiona's discarded backpack and knocked at her daughter's bedroom door. "Fi? You OK?"

"Yeah."

"You don't sound OK. What's going on?"

"Nothing" came the muffled reply.

Slowly, Kelly opened the door and peered inside. Fiona was lying across her bed, her face buried in her pillow. She must have kicked off her shoes, and her feet hung over the edge. Kelly walked over to the bed and sat down. "Doesn't look like nothing." She reached out and tugged at a piece of Fiona's hair. "Tell me what's going on."

"No."

God grant me the patience, Kelly prayed silently. With everything that was going on, the last thing she needed was her normally even-keeled daughter to have a mental breakdown. Kelly's shoulders were only so broad and so strong.

"Come on, Fiona. Talk to me."

To Kelly's surprise, Fiona pushed herself upright and faced her. She hadn't expected her daughter to give in so easily. Her face was pale and blotchy. Fiona had never been a crier, so that alone alarmed Kelly.

"That's just the problem." The hurt in Fiona's voice pained Kelly. "No one will talk to me!"

Kelly frowned. She knew that she hadn't told Fiona much about the situation with Zach, but there wasn't much to tell. Not yet. And she had arranged for Fiona to have people around her so that she wasn't alone. First Charlotte, and then her mother.

"What do you mean?" Kelly asked. "I'm talking to you, Fiona. I just don't know what to say."

"Not you!" Fiona said. "At school! Everyone just stared at me and whispered behind my back. I could hear them. And even Molly won't return my text messages."

"Maybe you're imagining it."

"No, Mom. I'm *not* imagining it. Jenny avoided me at lunch, and we *always* eat lunch together. And Molly wouldn't even look at me. She's been weird ever since the sleepover anyway, but now? She's, like, angry with me or something."

"I'm sure she's not angry with you," Kelly said, trying to reassure Fiona. She knew that girls could be cruel, but she wasn't prepared for this. Not now. She had too many other things to worry about. Junior high school girl drama wasn't on the list. Still, Kelly also knew that Fiona didn't ask for much, and clearly, she needed her mother at the present moment.

"Nothing happened at the sleepover, right?" She wondered if there had been a little spat. Sometimes when too many girls got together, someone was the odd person out. And with Molly being the newest to the small, little clique, she would most likely have been the one pushed outside of the circle.

But Fiona gave her a puzzled look and groaned. "Seriously?"

"Yes, seriously."

"No, Mom." Fiona rolled her eyes. "Nothing happened at the sleepover," she said, mimicking her mother's tone.

"Everyone got along, right?"

Another eye roll.

"Well, I'm sure it's nothing." But Kelly wasn't certain about that at all.

"She's just acting so weird. And I know it's about Zach."

Kelly bit her tongue. She wanted to tell her daughter that she was being ridiculous. That she was imagining things. That people would not avoid her because her older brother had overdosed. But Kelly knew that would be a lie. People did hurtful things to other people all the time. It didn't matter whether the victim was thirteen years old or thirty-three.

Her heart ached for Fiona. Why did her daughter have to learn such a hurtful lesson about people's willingness to cast judgment on others who were down on their knees? It was a lesson that Kelly had learned only a few years ago during her divorce. Prior to that, she had lived under the illusion that people were innately good. After all, God made man, right?

But she had quickly learned that God may have created man, but the devil fought hard to own their souls.

It was a lesson that Kelly never wanted her daughter to learn.

"Oh Fiona," she sighed, reaching out to brush back a stray strand of hair.

"Everyone knows about Zach." Fiona scowled. "*Everyone.* He just ruins everything."

Kelly placed her hand on Fiona's back and gently rubbed small circles, a gesture that had always given her comfort when she was younger. To Kelly's relief, Fiona didn't tell her to stop. "Nothing is ruined, Fiona," she said softly. But Kelly hadn't thought about the chain reaction of people learning about Zach's overdose. She hadn't considered that her daughter would, once again, become collateral damage.

"It's so embarrassing!" Fiona said, her voice angry. "Why did he have to be my brother?"

"Fiona—"

But Fiona spoke over her. "Why couldn't he just be normal, you know? Like Jenny's brother. He doesn't even beat her up! But no! I had to have the loser drug addict who just makes my life miserable."

"I . . . I'm sure it will blow over, Fiona. These things always do." Even as she said it, she knew she didn't sound convincing. To a thirteen-year-old, drama like this never blew over. At least not fast enough to appease an already-insecure teenager. And the damage could certainly linger far longer than the actual situation.

For Fiona's sake, Kelly hoped not.

"Why'd he have to do this, Mom?" Fiona's scowl disappeared, replaced with something else, a new emotion that Kelly had never seen on her daughter's face: raw anger. "Why? I mean, it's so stupid!" And then the final words that Kelly had suspected were coming. "I hate him."

Just the way that Fiona stressed the words "stupid" and "hate" hurt Kelly's heart. Yes, it was stupid. But how could Kelly explain that to her daughter? People often did stupid things for even stupider reasons. Now, Zach had to suffer the consequences. The problem was explaining why Fiona had to suffer, too.

"Look, I'm wrapping up some stuff downstairs and then heading over to the hospital," Kelly said, hoping that her voice sounded more cheerful than she felt. "Why don't you come with me? We could stop by Friendly's afterward for a quick bite."

Fiona, however, shook her head. "No way. The last person I want to see is Zach."

"Now, now." Kelly gave her a stern look. Whether or not Fiona was suffering, as a mother, Kelly still had to draw the line somewhere. "Let's try to be a little compassionate, OK? He's going to have a rough road ahead of him." She didn't add: *If he comes out of the coma and doesn't have brain damage.*

But Fiona wasn't having any of it.

"What about me?" Fiona's eyes widened. "Everything is always about Zach and what he's going to have to go through. What about me? I mean, first Dad and now Zach. What's next, Mom? They're like energy vampires, just sucking the joy out of everything. I can't stand it anymore."

Energy vampires. Kelly knew the feeling.

"I promise you, Fi, it will get better," she said softly as she wrapped her arm around Fiona's shoulders and held her. "It has to."

For a long while, they sat like that, the two of them holding each other. Words didn't need to be spoken. The silence said it all.

CHAPTER 20

On Friday morning, when Kelly walked into the ICU and approached the nurses' station, one of the nurses looked up. There was an expectant expression on her face, and, when she saw Kelly, she smiled.

"Good news, Ms. Martin," the nurse said. "Zach woke up just an hour ago."

Kelly felt her heart skip a beat. "He did?" Why hadn't anyone called her? "Oh! May I go see him?"

The nurse shook her head. "Not just yet. The doctor's in with him."

"Was he talking? Did he say anything? Is he OK?" The barrage of questions came in rapid fire.

"I wasn't here, Ms. Martin. I'm sorry." The nurse gave her an apologetic shrug. "But he sure seemed alert enough when the doctor arrived."

Thank the good Lord, Kelly thought. *Zach awoke at last!*

While she hadn't doubted the doctor's encouragement that Zach would, indeed, wake up, she had worried that, perhaps just this once, the doctor would be wrong. Oh sure, she knew that doctors tended to be more pessimistic, not wanting to raise anyone's hopes. While his positive outlook for Zach had given her the optimism she had been looking for, she still feared the worst. Ever since Zach had arrived at the hospital, Kelly hadn't been able to shake the idea that he wouldn't wake up. What would she do then? How would she deal with accepting that?

How would she live, knowing that if she had tried just a little harder, he might not have overdosed? As was the case with any mother, worry became a permanent fixture in her life once she had given birth to her first child.

Now, however, Kelly could breathe a sigh of relief. He had awoken, indeed!

As quickly as her elation overtook her, Kelly felt the subsequent wave of panic. Even if he was awake, no one had said whether or not Zach had suffered any brain damage. He could be conscious but without all of his faculties. Maybe he lost his memory or his ability to speak properly. She began to fret, pacing in the hallway as she wrung her hands and worried about the next mountain to climb.

Please God, she prayed. She stopped pacing long enough to close her eyes as she stood outside of Zach's hospital room waiting for the doctor to emerge. *Let Zach be fine. Place your healing hand upon my son and help give him the strength to fight these demons, once and for all.*

Her thoughts were interrupted by the sound of a machine beeping rapidly from the hospital room across the hallway. Several nurses jumped into action, hurrying into the room while someone grabbed a phone and, from the sound of the conversation, paged a doctor. The term "asystole" was used, and, while she wasn't familiar with its meaning, she understood that whoever was in that room was flatlining. Wide-eyed, Kelly watched the medical personnel checking the equipment and lines until someone, mercifully, shut the door.

The noises from the room lingered in the air long after the door closed. Kelly had felt the urgency in the medical team's actions, their focus on the individual tasks at hand. To these doctors and nurses, the patients were not just bodies in bed, but people. And, at the current moment, the person behind that closed door was the most important one on the floor.

Kelly had always given a lot of credit to people who chose a career in medicine. It took a different type of person to devote their life to saving others. Right now, Kelly was having a hard enough time saving just one life: her son's. She couldn't begin to comprehend the stress involved with saving the lives of strangers.

Especially without passing any judgment.

For a moment, Kelly stood there, frozen in place. How would she have reacted to saving Zach, knowing that he was a drug addict? What if Zach had been a drug dealer, ruining other people's lives, too? Did the doctors and nurses ever think about that when they were working on patients in emergency situations?

Kelly shuddered.

The door opened and three people walked out. The energy was gone from their steps, and they wore empty expressions on their faces. No one needed to say the words for Kelly to realize that the patient in room 318 had died. And yet, despite the blank looks, the medical team knew what had to be done and went about their business. Surely they had people to call: the doctors, the morgue, the family. Their work didn't stop just because the patient died.

That could have been Zach, Kelly thought as she watched them disappear into the area where the nurses worked. Immediately, Kelly felt tears well up in her eyes and a burning sensation at the back of her throat. What would she have done then? If Zach had died? How would she have handled losing her child to the dreadful darkness of drug addiction?

She moved a few feet down the hallway and leaned against the wall. She didn't want to remember hearing the beeps and panicked voices from that room. Whoever was lying in that bed, a sheet probably covering their head, had family, and that family would not receive the joyous news that Kelly had been given just moments ago, that Zach had awoken.

"Kelly."

At the sound of her name, she started. "Doctor!" She gave a weak smile and pressed her hand against her chest. "You startled me."

He laughed as he stepped through the doorway from Zach's room. "Sorry about that. You must've been deep in thought." He shut the door behind himself and didn't wait for her to respond. "Probably about the good news. I'm sure you heard that Zach regained consciousness." He paused and leveled his gaze at her, an open expression on his face. "I'm happy to report that he appears to be fine."

"Oh!" Kelly exhaled and, immediately, her chest felt lighter. Had she been holding her breath, waiting to hear those very words? "Thank God!"

"He's talking, aware of his surroundings, and, overall, in great shape."

She sensed a "but" lingering behind the doctor's words. "And?"

"Well." He paused and glanced around the hallway. No one was around, but he moved closer to her. "I'm not exactly convinced that the overdose wasn't planned, Ms. Martin."

It took a moment for his comment to sink in. Suddenly, her knees felt weak, and she was glad that the wall stopped them from buckling. "You mean he overdosed on purpose?" Even as she spoke, she couldn't believe her own words. "I . . . I don't find that likely. Not Zach."

And then she stopped short, her next comment—*Zach would never overdose on purpose*—on the tip of her tongue before she shoved it far, far away. How many mornings had she worried that Zach might actually do just that? How many mornings had she opened his bedroom door, fearful that she might find him hanging from the ceiling fan? She had worried about Zach attempting suicide, but she had suspected the wrong method.

Her shoulders sagged as if the weight of the realization were upon them. "Oh. I . . . I see."

The doctor reached out and touched her shoulder, a gesture of support that she found strangely comforting. "Kelly, hang in there. I've requested that one of our psychologists evaluate Zach. He'll undergo detoxification and then be put into a therapeutic environment under twenty-four–seven observation. Based on the results from the psychological analysis, we can take it from there."

"What does that mean?" she asked. "Take *what* from there?"

The doctor's expression was devoid of any emotion. Kelly wondered how many times he'd had to deal with panic-stricken parents, explaining the recovery process in layman's terms. Probably dozens if not hundreds. For the doctor, Zach was just another patient in a long line of troubled, at-risk teens. For Kelly, he was the only one that mattered.

"His treatment. As a minor, he'll be referred either to a drug rehabilitation center or, more likely, a teenage psychiatric program. Inpatient, of course."

"Oh. Yes. Of course." The words slipped out but Kelly felt dazed and confused, her mind wandering aimlessly as she listened to the doctor. She wondered how Todd would try to sabotage this new recommendation.

First, he'd fight the inpatient part; such was his determination to *not* send his son away. Heck, he had fought her on sending Zach to a one-week sleepaway camp when their son was ten years old! And the only reason she'd been able to convince Todd to send Zach to that one inpatient rehabilitation was because Zach had played hooky from school and broken into Todd's house, spending the day drinking all the gin in the liquor cabinet. A police officer had investigated when he saw the front door open and found Zach passed out on the kitchen table.

Even Todd couldn't argue with the long arm of Johnny Law.

Next, Todd would fight any diagnosis that included psychotherapy. *His* son wasn't crazy; *that* specialty was reserved for Kelly. No, Todd would never support Zach going into a psych program for fear that his son would be labeled, much the same way that Todd labeled Kelly.

Finally, there was the money issue. Oh, how Todd fought paying for anything extra. He already *gave* her child support—$271 a week, to be exact. When Fiona wanted to take dance lessons, Todd refused to pay. When both kids wanted cell phones, Todd cried poor. And yet, he'd always appear at Fiona's dance recitals or call the kids on their cell phones. The inequitable distribution of his financial contribution, masked under the guise of child support, disgusted Kelly.

Kelly sighed. Yes, she'd have to fight him tooth and nail on all of these issues. But the time for being walked over, like a ratty old doormat, had ended. Once again, she needed to turn on her autopilot and go through the motions, one step at a time, in order to save her son.

The doctor reached into a folder that he carried. "Here's a list of facilities that you might want to start contacting," he said as he handed a white sheet of paper to her. Kelly scanned the list of names, all bubbly and bright as if they *weren't* the last place on earth most people would want to visit: Sunrise House, Rosewood Wellness Center, Diamond Detox, Ocean Breeze Manor.

She folded the paper and put it in her purse. "Thank you."

The doctor's eyes fell to his cell phone. "If you'll excuse me," he said and then quickly walked away.

Kelly watched him for a minute, wondering what he really thought of patients like Zach. Surely he must've grown immune to the senseless way so many people threw away their lives, all because of drugs. But Zach wasn't just another drug-addicted person. He was her son.

She turned toward the door of Zach's hospital room and took a deep breath before she opened it and entered.

"Hey you." She smiled at him, hoping that her voice didn't divulge how nervous she felt. Crossing the room, she started to reach for him. All she wanted was to touch his arm, a reassuring gesture, but he turned his face toward the wall. "Zach?"

"Leave me alone."

She frowned. For a long moment, she stood there, frozen in place, as she tried to comprehend how he could just tune her out. Didn't he know how worried she had been? Didn't he care that she hadn't slept in days? His rejection wounded her deeply.

Despite his rebuff, Kelly finally moved over to the chair by the window. She set her purse on the floor and sat. He continued staring at the wall, the back of his head turned toward her. The silence intensified to the point that it was deafening. But Kelly refused to break it. If he didn't want to talk, that was fine by her. Just being able to sit there and watch the gentle rising and falling of his chest as he breathed was enough. And one day, maybe—just maybe—he'd remember that she had sat there with him, refusing to honor his request and staying by his side.

CHAPTER 21

Later in the afternoon, Kelly reluctantly left Zach's side. He hadn't spoken to her at all, and Kelly had hoped he might say something—anything!—to her before she had to leave. She wanted to be home when Fiona returned from school. It was the one degree of normalcy that she could provide for her daughter. Besides, with the new information from the doctor, Kelly needed to make some phone calls. Long ago, she had discovered that information was the best weapon against Todd's passive-aggressive behavior toward Zach's rehabilitation.

She was seated at the kitchen table, her laptop, a pad of paper, and her cell phone spread out, her tools of choice, as she researched the list of facilities that the doctor had given to her as well as additional options for psychiatric care that might suit Zach's needs. But every single website for dual-diagnosis care clearly stated it was for adults only.

"Kell? You home?"

Kelly didn't look up. "In the kitchen, Charlotte."

Charlotte entered the room, and, after placing her phone on the table, she sat down across from Kelly. "I saw your car and thought I'd stop in. See how you're doing."

Kelly sighed and shut the top of the laptop. "I'm hanging in there. Did you see my text?"

Charlotte nodded. "I sure did. Thought I replied, too." Quickly, she waved her hand. "Sorry. I know you've more important things on your mind than replying to every text." And then she smiled. "That's great news, though. I bet you're over the moon with relief."

"I am." But Kelly didn't feel over the moon with anything. "The problem is that the doctor thinks Zach did it on purpose."

Kelly thought from Charlotte's reaction that her friend hadn't seen that one coming. Charlotte leaned forward. "What do you mean that he did it on purpose?"

Kelly took a deep breath, then simply said, "He *wanted* to overdose."

"Oh sweet Lord!" Charlotte let her body flop backward into the chair. She stared at Kelly, her eyes wide and her mouth opened ever so slightly. "I'm so sorry, Kelly. That's . . . that's just terrible."

"That's not the worst of it, unfortunately. The doctor says Zach needs a dual-diagnosis facility or something like that. A place that handles addiction and psychiatric problems," Kelly explained, gesturing toward the pad of paper covered with her handwriting. Notes. From all of the different places she had called.

"Because . . . ?"

Kelly sighed and rested her cheek against the palm of her hand, her elbow on the table and her eyes staring at the laptop. "Either the addiction is feeding the depression or the depression is feeding the addiction. He needs both disorders treated, not just addiction."

Charlotte narrowed her eyes, clearly not understanding why this was a problem. "So find a facility, then."

She made it sound so simple. But Kelly knew otherwise. "There aren't any. Everything is for adults. I can't find any inpatient facilities for teenagers. It's like no one wants to touch them."

"That's ridiculous."

Kelly nodded. "I agree. This has been the problem all along. When Zach first started showing signs of depression, no one would see him without us paying a fifteen-hundred-dollar fee, and that was only for the evaluation, not even the care! Insurance paid for nothing."

Charlotte responded by shaking her head.

"I've called about six of these facilities today, but not one of them will take him, either because he's possibly suicidal or because he is dual diagnosis. The one place that *would've* taken him, right here in New Jersey, says they won't because he's demonstrated violent behavior." *That* phone call had been a terrible blow for Kelly. It was a state-funded inpatient rehabilitation center that the doctor had suggested she should call, but they didn't take teenagers like Zach, the ones who punched holes in the walls or shoved their mothers. Why had she told them the truth? She'd know better, next time.

"How, exactly, do these people expect the kids to get better?"

That was what Kelly wanted to know. If no one would treat them, would these afflicted teenagers have any future? "I just don't know," Kelly said at last. She felt powerless. Was it possible for her to help Zach if no one would help *her*?

"Have you called the insurance company directly?"

And that was the crux of the problem. "They won't speak to me."

"What do you mean, they won't speak to you?"

"I'm not on the policy."

"Oh for crying out loud!" Charlotte made a face, her expression hard and fierce. "So you can't even talk to them about your son's care?"

"Welcome to the world of raising a child after a divorce."

"That's insane, Kelly. You can't count on Todd for this. You *need* to be in charge."

Kelly knew that Charlotte spoke the truth. She hadn't thought that part through when she divorced Todd. She had been so anxious to just get away from him that she practically agreed to anything. In hindsight, Kelly knew that her lawyer did a grave disservice by not advising her to fight for full custody. With Todd's own addiction issues, Kelly could have won. But that would have cost money. A lot of money. And the lawyer knew that money was the one thing Kelly *didn't* have—and Todd was willing to spend *his* money to ensure she didn't get any of his.

Money. The root of all evil and the number one reason that Kelly hadn't received the best counsel. No, life and fair didn't go together at all.

The front door opened. Both Charlotte and Kelly looked down the hallway in time to see Fiona drop her backpack on the floor and trudge into the kitchen. She wore a long face and her shoulders sagged.

"What's up, kiddo?"

Fiona gave her a look as she slid into an empty chair. "Molly still won't talk to me, Mom," Fiona said. "I just don't understand it."

"Do you want me to call her mother?"

"No!" It came out quick and forceful.

"Molly Weaver?" Charlotte asked, curiosity obviously getting the best of her.

"Yeah." Fiona sounded miserable.

Kelly got up, hurried over to the refrigerator, and poured some orange juice into a glass. She walked back to the table and set it next to Fiona.

Kelly watched as Fiona downed it in three long, healthy gulps. "I wonder what's bothering Molly."

Charlotte rolled her eyes. "If she's like her mother, it could be anything."

Kelly suppressed a laugh and shot Charlotte a teasing, but cautionary, look.

"The only thing is that she's not talking to anyone," Fiona said, pushing the empty glass away from her so that she could lean her elbows on the table. "And she went to the nurse twice complaining of headaches. Jenny told me so."

That sounded hopeful. *At least Jenny was talking to her,* Kelly thought.

"Well, ladies," Charlotte said as she stood up. "I hate to leave this joyous party, but I have to show a property in thirty minutes." She reached for her smartphone and checked the home screen before putting it into the pocket of her open jacket. "Kelly, if you need anything, let me know. If you need to go to the hospital later, I could pick up the kiddo and take her to the Famished Frog or something." She winked at Fiona as if conspiring with her. "I don't do Friendly's, though."

"Me, neither!" Fiona said. Lighting up, she turned toward Kelly. "Oh please, Mom!"

For a split second, Kelly almost declined. Fiona hadn't visited her brother at the hospital yet. And now that Zach was being moved onto the psychiatric floor, Fiona could. But before Kelly opened her mouth to say *Thanks but not tonight,* she realized that forcing Fiona to visit Zach helped no one—not Fiona and certainly not Zach.

One look at her daughter's anxious eyes and Kelly understood that what Fiona needed was the ear of a sympathetic adult, someone just like Charlotte who would take her out and talk to her. *No,* Kelly corrected herself. *Listen* to her. An empathetic ear would do far more for Fiona than being dragged to the hospital on a Friday night.

"If you're sure . . . ," Kelly began slowly. She hated to infringe on Charlotte's Friday evening. "I mean, don't you have any plans?"

Giving a little laugh, Charlotte nodded. "I sure do." Once again, she winked at Fiona. "Now, anyway."

Kelly watched as Fiona beamed, a genuine look of happiness that warmed her mother's heart, while Charlotte told her to be ready by six thirty. The one thing that her daughter needed, and her best friend had realized it. Not Jackie, not her mother. But Charlotte.

While people couldn't pick their family, Kelly prayed a silent thank-you to God that she *was* able to pick her friends. She had chosen a good one when she had selected Charlotte.

CHAPTER 22

On Saturday morning, from the moment she woke up, Kelly's cell phone didn't stop ringing and buzzing. Apparently the word had spread, and suddenly people felt it was socially acceptable to reach out to her. Or, perhaps, they just wanted the inside story to repeat at their next gathering.

After showering and getting dressed, Kelly headed for the kitchen. Coffee. She definitely needed coffee. And she'd have to drink it black because she hadn't gone to the grocery store all week.

Most people who knew her well would've texted her. Kelly preferred avoiding the phone. It took too long and, on regular days when her life wasn't in crisis overload, she focused on working, her attention riveted to her computer screen. For Kelly, talking on the phone was reserved for her family, Charlotte (who knew to keep it short and sweet), and emergencies. Anyone else who called clearly didn't know her very well at all.

She began to pour water into the coffeepot when her phone buzzed again. Ignoring the noise, Kelly reached out and turned her phone upside down. She could respond to emails and texts as well as listen to voice messages later.

The previous evening, she had finally left the hospital at nine o'clock. Zach's mood hadn't improved, especially when his precious father hadn't shown up. Zach still refused to talk to her. Kelly felt conflicting emotions—hurt and angry—and, knowing that neither one was healthy for her or Zach, she finally leaned over, kissed him good night, and left.

When she had returned home, Fiona and Charlotte were sitting on the sofa, watching a movie. For a long moment, Kelly had stood in the doorway, quietly watching them. Everything looked so normal. Anyone else who witnessed the tranquil moment would never have suspected the behind-the-scenes drama from the past week.

Kelly's heart had felt nothing but enormous love for her daughter and her friend.

When the coffee finished brewing, Kelly poured herself a cup and stirred in a generous amount of sugar to hopefully kill the bitter taste that milk normally hid so well. Only then did she reach for her phone.

Nine texts, two voice mails, and three emails.

It was better than she had expected.

Quickly, she scanned the text messages first. Her brother, her cousin, three women from church, a few colleagues, and Debbie.

Kelly groaned when she saw the message from Debbie.

> I'm dropping off a lasagna for you and Fiona. If you need anything or I can help in any way, just ask.

Why did people always think food was the magic solution to everything bad? As if food would make the pain go away.

What *would* make the pain go away was if Molly would talk to Fiona or, even better, if Debbie made good on her empty promises to have Fiona over at *her* house. Instead, she wanted to stop by to drop off food.

Immediately, Kelly sighed and silently apologized. She should be grateful that Debbie was dropping off something. Even if Kelly hated lasagna—only casseroles were worse in her book—the truth was that she had to feed Fiona, if not tonight then tomorrow night.

And maybe, just maybe, Debbie was sincere and not just trying to find out what had happened so that she could spread the gossip around town. Maybe Debbie wasn't trying to weasel her way into the situation to make herself look more interesting. Or important.

No. Kelly chastised herself for feeling so cynical. She needed to presume that Debbie was, indeed, sincere and not trying to capitalize socially on Zach's overdose.

"Fiona?" Kelly called up the staircase. "You awake?"

The sound of her daughter mumbling from behind her closed bedroom door affirmed that she was, indeed, awake.

"I'm heading to the hospital. They're moving Zach to another room sometime today and I want to be there." Kelly paused, waiting for some acknowledgment, but she heard nothing. "Fiona?"

"OK! I heard you!" came the snappy reply.

"Call Grandma if you need anything, OK?" Pause. "OK?"

"Yes!"

The hospital was only a short drive from her house, but Kelly kept glancing at the clock on her dashboard. She hoped that she hadn't missed Zach being moved to the new children's psychiatric floor. She wanted to be there with him, even if he wasn't too thrilled with her presence.

She couldn't understand why he harbored such resentment toward her. She had always been there for him, always supported him. While it was true that she'd been the more consistent of the disciplinarians—perhaps the only disciplinarian—she also knew that children needed it. It was the only way that they could learn self-control and, later, self-regulation, two things that were core to their assimilation into society as grown-ups.

Todd, however, had fought her on disciplining the children.

Or, rather, Zach.

Which had made Todd the hero and Kelly the villain.

Kelly shook her head, disgusted that everything was increasingly becoming clear. Certainly Zach's affinity for his father was what drove his behavior. He emulated his father's reliance on drugs. Unfortunately, Zach had taken it a step further; using as a coping mechanism had turned into addiction that completely controlled him. If nothing else could be said about Todd, at least he was a somewhat functional alcoholic, holding down a job without letting gin ruin *that* aspect of his life.

After parking her car, Kelly hurried across the road and dashed up the front steps into the hospital. She checked at the front desk to learn whether or not Zach had been moved from the ICU yet.

He hadn't.

Kelly made her way through the first part of the old main building to another area on the first floor, where she waited to be buzzed inside the ICU.

"Good morning, Ms. Martin," a nurse greeted her cheerfully.

"Good morning. How's Zach today?" she asked as she paused near the nurses' station.

"He's awake."

Two words. No emotion. Clearly, he was still sullen and angry. The doctor had explained that Zach would go through a period of hostile reactions to everyone and everything. After all, he was forced to quit cigarettes, drugs, and alcohol cold turkey. Withdrawal was never fun, but to quit all three at once was definitely enough to make him beyond miserable to be around.

It was, as the doctor said, to be expected.

"Any idea when he's moving to the psychiatric floor?" Kelly asked. She knew that she needed to return home for at least part of the day. Just because Zach was in the hospital didn't mean that she needed to stop mothering Fiona. Plus, she needed to run to the grocery store and catch up on her emails. But she wanted to be there when Zach was transferred.

"As soon as a bed is available," the nurse said in that typical noncommittal way that medical professionals used. But she gave Kelly a smile, and that helped warm her evasive words. "We'll let you know."

Walking into Zach's room, Kelly was immediately struck by how oppressive the air felt. When he had been in the coma, the room had felt sterile and bright. Now, however, with Zach awake, the lights were dimmed and the television was on, without sound for some reason, and there was something discomforting about the mood in the room.

She set down her bag on the counter near the sink, the noise causing Zach to roll his head on the pillow to look at her.

"How you feeling?" she asked.

The corner of Zach's mouth twitched, conveying his disappointment at her return. *Perhaps,* she thought, *he was expecting Todd?*

She moved over to the side of the bed and leaned over to brush back his hair. "What do you think about a shower, Zach?" Somehow she summoned a smile that she plastered on her face. "I bet the nurses would let you take one, and, to be honest, it would make you feel better."

She had almost said that he needed it but thought better of it. She didn't want to say anything that could be misconstrued as putting him down. He had a big enough battle ahead of him; she didn't need to add to his burdens.

"Where's Dad?"

Good question, Kelly thought. She wondered if Zach ever asked for her. "I'm not certain. He'll be here, though. I'm sure."

"When can I go home?"

If Kelly had her way, he wouldn't come home until he had been clean and sober for long enough that she didn't have to live in fear of a relapse. She didn't want to be afraid of what he might do. In a way, she hoped that this overdose might prove to be a blessing in disguise, an answer to her prayers.

"I don't know," she answered at last. "Let's just concentrate on getting you better, OK?"

He made a noise, scoffing at her response. And then he turned his head to stare at the television, his eyes watching but clearly not seeing or caring about the program.

His indifference to her presence hurt. For a moment, Kelly contemplated walking out of the room. *It would be so easy,* she thought, *to just leave and concentrate on my own things: Fiona, work, grocery shopping, chores. What did I do to deserve this type of treatment from my own son?*

"You know," she said slowly, trying to keep her tone even and not too critical, "I may not have been a perfect mother, Zach, but I *am* your mother." She paused, hoping that he might respond. When he didn't, she pressed her lips together, her hurt increasing. "And I love you, Zach. I don't know what is at the root of all of this, but I love you and I want you better."

"I'm better," he mumbled half-heartedly. "I'm still here, aren't I?"

"And I want you to *stay* here, Zach."

"Why?" He rolled his head and looked at her, his eyes blank and devoid of emotion. "What's the point?"

Kelly reached out and laid her hand on his arm. She half expected him to pull away, but he didn't. "Life, Zach. Life is worth living to the fullest. And whatever you're doing, this whole drug business, that's not living. It's dying. And whatever you think, it's not your time to leave this life." She paused. "You need to learn from all of this, change the trajectory of your future. That's what all of these people are here for, to help you do that." She gave him a soft smile. "And you can have joy again, Zach. Real, true joy. That's the life that God wants for you, and your mother, too."

For a moment, she thought he might say something—anything!—to acknowledge her impromptu speech. Maybe he might even agree with her, profess that he would change his life, give up drugs, and start living once again.

His eyes met hers, and she saw him swallow. She waited, hoping that he might open up to her, at last, about the reasons behind his choice to live in the dark shadows of evil rather than embrace the joys of life.

But Zach merely stared at her. Silence. He blinked once and then, to her surprise, he shut his eyes. His chest rose and fell, slowing down until she realized that he had fallen asleep, leaving her seated by his side, her hand still upon his arm, and a sad quiet filling the room.

CHAPTER 23

"Kelly? Kelly Martin?"

It was late afternoon. Zach was sleeping. He still hadn't been transferred from the ICU, a fact that frustrated Kelly. Getting Zach out of that terrible unit—intensive care—felt like the first step toward true recovery. But the hospital moved at its own pace, not Kelly's.

Just a few minutes earlier, Kelly had gone out to the main waiting room, where she could stretch her legs and check her emails. The wireless reception was better there. Plus, she needed to take a break from sitting by Zach's side. He still wasn't talking to her and, with him sleeping, she needed to escape, even if only for a few minutes.

She was surprised to hear someone call out her name. Looking up from her phone, Kelly saw a middle-aged woman with short, thinning brown hair and big gray eyes staring at her from behind wire-rimmed glasses. "Yes?"

The woman looked relieved, as if she had feared she had the wrong person, and approached her. "I was so sorry to hear about Zach. I wanted to see him, but I understand that, because it's the ICU, only immediate family can visit."

Kelly frowned, trying to place the woman's face. Did she know her? She didn't look familiar. *Perhaps she's one of his teachers,* she thought, and then immediately discarded that idea. Would a teacher bother visiting a student in the hospital? Especially a student who rarely attended class? If so, Kelly was touched by such a small act of support.

"I'm sorry," Kelly said in a kind voice. "You are . . . ?"

The woman grimaced, the color rushing to her cheeks as if she was embarrassed that Kelly didn't know who she was. "Oh of course. We haven't met, have we?" A nervous laugh escaped her parched lips, the beige lipstick she wore accentuating how dry they looked. "I'm Joan. Joan Stevens." The woman extended her hand to shake Kelly's.

But Kelly hesitated. She still didn't recognize the woman. "And you know my son how, exactly?"

"Zach?" The expression on Joan's face softened. This woman sounded as though she knew Zach rather well. And that surprised her, especially when Joan said, "Oh, he's such a dear. Always willing to help me out whenever he's over."

Kelly couldn't help but give her a puzzled look. What was she talking about? Zach hardly ever went anywhere, at least not when he was staying with Kelly. "Over where?"

"Our house." Joan paused and then gave Kelly a sideways glance. "You do know he spends lots of time at our house, don't you?"

"I do now." It came out much drier than Kelly intended. However, she couldn't help but feel an increasing sense of foreboding that, whoever this woman was, she didn't bring good news. "Although I'm surprised, really. He rarely goes out."

"Um." Joan nodded. "I wondered about that. Seems he might have been sneaking over under his father's watch, I suppose."

But Zach hardly ever went to his father's. In fact, his regular weekend visits were sporadic at best. A little red flag went up in the back of her mind, causing Kelly to realize how wide the chasm between her and Zach had grown. She didn't know her son at all.

"Well, I'm sorry to hear about what's happened," Joan said softly. "He's been such a great influence on my son, Michael."

Suddenly, the pieces came together. It was as if a kaleidoscope of splintered colors suddenly coalesced and formed a complete image, instead of variegated slivers of brightness. Kelly caught her breath. "Michael as in Michael Stevens?" She heard the terseness of her voice, a level of disdain that she almost felt ashamed of, given that Michael was still a minor. And then she remembered where she was: in the ICU waiting room, her son recovering from a drug-induced coma that had, undoubtedly, been supplied to him by the son of the woman standing before her. Kelly felt as if she floated overhead, a surreal sensation, watching herself as she stiffened and shifted her weight away from the woman.

"He wanted to come see Zach, too," Joan continued, oblivious to Kelly's inner turmoil, "but I told him that was probably not a good idea."

Kelly's heart raced. She felt the walls closing in on her. Her vision was changing, too. At the corners of her eyes, darkness slowly shielded everything from view, everything except the woman, Joan Stevens, who stood before her with a sorrowful expression on her face, a face that Kelly desperately wanted to smack.

"So," Joan said, "how *is* Zach doing?"

Kelly pressed her lips together and stared intently at Joan. "I'm afraid that this just isn't a good time, Joan," she managed to say with as much forced civility as she could muster. She wanted to yell. Wanted to shake this clueless mother. But if she lost her self-control now, she wasn't certain whether or not she would ever regain it. Especially with this woman. No, Kelly's current state of mind made this a bad time to address the evils that lurked in Joan Stevens's house. But oh how Kelly wanted to speak her mind.

"Is there anything I can do?"

A dozen responses raced through Kelly's consciousness. She remained speechless and simply stared at the stranger. It suddenly dawned on Kelly that Joan was either extremely bold or extraordinarily ignorant. If she was bold, Kelly had nothing to say to her. If she was ignorant, who was Kelly to educate her? Either way, Kelly found that words escaped her. And yet, she had to say something. Anything.

Perhaps it was the awkward silence that made Joan shift her weight and take a step toward the door. "Well, then, I . . . uh . . . I guess I'll just go," she said, her voice wavering under the intensity of Kelly's stare. "Unless you can think of anything you need . . ."

Suddenly, the fortress walls protecting Kelly's words crumbled. Her son, after all, was lying in a hospital bed in the intensive care unit because of this woman's son. As the barriers collapsed, Kelly rushed forward. "Wait!" She took hold of Joan's arm. "There is something you could do."

Joan's eyes widened. "Oh?"

"Answer me this one question," Kelly heard herself say, her voice sounding like someone else was speaking. "How can you live with yourself knowing that your son deals drugs and destroys lives?"

The color drained from Joan's cheeks, and she backed away from Kelly. But Kelly maintained her grip. "Let go of my arm," Joan hissed, jerking free from Kelly's hold.

"You know, don't you?" Kelly insisted, moving forward. "You know what your son does. If you don't, you should. Otherwise, one day this scene will repeat itself." Kelly gestured wildly around the waiting room. "You'll be standing here, flipping through year-old magazines, unable to read one word because you'll be frantic with worry, powerless to do anything but pray that *your* son hasn't suffered any brain damage after overdosing."

In a clipped tone, Joan snapped, "I have no idea what you're talking about." Just the way her eyes narrowed and her lips pursed told a different story.

And then Kelly remembered what Thomas had said about the school trying to expel Michael Stevens and his mother rushing to defend him, claiming that it was his right to attend public school. For the briefest of moments, Kelly wanted to fling that juicy tidbit of information at Joan, to let the woman know that she was well aware of Joan's lie. But she didn't. She had promised Thomas that she'd never share that confidential information, although she'd never envisioned actually meeting Joan Stevens.

In truth, Kelly realized that it didn't matter. Joan was either lying outright or in complete denial. Maybe a little bit of both.

"If you don't mind," Kelly said in a strained voice, "I'm going to ask you to leave. Your company is not wanted here."

"I can see that."

The hostility in the woman's voice, as if Kelly had truly offended her, infuriated Kelly. Somehow, however, she managed to restrain herself. She watched as the woman hurried out of the waiting room. Only when Kelly was certain that Joan had gone did she allow herself to collapse into a chair. She covered her face with her trembling hands and cried, a tidal wave of emotion that had been pent up inside for God knows how long suddenly streaming down her cheeks.

CHAPTER 24

"I can't believe you're making me go!"

Kelly stood at the bottom of the stairs, her hand on the banister as she stared at her daughter, who loomed over her in the stairwell. "Please, Fiona."

"My brother just overdosed and you want me to go to a stupid birthday party?" she practically screamed at her mother. "Are you kidding me?"

Covering her eyes with one hand, Kelly took a deep, calming breath. Only it didn't calm her. How could she hold herself together when everything else was falling apart around her?

"Fiona, please."

"Please what, Mom?"

She wasn't certain if she had reached the threshold of her stress limitations, or if it was Fiona's tone, but something pushed Kelly over the edge of the cliff. For a moment, she felt that same sense of tunnel vision that she had felt earlier when Joan Stevens had so casually popped into the hospital's waiting room as if she were an old family friend. "Stop it!" Kelly screamed, her voice far too shrill and loud. "Just stop it! For once, Fiona, stop fighting me. You *are* going to your aunt's house and you *are* going to attend this stupid birthday party if I have to drag you there myself!"

The color drained from Fiona's face.

Kelly grimaced, her jaw hurting from the pressure of clenching her teeth. She felt the tiny nerves in her arms twitching, a wild source of energy pulsating throughout her body and seeming to centralize in her shoulders. "I am sick . . . and tired . . . ," Kelly began, enunciating each set of words. ". . . Of being the punching bag . . . for everyone . . . in this family!"

"Mom . . ."

Kelly held up her hand. "Stop! Don't say a word, Fiona. Just go and get ready," she snapped, her eyes darting to the grandfather clock in the downstairs hallway. She needed to get back to the hospital. She had left earlier when Todd arrived. Just being in the same room with him was too much for her nerves at the present moment. But it was almost six. Cocktail hour. Surely he would have left the hospital already, especially since it was Saturday night. The bar beckoned.

"We're leaving in five minutes," Kelly said sharply before she walked away.

Retreating to the kitchen, her safe haven, Kelly hurried to the back door and let out the dogs. The poor things had been locked inside for the better part of two days. Normally, she could let them out throughout the day when she worked from home. She hadn't even reprimanded them for the accidents that stained the family-room carpet. They were, after all, collateral damage from Zach's overdose, just like Fiona was.

Immediately, Kelly felt horrible. That's exactly what Fiona was: collateral damage. She didn't want to go to her cousin's birthday party, and, in all honesty, Kelly didn't blame her. But Kelly also didn't want to leave Fiona home alone. Not on a Saturday night.

Stop it, she yelled silently to herself. *Stop putting other people first!*

She wanted to apologize to Fiona. She wanted to give in. But, for once, Kelly knew that she needed to stand by her decision. Just. This. Time. It wasn't any good for Fiona to sit at home alone, undoubtedly on Facebook or Instagram, apparently still experiencing a social blackout from her friends. *That* would only depress Fiona even more. No. Taking

Fiona to Heather's, no matter how unpleasant it might be for Fiona, was definitely better for Kelly. And that, unfortunately, was more important at the present moment. A little socialization would be good for her daughter.

Ten minutes later, the headlights from her Camry lit up the front of Jackie's custom-built colonial in Mendham.

"Please, Mom," Fiona whispered, her voice full of pleading. "Don't make me do this."

Kelly shut off the engine and opened the car door. "Grab the present, please."

"Mom . . ."

Kelly swung her legs out. "Look, Fiona, your grandmother will bring you home early. You don't have to stay long, but I promised your aunt, and Heather *is* your cousin, after all. Sometimes, when it comes to family, you just have to make an effort, Fi, even if it means doing things you don't really want to do."

Silently, Fiona got out of the car, carrying a pink gift bag that Kelly had somehow managed to fill with little presents for the newly turned sixteen-year-old: makeup, fun socks, some candy, and, of course, the obligatory gift card so that Heather could buy exactly what she wanted. It was the best Kelly could do under the circumstances.

Fiona followed Kelly up the steps to the enormous front porch, which Jackie had decorated with hay bales and cornstalks, orange and white balloons, and several pumpkins. Kelly felt a twinge of envy. She wondered what it would be like to have not just the money but the time to decorate for each season. What it would be like to have someone take care of her, rather than being the one who took care of everyone else.

"Hello?" Kelly called out as she opened the front door. "Jackie?"

"In the kitchen."

Kelly headed through the two-story foyer, stepping around the circular marble-topped table that held the tall vase of fresh flowers—orange and white roses, of course—and made her way toward the kitchen at the back of the house.

It wasn't so much a kitchen as a huge gathering room. Everything had been customized to Jackie's specifications: tumbled marble floors, white cabinets, granite countertops, and a professional stove that would make any five-star restaurant's chef green with envy. The ironic thing, though, was that Jackie never cooked. While she had all the trappings of a culinary savant, in reality she always catered her parties or ordered in when people came over. Even when she hosted holiday meals—which was every gathering, since Kelly's house was too small to accommodate the entire family—Jackie avoided cooking in her own kitchen.

Music played from the hidden speakers in the ceiling, and Kelly noticed the girls sitting on the leather sectional, all peering over Heather's shoulders at whatever was on her cell phone.

Heather looked up and glanced from Fiona to Kelly. "Hey, Aunt Kelly." She stood up and skipped over to give Kelly a hug.

"Happy birthday, Heather."

Fiona mumbled something under her breath that sounded like a similar greeting.

"Thanks!" She gave Kelly a big grin. "Can you believe I'm getting my permit next week?"

"I'm getting off the roads!" Kelly teased. In truth, she had forgotten that sixteen was the age for driving. Fiona would only turn fourteen in January, and Zach hadn't even bothered getting his permit or license, so she hadn't experienced the whole teenage driving nightmare yet. "How's your mother taking that?"

Heather shrugged. "OK, I guess."

Kelly glanced at Fiona and then back at Heather. They were as different as apples and a puddle of mud, Fiona being the mud puddle at the present moment. Heather wore her dark-brown hair short and stylish while Fiona was more into the messy-bun look. And Heather always dressed as if she were about to go to the country club: clean, pressed, and presentable. Despite being a teenager, she never wore jeans or a sweatshirt like Fiona was wearing. Heather was certainly being groomed to live in Jackie's image: a good education, a good husband, and a good life.

Kelly wondered what type of life she was grooming Fiona to live.

"Hey you!"

Kelly looked up in time to see Jackie walk around the corner from the back hallway. There was a second kitchen back there, one that Jackie "used" when she had company so that the main kitchen didn't get cluttered with dirty plates and glasses.

They gave each other the obligatory air kiss.

"Hi there, Fiona," Jackie said, a strange tone to her voice. "Did Heather introduce you to her friends?"

Kelly wanted to point out that Heather hadn't even greeted Fiona, but she didn't want to make waves. Not today. Usually not ever.

She waited until Fiona, with a big sigh, followed Heather over to the sofa. "Mom's going to bring her home for me," Kelly said, although she suspected that Jackie already knew that. Her eyes scanned the wall, looking for a clock. The only one she saw was the digital clock over the oven. "I really have to get going. I'm sorry to just drop off Fiona and leave but . . ."

"No worries," Jackie said. "Reba and Tonya are coming over soon, too. You know, to keep me company."

Kelly nodded and started for the door, eager to get back to the hospital and Zach. "OK, great. Have fun and thanks again for inviting Fiona."

Jackie waved her hand dismissively. "That's what family is for, right? To be there for each other?"

And yet, as Kelly shut the front door behind herself, she realized that Jackie hadn't invited *her* to stay for appetizers or to socialize. Nor had she even inquired about Zach. Again. In Jackie's world, family was family only when it was convenient for her. That much her sister had made perfectly clear, even without having said a word. In fact, it was her silence about the most important things that spoke the loudest.

CHAPTER 25

Unlike the intensive care unit, the brand-new children's psychiatric floor had windows that overlooked the abundant trees that bordered the east side of Morristown. It had only opened a few months earlier and, to Kelly's dismay, every room was occupied. Prior to that, minors were sent to other hospitals for psychiatric issues. Kelly wasn't certain whether she was grateful that the Morristown hospital had dedicated a new area to treating minors in emergency psychiatric situations or whether it depressed her.

Were there so many children battling these demons that they needed their own floor?

Upon getting buzzed into the secured area, Kelly was greeted by the nurses as if they had already met her before. Their warm words of encouragement helped bolster Kelly's spirits as she checked in, leaving her personal belongings with security before getting patted down by a guard.

Clearly, safety precautions were taken seriously on the psychiatric floor.

Kelly walked down the hallway, escorted by a nurse, cringing as she heard a young girl screaming from behind a closed door. The nurse never skipped a beat, apparently already immune to the ranting and raving of young people battling mental illness.

"Here you are," the nurse said as she knocked on the door but immediately opened it. "Zach? Your mother's here." The nurse's voice sounded just as sunny and bright as the room.

Kelly frowned, eyeing the windows that overlooked the east section of town. She worried that the morning sun would beat through the panes and heat up the room too much.

But it was evening now, and the room felt cool enough.

"How're you feeling?" she asked Zach as she adjusted the blinds.

"Where's Dad?"

She fought the urge to roll her eyes. Why did he always ask for Todd? Did Zach think his father could save him this time? Sweep him away from the hospital and return him to home, where attending an outpatient rehabilitation program would temporarily solve all of his problems? Todd's Band-Aid fixes to problems might have panned out in the past, but Kelly suspected she had enough ammunition with the doctors' involvement that it wouldn't happen this time.

"I'm sure he'll be here soon." The moment she said it, she remembered that it was Saturday night. In all likelihood, Todd would be at the local bar, drowning his sorrows over a gin and tonic. She wondered if Zach realized that. "Was he here earlier?"

"Yeah. He said he'd be back later."

She made a noise, a hmm sound, and lowered the final shade.

"What's that supposed to mean?"

Kelly ignored his question; it wasn't worth arguing with Zach. "It's a nice room, don't you think?"

"A floor full of crazy people."

"Don't say that," she chastised gently. She was disheartened by Zach's foul mood. For someone who had almost died choking on his own vomit, it was clear that he didn't appreciate the second chance at life. "Do you realize how fortunate you are?"

He glared at her. "Fortunate? For what?"

"For being alive, Zach." She moved over to the faux leather chair next to his bed and sat down. Leaning over, she reached for his hand, half expecting him to pull away. He didn't. "You have a chance to start over, Zach. Do you know how many kids don't have that chance?"

"A chance for what? To keep screwing up?" The already-angry expression on his face grew even darker. "To fail just one more time at rehab? I'm only seventeen and all I'm good at is failing!"

"That's not true—"

"I can't even overdose correctly," he mumbled.

Kelly froze. There it was, exactly what the doctor had suggested the previous day. Zach *had* tried to overdose with the intent of never waking up. And Kelly found that she resented knowing that Zach considered *not* dying a failure.

As usual, Zach thought only of himself and not of the suffering he put other people through.

His selfishness shouldn't have surprised her. She had attended enough family sessions at the different outpatient rehabs he had attended over the years. Addiction and self-absorption went hand in hand. The world revolved around the addict and the continual need to satisfy the cravings for their drug of choice. And that was something Kelly just couldn't understand. How some people could be such givers while others focused only on taking.

But what bothered her even more was the hopelessness that he felt. When had life stolen hope from him? She stared at her son, the anger and irritation giving way to a new emotion: despair. He may not have had the perfect life, growing up with an alcoholic father and enabling mother, but she had tried to protect him as best she could. No mother ever looked at her newborn baby, swaddled in the soft, little baby blankets while sleeping in her arms, and wanted *this*. If only she could go back in time, hold him in her arms again, and protect him from the harsh realities of the world. How had she failed to prepare him for facing such ugliness?

Outside the door, someone approached the room. Kelly looked up, thankful for the distraction.

"Ms. Martin?"

Kelly stood up and greeted the young man wearing blue scrubs with a simple, "Yes?"

"We need to ask that you step outside for a few minutes," the man said. He gestured toward Zach.

She hesitated.

"Bath time," the man explained with a nod toward Zach.

The thought of a man bathing her grown son startled her. She looked from the man to Zach and then opened her mouth as if to say something. But she noticed a woman enter the room, pushing a cart holding a pink plastic container filled with soapy water on the top and folded white towels stacked on the lower rack.

"Hey Zach!" she said in a cheerful voice. "Ready to get cleaned up? It's Saturday night!"

Zach rolled his eyes.

"I'll just be outside for a bit, OK?" Kelly said to Zach, not expecting him to respond. She wasn't disappointed.

Her chest felt heavy as she wandered out of his room. The floor layout was different than the ICU, and she had to walk around the corner to find the waiting room. But it was small and felt claustrophobic. So she collected her purse from security and left the area, knowing full well that she'd have to go through the inspection process all over again when she returned.

As she passed through the double doors, leaving the children's psychiatric section, she noticed a man walking toward her. It took her a moment to realize that it was Thomas.

"What are you doing here?" she asked, immediately embarrassed that her voice sounded surprised but not in a good way. "I'm sorry. I meant, you know, it's Saturday night and . . ."

Thomas held up his hand to stop her. "No worries. I was just leaving the school and wanted to check in on Zach."

Kelly frowned. For a split second, she didn't believe he was telling the truth. "You were at school? On a Saturday?"

"We've got a big game tomorrow, remember?"

"Oh." She felt the heat rise to her cheeks. For a split second, she had thought that maybe, just maybe, he had stopped by to check up on her and, in the brief moment, the thought had not been unpleasant to her. Embarrassed, she averted her eyes.

As if he sensed her discomfort, Thomas cleared his throat. "So, uh, how's Zach doing today? I heard that he was out of the coma. That's great news!"

She nodded. "They moved him up here this afternoon." And then, realizing the idiocy of her statement, Kelly shut her eyes and shook her head. "Which you obviously know." What was wrong with her? "I'm sorry I didn't contact you."

Thomas chuckled under his breath. "Hey, I get it. You're under a lot of stress, Kelly."

"And how," she managed to reply in a normal voice. There was a long silence between them. He was staring at her, something intense in his expression that gave her the unusual conflicting feelings of nervousness and excitement. "He's getting cleaned up," Kelly said, gesturing toward the doors. "But I don't think you can go in anyway. They're really strict and"—she gave him a sideways glance—"the nurses don't look like they have children old enough to be on your team. Yet."

He laughed.

She liked the sound. When was the last time she had made a man laugh?

He shoved his hands into the pockets of his coat. Kelly remembered he had done the same thing the other day before he left. "Well, I guess I better get going then." He took a step backward before he paused. "Unless you want to take a walk with me? To the cafeteria? I could use a little something before I head home. And, if you're anything like my sisters, you probably haven't eaten all day."

Sisters?

She must have looked at him with a quizzical expression, for he quickly explained, "Whenever their kids get sick, they don't take care of themselves. You know, putting their own needs on the back burner."

"I see."

Another pause and then Thomas raised an eyebrow. "So?"

Kelly glanced toward the double doors and then looked at her cell phone to check the time. It was almost eight thirty. Zach was in a terrible mood, and she had no idea how long the nurses would take. For a moment, she thought it would serve Zach well to have to wait for her return. Just as quickly, she felt guilty for thinking that.

"I . . . I don't know," she said softly. "I mean, what if they come out looking for me?"

Thomas nodded and took a step backward. "I totally understand."

But then, just as quickly, Kelly realized how true Thomas's statement was. She always put herself on the back burner. And, even if it was just a hospital cafeteria with mediocre food and lots of strangers milling about, when was the last time she had gone anywhere in the company of a man?

"Then again, I *am* a little hungry," she said quickly as she moved forward, her pace slow and hesitant.

Thomas tried to hide a smile. He stopped walking, waiting for her to join him.

Kelly pulled her purse strap over her shoulder and hugged the bag closer to her body as if protecting herself from something. In silence, they walked down the corridor toward the elevator. But, for once, Kelly found herself realizing that silence didn't have to be a bad thing. There was something comforting about being near Thomas and not having to speak. She let him press the elevator button, standing quietly beside him and wondering if, just maybe, he had stopped by the hospital to see her just as much as to find out about Zach, after all.

CHAPTER 26

Kelly carried her red tray to an empty table and then paused, glancing over her shoulder to see if Thomas was behind her.

He had paid for her food, and she felt nervous about that. In her world, men paid for dates and wives. She wasn't either of those to Thomas, and she worried that he would think she had expected him to pay. But she had reached for her wallet before he made a face and shook his head at the cashier. Maybe he was just a kind man. She wasn't used to that.

"Is this OK?" she asked, hating how nervous she felt.

He scanned the room, and his gaze fell upon a table farther away from people. "How about there instead?" He started walking in that direction but slowed down so they could walk together. "More private to talk without people overhearing."

After setting down her tray and taking a seat, Kelly looked around. The cafeteria wasn't too busy, which didn't surprise her since it was a Saturday night. She wondered how many visitors had come earlier in order to leave for whatever they had scheduled for the evening. Most people made plans for Saturday evenings, unlike Kelly.

Charlotte usually had dates, and her mother often went out with some of her friends. They liked to play bridge at each other's houses, at least once a month.

But tonight, Kelly was seated at a table with Thomas.

She felt a fluttering sensation and wondered if anyone in the cafeteria thought they were a couple. Surely they looked like it, for Thomas had taken a seat, not across from her, but beside her. That, too, made her feel out of sorts.

"So." He placed his paper napkin on his lap. "How's Kelly today?"

"Who?"

He laughed. "I bet that's not far from the truth," he said. "Well, you aren't lost in the mix with me."

It was true. Everyone focused on Zach, but no one, except Charlotte, inquired about her. With all of her time being eaten up at the hospital and dealing with Fiona, Kelly *did* feel lost. She wondered why the health-care system didn't realize that the caregivers might need some help, too. Someone to talk to or even just a shoulder to lean on.

"I had an interesting visitor earlier today," she said as she poked at her garden salad with her plastic fork.

"Oh?"

"Michael Stevens's mother."

Thomas froze, his fork in midair. "Come again?"

She nodded. "That's how I felt."

He set down his fork and stared at her. Kelly felt a moment of unease with such scrutiny. "What did she say?" He paused before adding, "If I may ask."

She appreciated his caution. They were, after all, practically strangers. But she had brought up the subject. "Of course. That's why I mentioned it." Was that why? Or was it that she needed to tell someone and had no one else to talk to? It dawned on her that she might have crossed a line by imagining it was OK to confide in Thomas. What did she know about him anyway?

"So?"

Kelly shook her head and gave a skittish laugh, deciding to back-pedal a little. "Well, I don't want to bore you with all of the details, but I was rather surprised by her showing up."

"I can imagine." He took a bite of his food, a beef stroganoff that didn't look very appetizing to Kelly. "Go on."

Startled that he was pressing her for more information—that he actually appeared interested—Kelly tried to explain without going into too many details. "Well, it appears that Zach hung out with Michael more than I realized." She knew that sounded bad, so she quickly added, "I suspect he went over there when he stayed with his dad, or maybe he even snuck out when I wasn't home."

Thomas nodded and looked at her expectantly, clearly wanting her to go on.

Kelly wasn't used to a man being interested in what she had to say. During their marriage, Todd had always complained that she was boring or took too long to tell stories. He hated that she focused on details instead of just getting to the point. Clearly, Thomas wasn't like Todd, something Kelly had suspected but found hard to navigate. "I have to admit that I wasn't very appreciative of her visit," she admit-ted. "Joan—that's her name—asked if there was anything she could do and . . ." She hesitated, not wanting to make herself look bad but knowing that she needed to speak the truth. ". . . Well, I'm afraid I snapped a little."

Thomas's mouth twitched as if he wanted to smile, and he raised one eyebrow in a questioning sort of way.

"OK," she said with a sigh. "I snapped a lot."

He laughed. "I think you have that right, Kelly. Don't feel ashamed."

"But I do," she said. "She was offering support and I turned it around, Thomas. I made it about Michael and how he has influenced Zach." She slouched in the chair and began picking at the salad, moving a tomato to the side and spearing a black olive. "Maybe she didn't know about Michael. Maybe she is a nice person."

"Maybe."

She frowned. "But I wasn't very kind, and I'm not even certain if I feel bad about it."

"That's understandable."

She raised her eyes and stared at him. "Is it? Does a bad situation excuse bad behavior?"

He set down his fork and studied her for a long moment. "I'm not certain that's even a valid question, Kelly. We both know that she is aware of Michael's problems. At least I know because of what I was privy to."

Kelly nodded, remembering that she had wanted to use that information to confront Joan, but she hadn't wanted to throw Thomas under the bus.

"So, you have that in your favor. Couple that with the enormous amount of stress that you have been living with." He tapped his finger on the edge of the table. "Zach's problems didn't just appear on Wednesday morning. There was a buildup, months, if not years, of stress and pressure that you've been living under. I know he's been to rehabs and nothing has worked."

For a moment, Kelly wondered *how* he knew that—Todd had only agreed to Zach attending rehabs when it didn't conflict with the autumn football schedule—and then she realized that, as the football coach, he might have been alerted anyway.

"So all of that led up to Wednesday morning. And here you are, three days later, and a stranger ambushes you at the hospital, offering help." He gave a slight shake of his head. "It sounds nice on the surface, but perhaps it was self-serving. A way to assuage her own guilt at the situation." He pursed his lips. "A way of reassuring herself that *her* son is OK when one of his friends—"

Kelly scoffed at the word.

"Is not. The people who aren't involved, the ones with no guilt, they tend to stay away. It's like when people see an accident on the highway. They all slow down to stare, their impatience at having been trapped in bumper-to-bumper traffic immediately forgotten when they see the wreck and they think, 'Thank God it wasn't me.' Right?" He didn't wait for her to respond. "It's the same thing. Some people are drawn to disasters, almost as if to reassure themselves that they are survivors. But, usually, they don't like to get involved. The silent bystanders."

"That's a little morbid, don't you think?"

"It's the truth."

But was it? She immediately thought about Jackie. Were they so different, Thomas's car-wreck analogy and the way that her sister avoided the situation? She'd only inquired about Zach once, as if ignoring the subject would make it go away and not taint her own family. Perhaps that was Jackie's way of reassuring herself that she was untouched by the accident known as substance abuse.

"I'm not so sure," she said slowly, feeling timid about contradicting him. "During my divorce, people disappeared in droves. And while Zach's been fighting this addiction, my circle has shrunk even more. Based on your philosophy, I should've been inundated with people wanting to reassure themselves that they were OK, instead of being treated like divorce and addiction are contagious."

He gave a little shrug. "I haven't ever been married, so I can't speak about the divorce part, but I can speak about the addiction. People stay away because they *are* afraid it's contagious. And what they don't realize is that it's happening in most parents' houses, right under their noses. Parents take a little extra Percocet after having a knee or shoulder surgery, even though they're no longer in pain. Rather than get rid of the extra medicine, they keep it 'just in case.' The kids find that stuff—their father's Vicodin or their mother's Xanax—and they use it. Those people might be staying away because they know it hits just a little too close to home."

She leaned toward him, wanting to believe what he was saying and yet terrified that it might be the truth. "Do you really think so?"

"Oh I know so."

She gave him a quizzical look but didn't ask the obvious question.

Thomas wiped at his mouth and set the napkin back on his lap. "It's easier to ignore the truth than to face it, Kelly. I'm not certain why some people live in denial and avoid the truth. But I'm certain that Joan Stevens, who is well aware of her son's situation, came here as a way of reassuring herself, on some deep, subconscious level, that her son is OK while yours is not. A parent in denial of their children's addiction, or even the possibility that they *could* ever use drugs, will remove themselves from the situation as if distance will shield them, but a parent who is aware that there's a problem may look for reassurance that their child isn't as bad as someone else's. And believe me, there are more people out there in your shoes than they like to admit. It's a problem hidden in the shadows of their dark closets, if you ask me."

Thomas's words made sense. And still, Kelly knew that she needed time to digest this. It was too much to take in at once.

"I'll have to think about that," she said in a soft voice.

Thomas picked up his fork and stabbed at his food once again. "In the meantime," he said, taking a small bite and then making a face, "this is terrible." He laughed and looked at her as he pushed away his plate. "I can't believe a hospital can serve such food. Shouldn't they be the mecca of nutrition?"

Kelly smiled. "It does make one think." She slid her salad over toward him. "Try this. You can't go wrong with a simple garden salad."

He hesitated and then took her up on the offer, spearing a piece of lettuce. For a few long moments, they shared her salad in silence. It was a comfortable silence, not awkward, and Kelly found herself feeling a kind of serenity in Thomas's company that she hadn't experienced in a long time. She savored the feeling for as long as she could.

CHAPTER 27

At exactly eight o'clock the next morning, Kelly's cell phone rang. Normally she would know who it was: Jackie. If there was something important to discuss, Jackie would wait until eight in the morning before making that phone call. Not 7:59. Not 8:01. Eight o'clock on the dot. Earlier than that was an invasion of privacy, but after that, she feared the risk of missing Kelly.

But with Zach in the hospital, Kelly heard the phone ring and felt a moment of panic.

For the first time in months, Kelly had finally slept well. Just the knowledge that Zach was in a safe place and being monitored by trained professionals helped ease her mind enough to drift off without worry. She didn't have to fear that he was sneaking out at night or doing drugs by himself. Nor did she have to worry that he was going to kill himself, whether by choice or accident. In fact, with Zach in the hospital, she almost felt as if she didn't have to worry, period.

On Sunday morning, however, with her cell phone ringing so early, Kelly immediately panicked. Was this the dreaded phone call? What if he had found his way into a medicine storage room? How did the hospitals keep track of their meds anyway? What if Zach had escaped? What if he had killed himself there?

In that moment, Kelly realized that she had found a false sense of comfort over the past few days with Zach under twenty-four-hour medical care. And she also realized that there was a long way to go before she could allow herself that fantasy of comfort again.

Without looking to see who called, Kelly grabbed the phone and answered it with a hurried "Hello?"

"Kell?" It was Jackie. She must have sensed the anxiety in her sister's voice. "Everything OK?"

Relieved, Kelly sighed. She shut her eyes and lay back into the pillows. "I thought you might be the hospital calling. Sorry."

"At eight in the morning? Why on earth would they call you so early?"

Kelly almost smiled at her sister's obliviousness. Rather than remind Jackie that Zach had overdosed and was under round-the-clock surveillance—for more than just medical reasons—she merely replied, "*You* call me that early."

"I'm your sister."

Kelly rolled her eyes, but in a good-natured sort of way. She wished that Jackie could be like this all the time: casual, light, and sisterly. If only she would drop that air of superiority, perhaps they could actually be friends. "This *is* true," Kelly said. "Some days that's a good thing."

Jackie laughed, but it was off. Not 100 percent real. That was Kelly's indication that something was, indeed, wrong.

"So, what's up?" Kelly asked the question cautiously. "Everything go OK last night?"

And then she heard it: Jackie's sigh. That's how it always started: with a sigh. As if her bad news caused her personally to suffer by having to share it. But, whenever Kelly heard that sigh, she knew that Jackie's pain was superficial. Even though Jackie made it seem like she was troubled, she really wasn't—she just wanted to spread gossip, even if it hurt the person she was telling it to.

"Well, that's just the thing," Jackie started, her words slow and spoken with a little edge. "No, things weren't so great last night."

Kelly shut her eyes, waiting for the bomb to drop. Slowly, she counted as she waited. One . . . two . . . three.

"I hate to have to tell you this, but Fiona was"—Jackie paused as if looking for the right word—"well, frankly, she behaved rather poorly, Kelly."

Immediately, Kelly's eyes opened. *That* was the last thing she expected to hear. "Excuse me?"

"I'm sorry to have to tell you this, but she conducted herself like a selfish little brat."

From the way she said it, Jackie didn't sound sorry at all. In fact, her sister sounded rather smug about it, as if proving her prediction from the previous week held true: Fiona, too, had fallen apart, following in the footsteps of her father, brother, and even Kelly.

A wave of fury washed over Kelly, and she felt her blood race, her hand beginning to quiver as she tried to hold her tongue to keep from lashing out at her sister.

"She sat on the sofa, hugging a pillow to her chest," Jackie continued, oblivious to the hatefulness in her own voice. "Heather went over to her—not once but twice!—to try to include her with the other girls. But Fiona just sat there. Her behavior was just awful, Kelly."

"I really can't believe I'm hearing this."

Jackie missed the point. "Exactly. All of the girls were talking about it. They were just appalled that Heather's own cousin would behave like that."

No, Kelly wanted to scream. *They should be appalled that I made my daughter even go there!*

Jackie's words continued to send daggers through Kelly's heart. "She's become a very cruel and selfish little girl. Fiona really owes Heather an apology for behaving that way, especially after Heather was so thoughtful as to invite her in the first place."

Suddenly, Kelly saw everything far too clearly. Jackie had invited Fiona not for Heather's sake but for her own. Heather probably hadn't even wanted Fiona to attend her little gathering. Under the guise of inclusion, Jackie had invited Fiona in the hopes—whether conscious or subconscious—that Fiona would finally do something wrong and give Jackie the ammunition to have something to complain about. Kelly could imagine her sister lying in bed in eager anticipation of making this phone call, practically salivating as she role-played in her mind how she would, once again, prove to Kelly how inferior her children were, all the while presenting the face of being a nurturing aunt.

"Jackie, you do realize that Fiona's under a lot of stress right now," Kelly said at last. She couldn't believe how calm her voice sounded. Inside, she was seething. "Or did that happen to slip your mind? You know, the stress of her brother overdosing?" She heard the edge to her own voice and, for once, she didn't care. "He's in the hospital? He almost died? Did you forget about that?"

"Then maybe she shouldn't have come at all," Jackie snapped.

Kelly clenched her teeth. "Right, Jackie. And I can only imagine how that would have played out. How Fiona was so cruel and selfish to not show up for Heather's birthday party."

She thought she heard her sister gasp. It bolstered Kelly's courage to finally speak her mind.

"You know, I'm more than a little tired of this game, Jackie. *Your* game." Her words came rushing out of her mouth, fast and furious, like water bursting through a broken dam. "We all get the picture, Jackie. *I* get it. Everything about you is better. Your house. Your children. Your life. But what I don't get is why you feel the constant need to keep reminding everyone. Makes me wonder what you are hiding—that the only way you can feel better about yourself is to make others feel worse about themselves."

"How dare you—"

"No! How dare *you*!" Kelly shouted. "How *dare* you bother me with such self-centered, myopic, and mundane issues when you know what I am going through. And, by the way, Fiona, too! Zach *is* her brother." Furious, Kelly hung up on her sister. Oh, she was certain to hear about it later from her mother, who would want her to apologize. Kelly was forever apologizing, and most of the time she had no idea why.

"To keep the peace, dear," her mother would say. "Sometimes you just have to be the bigger person."

She never thought to ask why Jackie never apologized. In hindsight, Kelly knew the answer: Jackie just wasn't *capable* of being the bigger person.

Well, regardless of what her mother wanted, Kelly would never apologize for this altercation. In fact, the way that she was feeling now, Kelly didn't care if she *ever* spoke to Jackie again.

For once, Kelly felt a sense of dignity for having stood up to her sister at last. She had much more important battles to fight at the current moment, and her sister's pettiness was not going to stop her from focusing 100 percent on both Zach and Fiona.

But first, before calling the hospital to see how Zach had fared the previous night, Kelly knew that she had something just as important to do.

She set her cell phone on the nightstand and got out of bed. She knew that Fiona was still sleeping but also that it was important for her to talk with her daughter. It wasn't that Fiona *needed* an apology; it was more that Kelly *needed* to apologize.

It was only when she made her way into the hallway and headed to Fiona's room that Kelly realized that, once again, her sister hadn't inquired about Zach.

CHAPTER 28

Later that afternoon, Kelly sat by Zach's hospital bed, staring out the window, wishing that he would talk with her. He hadn't said one word since she had arrived, and Kelly had run out of things to talk about. Holding one-way conversations had never been her specialty.

She had let Fiona stay home alone again, reminding her to lock the front door and not let anyone in. It wasn't that Fiona had never stayed on her own, but Kelly found herself continually replaying the morning's conversation with Jackie, which only added to her guilt. Why hadn't she protected Fiona better?

Outside the open door of Zach's hospital room, Kelly heard a commotion. At the same time, her phone chimed. A text message. At first she thought it might be a reply from Thomas. She'd sent him a message earlier to update him about Zach. They'd sent a few messages back and forth, his last one a witty comment about stopping by later with something for her to eat so that she didn't suffer with more cafeteria food. She'd smiled at that text, and now she wondered if he'd sent her another message.

To her surprise, she realized that the thought did not displease her.

Turning her attention away from the window, Kelly reached for her phone and then stood up, carrying her cell with her as she went to shut the door.

Her hand was on the door, and she began to close it. Her eyes caught the first line of the text:

Mom, call me! There's an ambulance—

At the same time, she heard a familiar voice: Debbie Weaver.

For a long moment, Kelly felt that same surreal out-of-body experience that she had felt earlier that week. She was floating above her body, observing herself as she looked up and made eye contact with Debbie, who was sobbing while following a hospital bed being pushed in Kelly's direction. Her eyes trailed to the small, round face of the child, so pale and white, in the bed: Molly. And then she returned her attention to the cell phone.

> Mom, call me! There was an ambulance at the Weavers. Jenny texted me that something happened to Molly! I told you something was wrong. Can you find out what happened? Please???!!!

The attendant pushed the bed past Kelly, and Debbie averted her eyes.

"Debbie! What's going on?" Kelly said, leaving the safety of Zach's room to follow them.

But Debbie merely shook her head and held up her hand for Kelly to leave her alone.

Stunned, Kelly stopped walking and stared at the back of Debbie's head. She felt a sinking feeling. No one ever wanted to see a sick child. And then it dawned on her that Molly wasn't at the hospital because she was sick or injured. She was on the same floor as Zach: the psychiatric floor.

She leaned against the door frame, watching as the attendant rolled Molly's bed into a room just three doors down the hallway. Whatever was going on, Kelly would find out soon. If Molly had been admitted to the children's psychiatric floor, she wouldn't be leaving anytime in the near future. And Debbie couldn't avoid Kelly forever. But Kelly understood the need for time, especially if there was a crisis. Whatever trouble Molly was in, she needed her mother now. Kelly knew better than to interfere.

"Was that . . . ?"

Kelly glanced over her shoulder, surprised to see Todd walking toward her, two cups of coffee in his hands. "Hmm?"

"That looked like Weaver." He handed Kelly one of the coffees. "Debbie Weaver?"

Taking a coffee cup, she wrapped her hands around it, the heat seeping through the sides and warming her. "Really? I hadn't noticed." She wanted to give Debbie some privacy. Surely God would forgive Kelly that one little white lie.

Turning his attention to the open door, Todd peered inside. "How's Zach?"

"Sullen. Quiet. Angry." Of course, now that his father was here, surely Zach's mood would improve. "The usual."

Todd frowned and pushed past her. "Hey sport," he called out cheerfully as if he were greeting his son after coming home from work. "How you feeling?"

"I want to go home" was Zach's only reply. His flat tone and blank eyes surprised Kelly. Normally he lit up whenever his father was around.

Todd sat down in the chair by Zach's bedside, the one that Kelly had occupied moments earlier. He reached out and gave Zach's arm a playful nudge. "You can't come home just yet, Zach."

"Why not?"

Kelly sipped at the coffee, watching the exchange between father and son. *Yeah, Todd,* she thought. *Why not?*

"Well, uh . . ." Todd glanced at her as if seeking her help. But Kelly remained silent, waiting to see how Todd handled this. "Well, you know that everyone is really concerned about you."

While she was grateful that Todd cared, Kelly hated how, whenever he talked with Zach, regardless of the circumstances, his tone became so fatherly, a mixture of compassion and tenderness. Sometimes Kelly wished that he would be a father, even when the fatherly thing to do was to take off the kid gloves.

"And the doctors want to keep you here for a few more days until you're feeling better."

Zach turned his head away from his father. "I'll never feel better."

"Don't say that."

"They had a psychiatrist in here," Zach mumbled.

Todd snapped his head toward Kelly. Had the daggers that he shot at her been real, Todd would have killed her twenty times over. "Is that so?"

Kelly frowned at him. "I didn't know that, if that's what you're thinking."

Narrowing his eyes, Todd glared at her.

But Zach reached up and grabbed his father's arm. "Am I crazy?"

"No, no, of course not," Todd said quickly, returning his attention to Zach. "You're not crazy." He gave a little laugh. "Why would you say that?"

"I don't want to be crazy," Zach said softly, shutting his eyes as if he wanted to sleep. "Mom's crazy."

Kelly caught her breath. She felt as if the air escaped her body, that she couldn't breathe at all. A viselike feeling tightened around her heart, and she stood there, frozen in place as if she were nothing more than an object in the room.

Todd gave an uncomfortable chuckle. "Your mother's not crazy."

"That's what you always say," Zach countered.

"Now, now." Another nervous chuckle. "I never said that."

Zach's eyes opened, and he moved his head to stare at his father. "Yes you did. All the time. That's why you hate her so much."

"I don't hate your mother—"

"Yes you do!" Zach's voice was rising, becoming louder. "You always told me that I didn't have to listen to her. That she was crazy." His eyes narrowed. "And stupid. Like all women." His voice dropped. "Like Fiona, too."

Kelly began to step forward, intending to shut down this conversation, but she didn't have to. She felt the presence behind her before she saw the doctor walk into the room. A young woman with dark skin and sharp eyes. Kelly glanced at the identification badge around the woman's neck: Dr. Anja Kumpoor. She wondered how long Dr. Kumpoor had been observing this lovely family exchange.

"Zach?" the woman said softly. "Everything OK here?"

Todd cleared his throat. "He's fine. Just confused a little."

"No!" Zach practically shouted the word. "I'm not confused. *You* are."

The woman stepped forward and glanced at one of the machines hanging from a pole behind the bed. "Maybe it's time to get some more medicine for you, Zach." She glanced at Todd. "If you don't mind, I'd like a moment alone with Zach."

The color rushed to Todd's cheeks. Kelly pressed her lips together, watching as Todd scowled at the woman. She braced herself for what she figured would not be a pretty scene. If there was one thing Todd hated more than anything else, it was being humiliated by a woman.

"I do mind," Todd snapped. "I want to speak to the doctor. Do you know where he is?"

The woman tilted her head and faced Todd, her arms crossing over her chest. Zach's lips twitched, almost as if he was going to smile, but he merely looked away.

"As a matter of fact, I do know where the doctor is, Mr. Martin."

Todd gave her a look of superiority, as if pleased by her response. "I'd like to speak to him."

Inwardly, Kelly groaned. She knew exactly what was coming.

"You are speaking to him. Or, rather, her."

Todd bristled. "I meant the real doctor."

Dr. Kumpoor raised an eyebrow. "You mean a real male doctor? Or perhaps a real white doctor?"

"I meant a real medical doctor," Todd snapped.

"Todd!"

His eyes flickered in Kelly's direction.

"That's rude," Kelly said.

Todd started to retort, his fight shifting from the doctor to Kelly, but he didn't have a chance. Two men appeared in the doorway. Kelly wasn't certain how security knew, but somehow Dr. Kumpoor, the very female and very not-white doctor, had managed to summon them. Within seconds, Todd was escorted out of the room, thankfully without too much of a fuss. Kelly glanced at Zach, who met her gaze for the first time since his arrival at the hospital. There was a softening in his expression as he stared at her.

It unnerved her.

"I'll . . . uh . . . I'll leave you two alone," Kelly managed to say and slipped out of the room, still stunned that Todd had finally been put into his place, not only by a female Indian doctor but also by his son. There were, indeed, firsts for everything after all.

CHAPTER 29

In the waiting room, Todd paced back and forth, angrily searching for something on his cell phone. Kelly hesitated at the doorway, not wanting to enter the room and be subjected to Todd's rage.

"What was that, Kelly?"

Too late, she thought. He had noticed her standing there. "What was what?"

"That crap in Zach's room! What have you been telling him?" Before she could answer, he snapped, "You're not supposed to bad-mouth me to Zach!"

But it's OK for you to belittle me in front of him? she wanted to ask.

"I can assure you, Todd, that I haven't said a word about you to Zach," she said with as much civility as she could muster.

"Then where would he learn such . . . such nonsense? That I hate you?"

"Maybe from observing you?" she managed to say, her voice sounding surprisingly strong. "Did you ever think about that?"

"Pssh!" He waved his hand at her dismissively as if she were indeed crazy. "You have no idea what you're talking about, Kelly!" *Kell-lee.* There it was, that condescending tone once again. Whenever he didn't like what she was saying, it was so much easier to just put her down.

But this time, Kelly wasn't about to take it.

"I've just about had it with you, Todd," she snapped. "For years, you've done everything in your power to push me down, make me feel like a big, fat zero. And once you got me to that point, you got your jollies by pushing me further into the ground." She moved toward him with such speed that he took a step backward. "How many times have I said to you that you can't just flip a switch and turn Zach into a mature, responsible adult? It has to be learned, and not overnight. Over time, Todd. But you were too busy putting me down in order to build up your own self-esteem."

"Oh shut up, Kelly!"

"No, *you* shut up." She pointed her finger at him. "I may not be a perfect mother, but don't you stand there pretending you're the perfect father! That boy looked up to you. For all these years, he looked up to you. And what did you teach him? Disrespect women. Disregard authority. And, most importantly, dodge reality. Only he didn't do it just through booze; he added drugs to the mix."

His eyes bulged from his puffy, red face as he glared at her. "You *are* crazy!"

"And why should he seek any help for feeling down and out, right, Todd? After all, having any form of depression would mean that he was crazy, just like me, right?" She straightened her back and squared her shoulders as she faced her ex-husband. "Certainly Zach would much rather be like you than like me. So instead of getting help, he coped by mimicking you."

"You're crazy—"

"Kelly?"

They spun around at the sound of her name. For some reason, she wasn't surprised to see Thomas standing in the doorway, holding an envelope and a football.

He glanced at Todd. "Everything all right here?"

Todd glared at the intruder. "Who's asking?"

Kelly was about to respond that it was none of his business, but Thomas stepped into the room and positioned himself between her and Todd. "Coach Keates from the high school." He glanced down at the items he held. "Wanted to stop by to see Zach and to drop these off." He turned his attention to Kelly. "When I told the team that Zach was doing better, they all wanted to come visit him. Unfortunately, I had to tell them that visitors aren't allowed right now."

Somehow she found the fortitude to smile. For the life of her, she couldn't imagine why. Zach had been on the team three seasons, but this year hadn't made it through last summer's practices. Yet another concussion had forced him to withdraw from the team before the first game. So why would the team be so eager to visit her son? "Thank them for Zach."

Thomas nodded. His eyes flickered in Todd's direction as he set down the football and card on a chair. Something dark crossed over his face, and he straightened up, squaring his shoulders as he stood his full height and positioned himself so that he was closer to Kelly than Todd. "If I may ask," he said, directing the question to Kelly, "what's the latest?"

"We're waiting for the doctor."

Todd made a noise and turned away from the two of them. He glanced down at a table full of old magazines, which he shuffled around as if looking for something to read. But Kelly could tell that he was focused 100 percent on her conversation with Thomas.

The coach must have noticed her gaze flicker in Todd's direction. "Maybe I should go," Thomas said.

Immediately, Kelly shook her head. "No, please don't." What she couldn't tell him was that the last thing she wanted was to be alone with Todd. However, she reminded herself that Thomas was a stranger. "I mean, you don't have to," she added softly.

For a few long seconds, the room was silent. Thomas stood there, his hands thrust into the pockets of his jacket while Kelly wrapped her arms around herself. She didn't know this man and had nothing in common with him other than Zach. And, in truth, how much in common was that?

"How was the game?" she asked at last. She could remember from growing up with Eddie that talking about sports was always an icebreaker with his friends.

"We won, twenty to fourteen."

Kelly managed another smile. "That's great."

"They did it for Zach," he said in a soft voice. "I know he couldn't play this year, but they still really look up to him."

She glanced over her shoulder at Todd and then gestured toward the door. Thomas must have understood her silent message and reached out to take her arm, gently guiding her from the waiting room. For a moment, the pressure of his hand on her arm made her shiver. When was the last time anyone had touched her in such a chivalrous way? Embarrassed, she averted her eyes and prayed that her cheeks hadn't pinked up.

Outside the waiting room, Kelly leaned against the wall. Thomas stood in front of her, resting one hand on the wall about a foot from her. His back was toward the doorway as if blocking her from Todd's view. There was something protective about his stance, and Kelly felt a bolt of energy course through her veins.

"The doctors think that Zach did it on purpose," she whispered so that Todd couldn't hear her confiding to the coach. In truth, she wasn't certain why she *was* confiding in him. Perhaps it was because there just weren't many people she *could* confide in. Too many people had let her down. Instead, she chose to live her life by not succumbing to the demanding images of society. Living an honest life was lonely, she had realized long ago. "He told me on Friday, before they moved him to this floor."

Thomas remained silent, digesting her words. That gave Kelly the opportunity to study his face. She couldn't help wondering why, exactly, he was at the hospital again. And on a Sunday, nonetheless.

But this was the third time he had come to see Zach. Surely he could have sent the football and card with someone else.

Her thoughts were interrupted when Thomas cleared his throat. "I'm sorry, Kelly."

"I just don't understand why. I mean, I know the divorce was tough on Zach, but this?"

Thomas let his hand slide down the wall and rest upon her shoulder, giving it a gentle squeeze. "Look, he's in great hands now, Kelly." He let his eyes scan the floor. "This whole children's psychiatric floor is brand new. They never had it before, you know. Just opened last year." He made a face and returned his eyes to meet hers. Only then did she notice that his hand was still on her shoulder. "Before that, the children were kept in the purple zone."

"Purple zone?" She gave him a quizzical look.

"That's what they called it. You know, isolation? You couldn't even get back there unless you were escorted by security." He must have realized his hand rested on her shoulder, and he quickly removed it. "The kids were kept there for days until they could go to St. Clare's for treatment. It was awful."

"How do you know so much about it?" she heard herself ask and almost apologized for sounding so nosy.

"Do you think this is the first time I've visited a player in the hospital?" He leaned forward so that his lips were just a few inches from her ear. "Zach is very special, Kelly, but his problems are not unique to him."

"Ms. Martin?"

They both looked up and, before Dr. Kumpoor could say anything else, Todd poked his head out of the doorway. Kelly watched his reaction, first when he saw Thomas standing so close to her, and then when he recognized Dr. Kumpoor. Based on his reaction, Kelly couldn't tell which bothered Todd more.

Thomas shoved his hand into his pocket and backed away from Kelly. "I best get going," he said. And then, as if having a second thought, he mumbled in an awkward manner, "Maybe you could let me know what she says?" He pressed his lips together and shuffled his feet as he backed away. "I mean, if you felt like it, I'm around to listen."

She still had his business card. Was that what he meant? To call him? She nodded absentmindedly and stepped back into the waiting room. She paused at the door, turning to shut it but not before she noticed Thomas standing near the elevators. When the doors opened and he stepped inside, he turned around and, for just one brief second, their eyes met. He gave her an encouraging smile and lifted his hand, a wave goodbye, as the doors slid shut and, just like that, he was gone. But Kelly found herself thinking about him long after the elevator had swept him away.

CHAPTER 30

Dr. Kumpoor did not sit down, so Kelly followed the doctor's example and stood before the woman, her arms crossed over her chest. Todd, however, maintained his distance. If he was embarrassed by his previous behavior, he acted just the opposite: defiant, angry, and hostile. If Dr. Kumpoor was a psychiatrist worth even the paper on which her degree was printed, she certainly had figured out the chauvinistic dynamics at play in the otherwise empty room.

What Kelly wouldn't have done to be a mind reader.

"Mr. Martin," Dr. Kumpoor said slowly, acknowledging his presence before she directed her attention toward Kelly.

"How is he?" Kelly said. "Zach, I mean?" She didn't know why she said that. Nerves, perhaps. And she was nervous. She had never witnessed anyone put her ex-husband in his place the way that Dr. Kumpoor had just done. Calling security on him and having him removed from Zach's room made Dr. Kumpoor her new hero. Kelly definitely felt a bit inspired by the woman standing before her.

Obviously oblivious to Kelly's thoughts, Dr. Kumpoor inhaled and gave a little nod. "Fairly well. Much better than when Zach first arrived here." She glanced at Todd. "He's going through a bit of a withdrawal, from the drugs and alcohol. You'll notice that he'll be on a bit of an emotional roller coaster for a few days—"

Todd interrupted her. "When can he come home?"

Dr. Kumpoor ignored him. "But I get the sense that Zach is just that: an emotional roller coaster." She gave Kelly an empathetic smile. "He hasn't been easy, has he?"

Kelly lowered her gaze and stared at the floor.

"He admitted that the overdose was not an accident, Ms. Martin. And that changes things just a bit."

"Oh." She barely caught her breath.

The doctor, however, continued speaking. Clearly, she wasn't one to sugarcoat anything. "I noticed that he's had quite a few head injuries, and I'm curious as to whether he's experiencing early signs of CTE."

"CTE? What's that?"

"Concussions," Todd responded before the doctor could.

"Yes and no," the doctor corrected, but not unkindly. "CTE stands for chronic traumatic encephalopathy, which is a form of neurodegeneration—"

"What's that?" Kelly interrupted, her head spinning from all of the medical terms.

"A progressive death to brain neurons," the doctor explained. "Usually it's from repeated head injuries, and we're finding more and more instances where football players, even ones as young as Zach, demonstrate early symptoms of it."

Kelly glanced at Todd and then back at the doctor. "He's only had two concussions," she said. "Maybe three."

Dr. Kumpoor pursed her lips and glanced down at the file in her hands. "No, his records clearly show that he's had six." She looked up from the papers. "I'm surprised that a doctor signed off on him playing football again this year. It's probably lucky that he never made it into a game this season."

"Six concussions?" Kelly snapped her head toward Todd.

"You knew about them." Just the way that he said it, so dismissively, made Kelly try to think back.

Had she known about them? There was the one when he was playing Little League and the ball hit him in the head. And then the concussion during a freshman football game and, of course, the one this past summer during practice. When had Zach had three others?

"I don't remember six," she stated in a flat, firm voice.

"You forget everything important," he retorted harshly.

For what seemed like a long few seconds, Kelly felt as if time were suspended. Her breathing stopped, and she felt the pounding of her heart. Rage coursed throughout her body as she realized that he was lying. Six concussions? And she hadn't known about half of them. Had Todd's obsession with Zach's status as a high school football star led him to hide the extent of their son's injuries on the field? And, if so, was Zach's desire to live up to his father's expectations part of the reason for his depression and dive into despair?

What had Zach said just the previous day? That he failed at everything? He hadn't mentioned football, but maybe that was the driving force behind this last catastrophic event in her son's life.

The doctor's voice suddenly infiltrated Kelly's thoughts. She hadn't realized that Dr. Kumpoor was still talking.

"Anyway, I'm trying to arrange a spot for him at a wonderful facility in Arizona," Dr. Kumpoor was saying. "They provide equine-assisted psychotherapy, which, frankly, would be a wonderful experience for Zach."

Todd scoffed. "Equine-assisted psychotherapy?"

"Exactly," Dr. Kumpoor said as if Todd hadn't just insulted her recommendation with his demeaning tone. "Clearly, you've heard of the benefits for dual diagnoses among both teenagers and adults? Such a wonderful boost to self-confidence and self-esteem. And I think that would be very beneficial to Zach."

Arizona?

She felt rather than saw Todd's energy shift from belittling the doctor to suddenly paying attention to what Dr. Kumpoor said. "That's too far away," he said.

Kelly glared at him.

"And it sounds expensive," he added. "Insurance won't cover it."

"I'm not so certain about that, Mr. Martin," Dr. Kumpoor said. "You have a wonderful insurance plan. Didn't they cover everything in the past?"

Shaking her head, Kelly focused her attention on the doctor, not Todd. Inside, she was seething. But she needed to focus on helping Zach right now. She'd deal with Todd later. "Unfortunately not," Kelly said. She didn't want to add that she had run up far too much credit card debt paying for her court-ordered percentage of Zach's previous rehabilitations. All things considered, her job paid her well enough. And, of course, there was Todd's child support and limited alimony. But Kelly had her hands full paying the mortgage and Morristown taxes—which were absurdly high—as well as her other bills.

But the doctor persisted. "Are you certain?"

The way that Dr. Kumpoor emphasized the word "you" caused Kelly to catch her breath. She glanced at Todd. It was his insurance, after all. And, ever since the divorce, Kelly wasn't on the policy. Twice she had tried to speak to customer service, but they wouldn't disclose anything to her about the children's health insurance policy.

Todd cleared his throat. "They don't cover it," he confirmed.

Kelly noticed that the doctor stared at him, her dark eyes narrowing for just the briefest of seconds. Kelly couldn't help but wonder at Todd's amazing ability to so quickly create such hostile reactions in people. When he wanted to be charming, he could be. Kelly had witnessed that many times during their marriage. But when he wanted to be a complete miscreant, he could do that just as well and, unfortunately, just as fast.

"Well," Dr. Kumpoor said at last, returning her attention to Kelly. "Perhaps a phone call is in order to clear up that error." She turned to

Todd and, with an exaggerated wink, added, "Sometimes doctors have better luck with insurance companies than the policyholders."

Kelly noticed Todd scowl, but she didn't have time to deal with his unspoken but evident objections. "Can you tell me about this facility?" Kelly asked, hoping to release some of the tension in the room by redirecting Todd's attention to what was truly important: Zach.

The doctor nodded. "Yes, of course. There's a lot of research about equine-assisted psychotherapy and how it helps people communicate more. Patients work with the horses while therapists observe and, in some cases, talk with the patients. There is something about being around horses that helps the toughest patients open up." She tossed a glance at Todd. "You'd be quite surprised."

"It's too far away," Todd said.

"Perhaps, but maybe far away is a good thing."

Kelly couldn't agree more.

"Anyway, first things first." The doctor looked back at Kelly. "It seems that there are some issues bubbling under the surface. And, as I'm sure you are aware, Zach isn't the easiest communicator."

That was an understatement. Ever since kindergarten, Zach had been the master of shutting down. Prior to that, he tended to hold his breath until he passed out whenever he was upset and crying. Zach's communication strategies had always been to withdraw and disappear within himself, leaving everyone on the outside looking in, wondering what they could do to break down that iron wall that had few, if any, windows with a view inside Zach's world.

"I'm sure there are issues," Kelly admitted. "But he just refuses to talk to anyone."

"Well, I'll make some phone calls tomorrow when the facility opens up." She stared directly at Kelly. "You'll be here, I imagine?"

Todd spoke up. "You can call me with anything to do with insurance."

"That's between the two of you," Dr. Kumpoor said, never once looking at Todd. "In the meantime, I'm going to suggest that you both give Zach a bit of space. He's sorting through a lot right now, and I'm not certain visiting with him, at least tonight, is in his best interest."

Todd bristled. "That's my son."

"That's my patient," Kumpoor countered, emphasizing the word "my" as she corrected Todd. "And while he's under my care, my word is law, so either sit out here until morning or go home. Frankly, I don't care, but you will not be visiting with Zach until tomorrow, and only after I have talked with him again and deem a visit suitable for his state of mind." She leveled her gaze at Todd. "Got it?"

It dawned on Kelly that this was not the first time that Dr. Kumpoor had dealt with a Todd Martin. She remembered what Thomas had said about Zach. And, like Zach's, Todd's problems were not unique. He was just one example of many men who disrespected authority, especially in women, and felt that rules didn't apply to them.

"Thank you, Doctor," Kelly said softly.

The doctor nodded her head, gave Todd one more steely look, and then left the waiting room.

The air was heavy with tension. Kelly wished that she could have walked out with the doctor, but she hadn't thought about it in time. She glanced over at Todd, who was still stewing about the doctor's admonishment. It gave her some satisfaction because, inwardly, she was still stewing about the three concussions she hadn't known about.

When he made no move to leave, Kelly shrugged and started out the door. She wondered how long he would linger in the empty waiting room, and that was when she realized that, unlike her, Todd had no reason to return home. There was nothing for him there. No person or even a pet to greet him. It didn't make any difference to Todd whether he stayed at the hospital, hit the bar, or retreated to his small, little house on Elm Street. Regardless of where he went, no one would know the difference.

No one cared.

For the first time since she could remember, she actually felt sorry for her ex-husband. He had no one and, even if he found someone, that person would learn the truth sooner or later, and Todd Martin would still spend the rest of his life alone, a bitter man whose only friend in the world was bought at liquor stores and bars.

CHAPTER 31

When her phone rang on Monday morning, Kelly first thought it was the hospital calling her, and she panicked. But one glance at the clock told her that it was more than likely Jackie. Despite still feeling hurt by her sister's lack of compassion, Kelly found herself answering the phone. *What if it's an emergency?* she reasoned with herself.

"Hello?" she said as she pressed the phone to her ear. She had just finished dressing and was waiting in the kitchen for Fiona to come downstairs. While it was out of her way to drive Fiona across town to the middle school, Kelly had promised her that she would.

"Kelly," came the hurried, breathless voice on the other end of the line. "Are you still friends with that Debbie Weaver?"

"Good morning, Mother," Kelly said, surprised that it wasn't her sister.

"Well?"

Kelly didn't know how to answer the original question, so she responded with a simple question in return. "Why?"

"Her daughter's Fiona's age, and I just heard that she tried to kill herself."

Immediately, Kelly froze. *Kill herself? What could possibly make a thirteen-year-old want to kill herself?* "No, I hadn't heard that," she whispered, glancing toward the bottom of the staircase. Fiona was still upstairs. Maybe she wouldn't be going to school at all today. With everything else going on, Kelly didn't want Fiona to hear whispers in the hallways that Molly had tried to commit suicide.

"She tried to hang herself," her mother said, an incredulous tone in her voice. "Debbie Weaver walked in on her."

"What?" It wasn't a question of confusion but of disbelief. "What are you telling me, Mother? That thirteen-year-old Molly Weaver tried to hang herself?"

"That's exactly what I just said."

Kelly shook her head. She couldn't make sense of this conversation. Couldn't believe that what her mother was telling her might possibly be true. And yet, just the day before, she had seen the pale Molly being rolled down the hallway of the children's psychiatric floor at the hospital, her hysterical mother sobbing as she followed the hospital bed.

"Where did you hear this, Mom?"

"Your sister."

Kelly took a deep breath and exhaled. Of course. Jackie. Under normal circumstances, Jackie would have called her directly, but since they weren't currently speaking, especially after yesterday morning's phone conversation, Jackie had most likely called her mother, who, in turn, called Kelly to see if she had any information.

Well, Kelly thought, *they aren't learning anything from me.*

"I'm sure it's just a rumor," Kelly said quietly, refusing to admit having seen either Molly or Debbie the previous afternoon. "And I think spreading such gossip will benefit no one. Perhaps you should tell that to Jackie."

"If you hear anything, please let us know." Clearly, her mother hadn't been listening, although, to be fair, Kelly suspected her mother would hang up the phone and head right down to the church to pray for both Debbie and Molly. It dawned on Kelly that she hadn't heard whether or not her mother had done the same for Zach.

"Of course, Mom. Right away."

Another white lie. Kelly hung up the phone, disgusted with her sister and her mother. Was this how people had reacted to the news about Zach's overdose? A rapid game of telephone? Or, perhaps, it hadn't happened that way. After all, Zach was seventeen, not thirteen, and had a history of drug abuse. Maybe no one had really bothered to gossip about him. His past didn't make the gossip nearly as exciting as young Molly Weaver.

"Mom?"

Kelly looked up and smiled at Fiona. "Hey, sunshine. What do you think about playing hooky . . . ?" Her voice trailed off as she realized that Fiona, the normally stoic and strong Fiona, stood there with wide eyes and pale cheeks. "Honey? What's wrong?"

She didn't know why she had asked. She already knew the answer.

"It's Molly, Mom."

Patiently, Kelly stood there, waiting silently for Fiona to explain what she had learned.

"She . . . she tried to kill herself, Mom."

In three long strides, Kelly crossed the room and stood before her daughter. She placed her hands on Fiona's arms. "What have you heard, Fiona? Tell me."

"Jenny. Jenny texted me." She glanced down at the phone in her hand. "Something about Zach."

"You mean Molly."

"No." Fiona shook her head emphatically. "Zach, Mom. Our Zach."

"What are you saying?"

Fiona swallowed and met her mother's concerned but also confused gaze. "Molly's blaming herself for Zach's overdose."

None of this made any sense. "What do you mean? How could Molly have had anything to do with Zach's overdose?" For a split second, Kelly wondered if Zach had done something to Molly. She felt a wave of panic. Could he possibly have approached her? She could remember only too well how Eddie always teased her about her friends and pushed her toward inviting certain ones over. But Zach with Molly?

"I dunno. She just kept saying that it was her fault." Fiona stared at her, her eyes large and full of confusion. "Why would Molly do that, Mom?" And that was when Kelly noticed the tears filling her daughter's eyes and slowly spilling over.

Kelly pulled Fiona into her arms and held her. At thirteen years old, hadn't Fiona experienced enough heartache and emotional turmoil? How much more could she take? Kelly realized that there were limits to how strong people could be, and, clearly, Fiona had just maxed out.

"There now," Kelly cooed, letting Fiona cry against her shoulder. "It's going to be all right, I promise." Whether or not that was true, Kelly didn't know, but she had to give her daughter a glimmer of hope. A world without hope was far too dark a place for Fiona, and Kelly had to shield her from the possibility that things would *not* be OK, even if only for a few hours or days. "Maybe Jenny isn't getting the whole story right," Kelly said when she pulled away and stared down into Fiona's face. With her thumbs, she wiped away the final tears that stained her daughter's cheeks. "You know how people misunderstand things or even make things up."

"Jenny doesn't make thing up."

"Maybe not, but someone else might have."

"I don't want to go to school."

Kelly frowned.

"I can't. If people think that Zach did something to make Molly try to kill herself . . ." Fiona sniffled. "I can't take another day of people whispering about me or avoiding me."

And there it was. The truth.

At that moment, Kelly knew that she couldn't send Fiona to school. Her daughter was right. Even though Fiona had nothing to do with either situation, the other eighth graders would enjoy gossiping about it. Kelly remembered far too well her own years in middle school and how stressful it was to remain off the radar from public scrutiny.

Like the time when Cathy Jacobs had been flung onto the radar. After cutting school and drinking her mother's wine, she called one of her teachers, Mr. Seine, for help. He replaced the missing alcohol, but, when Mrs. Jacobs found out, she contacted the school. The story quickly grew from a small seed to a large vine that strangled the truth.

For the rest of the school year, Cathy had been a pariah. Kelly had felt sorry for her but succumbed to peer pressure and avoided Cathy. In hindsight, Kelly knew that Mr. Seine had been careless in how he handled the situation. But back then, all Kelly knew was that one of her favorite teachers had helped a student and gotten in trouble because of Cathy Jacobs. It was a defining moment for Kelly. For the rest of the school year, Kelly had wrestled with guilt every time she saw Cathy walking, alone, down the hallways. And she had made a promise to herself that she would never let other people pressure her into being someone she wasn't.

Kelly certainly didn't want her daughter feeling that sense of abandonment, especially over something involving Zach.

"Of course not," Kelly said at last. "You just stay home today, OK? I'll call Grandma and have her bring you lunch or, if you want, she can take you out." She leaned over and kissed Fiona on the top of her head. "Everything will blow over."

Fiona tilted her head and looked up at her mother. "When, Mom?"

Kelly didn't have the answer. She reached out and touched Fiona's cheek, a gesture of maternal grace. "I don't know when, Fiona. But I do know that it will."

Her daughter nodded, accepting her mother's honest response. She stepped backward toward the hallway. "I'm going upstairs for a bit," she said softly. "Do some studying, I guess."

Kelly nodded and then watched as Fiona turned around and headed toward the staircase. Only when Fiona disappeared upstairs did Kelly notice that she had left her cell phone on the counter. A wise decision, Kelly thought, figuring that Fiona didn't want to hear any more gossip from the people at school.

If only adults were half as wise, Kelly thought.

CHAPTER 32

From the moment that Kelly walked into the second-floor children's psychiatric ward, she knew that her morning wasn't about to get any better. Despite the sun shining outside and the air carrying a nice, crisp autumn feel to it, the inside of the hospital felt dark and heavy with tension from the moment she arrived.

"Ms. Martin, may I speak with you a moment?"

Kelly hadn't even been buzzed into the secured area of the floor when a man in a guard uniform stopped her.

"Is . . . is there a problem?"

The security guard approached her and glanced toward the waiting-room door. "There's a young man here, wants to see your son."

The hair on the back of Kelly's neck stood up. "A young man?" She looked toward the waiting room, but she couldn't see who was inside.

"I told him that only immediate family can visit, but he insisted on staying."

Kelly nodded, her exterior the picture of calm while her insides completely fell apart. There was only one "young man" who Kelly suspected would try to visit Zach in the hospital: Michael Stevens. "Thank you," she managed to say, and, taking a deep breath, she walked toward the waiting room.

He looked up as soon as she entered the room, as if he had been expecting her. His blond hair was disheveled and partially covered his wide, bloodshot eyes. The dark circles under them made Kelly wonder if he had been up all night, and that made her think he was wasted.

That thought angered her.

"Hey."

That was how he greeted her. Not a "hello" or "how's Zach?" or even an "I'm so sorry." Just "hey."

"What do you want?" She didn't care if her voice was sharp and edgy. That was how she felt.

"I . . . uh . . ." He shifted his weight on his feet. "I wanted to see Zach."

Kelly's eyes narrowed, and she glared at the young man standing before her. "Over my dead body," she heard herself say.

"Look, he's my friend."

"You're no friend." Kelly crossed her arms over her chest. "Not to Zach. Not to anyone."

Michael's shoulders stiffened, and he glared back at her. "What's your deal, man?"

"You are. Or rather, keeping you away from my son is my deal," she replied. "You have a lot of nerve showing up here, Michael."

He laughed, looking up at the ceiling as he did so. "Wow. You really *are* crazy."

Kelly caught her breath and, for a moment, considered retreating. Surely Zach had told Michael that. Or had Michael been over at Todd's house and heard Todd say it? Either way, Kelly knew that if she ran away from this conflict, she'd never stop running.

She took a step forward and uncrossed her arms. She pointed at him, not caring that her outstretched arm invaded his personal space. With some satisfaction, she saw him lean backward at the hostile gesture. "Do you have any idea what you've done to us? You ripped apart our family and have the nerve to come here expecting kindness? You pretended to befriend Zach and hooked him on drugs. Is that the only way you feel better about yourself? He was just an easy recruit and steady income for you!"

He took a step away from her. "That's what you think."

"That's what I know!" she practically shouted at him.

"Yeah, well, let me tell you what I know," Michael said, moving farther away from her. "If it wasn't me, it would've been someone else. His drunk daddy and crazy mommy couldn't have protected him from finding it."

The smug look on his face infuriated her. She had to remind herself that he was underage, and, despite wanting to slap that smirk, she wasn't about to give him the satisfaction of pressing charges against her. "Get out of here."

"The funny thing is," Michael said as he took a few steps toward the door, "he OD'd on drugs from your own house." He laughed, his eyes gleaming with delight. "He didn't need me at all for that."

Kelly stopped short. "What do you mean?"

Michael raised his eyebrows in a taunting manner. "Why don't you ask Molly Weaver?" And then he disappeared out the door, laughing to himself with total disregard for Kelly's last question.

Standing in the doorway of the waiting room, Kelly watched him pass the elevators. She wondered where he was going, and at first she didn't care. Her anger clouded her mind like a dense fog on a chilly autumn morning. And then she wondered if he was trying to find an empty med cart to steal drugs. Should she alert someone? It would be easy to not care, to think that Michael Stevens was not her problem. Zach was.

Just like that, another thought hit her. How many people had known about Michael Stevens's propensity for dealing drugs before Zach's involvement with him? What if someone—anyone!—had spoken up? Michael might claim that Zach would have fallen to the dark side without his help and, deep down, Kelly suspected that might very well be true. But if one person had stepped forward and spoken up, how many lives might not have succumbed to the savage cycle of addiction?

And why had Michael mentioned Molly Weaver?

Suddenly, she remembered that Michael had been at the house the night of Fiona's sleepover. A dark thought crossed her mind. Did the boys do something to Molly? Was that why Molly had tried to kill herself? Kelly held her breath. Had Michael done something to her and Zach knew about it? Was that what all of this was about?

Too many nefarious ideas flooded her head, and she had to lean against the door frame.

If only she had a support system, one that she could truly turn to. Her mother hid from the situation. Her sister disassociated herself from the inconvenience. Her ex added to the problem. And the doctors focused on the patient. There were few resources to help with the collateral damage of substance abuse, namely the rest of the family, who suffered in silence.

Kelly had never thought of herself as a strong person. During her marriage, Todd had torn her down. Nothing she had ever done was good enough. Her cooking, her cleaning, her parenting. Even her work. Nothing escaped his scrutiny and criticism. It started slowly, and Kelly hadn't even noticed at first. When she did, she had tried hard to correct whatever was wrong. But as the years passed, his complaints continued, and the kindness with which he pointed out her flaws began to change into a maliciousness that forced her to her knees.

She had lost her backbone.

And then, a few years ago, she had found it.

Perhaps it was how Todd treated Fiona, or maybe it was how Zach was mimicking his father. Either way, Kelly had looked into an imaginary crystal ball and seen the future for both of her children. It was bleak: full of heartache and pain for her daughter and a life of dishing out abuse by her son.

She had realized that she had to leave Todd, if for no other reason than for the children.

He had been caught off guard and, when he lost control of his marriage, Todd fought her tooth and nail.

During the years since the divorce, he continually berated her and belittled her ability to survive without him. But now, she saw herself as a fighter and a survivor. It was the only thing she *could* see herself as—for to admit that she was anything less would mean defeat.

And she had to persevere in order to save Fiona.

With her determination restored, Kelly hurried to the double doors and pressed the button to be admitted into the secured area.

"There's a young man," Kelly said to the security guard, a different one than she had spoken to earlier. She gestured in the direction in which Michael had disappeared. "He's wandering the halls. You might want to alert someone that he's a potential problem."

The security guard gave her a sideways look. "What type of problem?"

Kelly took a deep breath. "He's a drug dealer. Of prescription drugs."

The security guard seemed to contemplate what she was insinuating before he nodded once and, after escorting Kelly into the children's psychiatric floor, started walking toward the double doors while speaking into his security phone.

Kelly watched and felt a slim degree of satisfaction. Maybe they would catch Michael Stevens stealing some medication. Maybe he would be arrested and get sent to juvenile detention. Maybe his mother would wake up from her own stupor of denial and realize the truth about her son's propensity to destroy lives.

Or maybe they would just chase him out of the hospital.

Either way, Kelly felt empowered, just a little.

Until she turned to go into Zach's room and bumped directly into Debbie Weaver.

CHAPTER 33

"Debbie!"

The woman stood just outside of Zach's doorway, her face pale and her hair unkempt. She looked terrible. Her normally pristine clothes were wrinkled, and there was a stain on the front of her white blouse. Her eyes, usually so bright and piercing, appeared dull and lifeless. Clearly, she had not returned home since Molly's admittance the previous afternoon.

Catching her breath, Kelly covered her heart with a hand and forced a slight smile. "I didn't see you there. You startled me."

Debbie did not respond.

Uncertain what to say, Kelly hesitated. The woman appeared to be a shell of the high-strung socialite who usually paraded her superiority among others. Kelly had no idea how to approach the woman in her current state.

Perhaps just the truth, she thought.

Clearing her throat, Kelly crossed her arms over her chest as if she was cold and trying to warm herself. "I saw you yesterday," she said softly. "I wanted to come to you." She hesitated. *The truth,* she reminded herself. "But I wasn't certain you needed to feel pressured into answering questions yet."

Debbie opened her mouth as if to say something, but she immediately shut it.

"So the only question I want to ask is, How is Molly doing?" Kelly said with as much compassion as she could.

"How do you think?" Debbie replied in a hoarse voice that spoke of a sleepless night and hours of crying. "She's here, isn't she?"

Kelly nodded. "Yes, she is. But she's *here*." Kelly reached out and put her hand on Debbie's arm. "She's alive and she's being cared for."

The moment that her fingers touched the woman's arm she felt Debbie pulling away from her. It was sudden and fierce. "Don't you touch me!" Debbie hissed from behind clenched teeth. "Don't you dare touch me!"

The venomous tone behind the woman's words shocked Kelly, and, inadvertently, she took a step backward. "Debbie?"

"You! You and your . . ." She glanced toward the open doorway that led to Zach's room. "Your son! You caused this!"

"What are you talking about?"

Debbie moved forward, just one step, but it closed the distance between her and Kelly. Those empty eyes were suddenly filled with acrimony. "Your son stole my daughter's medicine!"

"Excuse me?"

"That's right." The expression on Debbie's face remained blank, no emotion. Even her voice was devoid of feeling. "He stole her medicine from her backpack."

Nothing could have caught Kelly more off guard than Debbie's accusation. "What are you saying? When would he have done that?" They weren't even in the same school. Zach had no access to Molly's backpack, which made Debbie's claim even more bewildering.

But Debbie didn't back down. Her mouth flattened into a tight line. Without any makeup, her skin looked older, and her wrinkles were accentuated. For the first time, Kelly saw her not as a social climber but as a real person, one who had problems just like everyone else.

"The other night at your house," Debbie said, her tone even and emotionless. "He stole it."

Last weekend? It seemed like months had passed since Fiona had invited her friends over. After Michael had left, Zach *had* gone downstairs to pilfer some of their pizza. But all of the girls' belongings had been upstairs. Could he have gone into Fiona's room and rifled through their bags while they were downstairs having pizza?

Kelly didn't think so. It had been minutes at best before the sweet scent of pizza had drawn him from his room.

"I don't understand," Kelly said, genuinely perplexed. "None of this makes any sense."

From what Kelly recalled, Zach hadn't interacted with the girls at all except when the pizza arrived. When would Zach have had a chance to steal the medicine? How would he have even *known* Molly had it?

And then Michael's words echoed in her head. He had made a comment about Molly. Kelly had thought that strange then, but now it made sense. She saw a vision of Michael walking into her house behind Zach and pausing to tie his shoe before he went upstairs to Zach's room. He had bent over at the bottom of the staircase, the exact same spot where Molly had thrown her bag just hours before, when she first arrived, and the exact same spot the girl had been frantically looking for something she had "lost" the next morning.

Suddenly, everything became clear.

Zach hadn't stolen anything. It had been Michael. Perhaps he had accidentally found the drugs that had fallen from Molly's bag when she tossed it on the floor that evening, but he had intentionally taken them.

Debbie was glaring at her with eyes narrowed and fierce. In that moment, Kelly knew that Debbie was looking for someone to blame, and Kelly resented it. "And why would that have caused her to try to hurt herself?"

"You can't just stop taking that medicine!"

Kelly remembered Molly searching for something in the morning when Debbie had arrived to pick her up. Surely she had known then that it was gone. "She should've told you that she lost it."

"She didn't lose it! Your son stole it."

"I don't think that's possible, Debbie."

But Debbie wasn't finished. "And knowing that he stole it and then almost died, she felt guilty. Guilty because of your son!"

A defensive wall began to form around Kelly. She couldn't let Zach get the blame for this. "I'm sorry you're going through this, but I'm not going to permit you to put my son into the crosshairs."

Debbie took a step forward and pointed her finger at Kelly's chest. "Your son is a drug addict, and you didn't warn me."

"Oh come on, Debbie. You knew. It wasn't as if I've hidden it from anyone." *A fact that had been a bone of contention with Jackie,* Kelly thought.

But Debbie shook her head, denying it. "Not like that. Dabbling in smoking pot is different than being a full-blown addict! I *never* would have let my child come over to your house if I had known. I'd never have exposed her to *that* sort of thing."

Kelly squared her shoulders. "That sort of thing?" She repeated Debbie's words. "Do you think that Zach is the only one?" Furious at the insinuation, Kelly remembered the words she had flung at her sister just the other day. "Those billboards on the highways about drug abuse are not there for just my son, Debbie."

"What's that supposed to mean?"

"Drugs are everywhere, Debbie. They aren't just sold on the street corners anymore." Kelly leveled her gaze at the woman. "Perhaps you ought to interview all of Molly's friends and their families. I can assure you that Zach is not the only person in Morristown who is caught up with substance abuse. In fact, most of the teenagers are getting their drugs from their own parents' medicine cabinets, not some shady person in a dark alley."

And then it dawned on Kelly that, if what Debbie claimed was true, the drug dealer in this situation was none other than Molly. Inadvertent, yes. But true.

"And why would Molly bring prescription medicine into my house?" Kelly's eyes flashed, realizing that, perhaps, the cause for Zach's overdose was the woman standing in front of her. "You say that I should've warned you about Zach? Why didn't you warn me that your daughter was bringing drugs into my house?"

"Medicine, not drugs," Debbie corrected too quickly.

"It's the same thing." Kelly felt her anger increase. How dare this woman blame *her*? "You should have told me, Debbie. You sent Molly to my house with a controlled substance. Not just one pill but an entire bottle. Why would you send that with a thirteen-year-old?"

Debbie took a deep breath, her chest rising as she did, and her eyes narrowing until they were nothing more than dark slits in her face. "What are you insinuating, Kelly? That I'm a bad mother? That this is *my* fault?"

Kelly knew too well how manipulative people could be, detracting from the real problem by spinning the argument onto themselves. She also knew that she had to focus on the real issue and not let Debbie make this argument about her. She had accused Zach of something terrible while omitting her own role in the situation.

"I never said any such thing, Debbie. But for a young girl to bring medicine into a person's house, don't you think she should tell the adult? Especially since you *knew* about Zach's issues with addiction." Kelly shook her head, trying to keep her voice steady. "I'm sorry that Molly lost her medicine, and I'm sorry that, for whatever reason, she didn't tell you, but you have no right to cast blame on my son."

"I'm casting blame where it lies." Debbie took another step forward, standing far too close to Kelly.

"Then be certain to look in the mirror when you do," Kelly heard herself say. "That's the only way you'll ever find true peace, Debbie."

"Ladies? Is everything OK here?"

Kelly glanced at the nurse. *Thank you,* she wanted to cry out. "Yes, I think we're finished." She managed to step aside, putting a little distance between herself and Debbie.

Debbie said nothing as she turned on her heel, the rubber soles of her sneakers squeaking against the hospital floor, and walked back down the hallway toward her daughter's room, leaving heavy tension in the air. Kelly suddenly felt weak; the confrontation had drained her, and she leaned against the wall for support.

CHAPTER 34

Kelly watched Debbie walk back to Molly's room, her head hanging down and her shoulders sagging. And yet, the sympathy that Kelly had previously felt for the woman quickly turned to anger.

How dare that woman speak to her in such a manner. They were both in the hospital, praying for their children's lives. Accusing Zach of stealing Molly's medicine was one thing. But to blame him—and by extension her!—for being the reason for Molly's depression-induced suicide attempt? Outrageous.

Even more important, Kelly was shocked that Debbie had sent her thirteen-year-old daughter to someone's house with medicine. A controlled substance at that! And why would she have allowed her daughter to have the entire bottle anyway? Why was it that everyone seemed to think substance abuse was only a problem for lower-income neighborhoods where people stood on street corners and sold illegal drugs? Prescription medicine was the drug of choice for the educated and middle- to upper-class people, something that had caught on with their children as well.

Kelly's mind was still whirling, all of these thoughts colliding, when she saw Dr. Kumpoor approaching from down the hallway.

"Ms. Martin, good news," the doctor said, obviously unaware of the exchange between the two women just a few seconds earlier. She reached out and touched Kelly's arm. "I just got off the phone with the Arizona facility, and a room just opened up. They've reserved it for Zach."

Kelly frowned. Arizona? Zach? It was hard to shift gears and concentrate on the doctor's words.

"Isn't that wonderful news?" Dr. Kumpoor said in an upbeat voice.

Shaking her head as if to clear the cobwebs, Kelly looked at the doctor, trying to focus. "I'm sorry. What did you say?"

"Are you OK?"

"Yes." She nodded.

But was she?

She tried to transfer her attention from Debbie Weaver's outrageous accusations to Dr. Kumpoor's update on Zach.

"No. I mean . . ." What did she mean? Had Debbie Weaver just accused her son Zach of having caused Molly's suicide attempt? Was that even possible? Or was it merely a strange dream? "The strangest thing just happened," she whispered to the doctor. "A mother . . ." But Kelly couldn't finish the sentence. How could she?

Kelly gave her head another little shake, the cobwebs still lingering there. It rankled Kelly's remaining nerves how so many parents did not hold their children, or even themselves, accountable for their actions. Why! Those parents sought blame from external sources rather than reflecting on the internal contributions to the problem. No wonder the children behaved so poorly!

And then Kelly froze.

A moment of clarity struck her, and the color drained from her face. Was she any different? Didn't she, too, fall into that category of shifting responsibility to other people? Hadn't she blamed Michael Stevens? Hadn't she gone to the school, expecting them to do something? Perhaps even to admit their own culpability? And yet, now she realized that, when it came to Zach and his problems, there was no one to blame but Zach himself. Not Todd. Not Michael. Not Molly. Not even the school. Hadn't that been what Michael Stevens had tried to tell her?

"Ms. Martin? Is something wrong?"

"Nothing, I'm sorry." Pushing her epiphany aside, Kelly forced herself to focus on what the doctor was saying. She'd have plenty of time later to ponder her sudden revelation. For the moment, however, Zach was more important. "So you were saying?"

"Arizona. The facility in Arizona. They've reserved a bed for Zach."

Kelly took a deep breath. "I can't afford that, Doctor. I thought I already told you that."

The doctor glanced down the hallway as if looking for someone before she leaned closer to Kelly. Lowering her voice, she spoke in a slow, deliberate manner. "Your insurance *will* cover it, Ms. Martin. In fact, your children's health insurance covers most of this."

For some reason, Kelly felt irritated. How easy it was for the doctor to think that insurance companies simply wrote endless checks for the expensive care that went along with substance abuse. "I'm quite sure I know what I've paid."

Dr. Kumpoor paused. "I'm familiar with this plan, Ms. Martin, and they do, indeed, cover this type of care. Perhaps you need to speak with them?"

"What do you mean?" Kelly blinked. Surely the doctor was mistaken. How many times had she had to scramble for money in order to pay, up front, for Zach's treatment? "That isn't true. I've had to pay out of pocket for every one of these facilities! Insurance paid for nothing."

The doctor pressed her lips together and stared at her. She seemed to be contemplating her next words very carefully. Finally, she said, "Parents paying up front for treatment versus the insurance company reimbursing the policyholder are two very different things, Ms. Martin."

"What are you saying?"

The doctor straightened up. "Exactly what I just said. The insurance company reimburses the policyholder. Are *you* the policyholder?"

Kelly felt her heart begin to palpitate as she realized exactly what the doctor had just told her. How many thousands of dollars had she spent? Thirty? No, almost double that, especially when she considered the interest rates and finance charges for using a credit line and charge cards to pay for Zach's treatments. Once she had contacted the insurance company, trying to argue with them about the fact that they covered none of Zach's treatments. And their response had been similar to Dr. Kumpoor's.

"Are you the policyholder?" the woman on the other end of the telephone asked.

"No, but I—" Kelly stammered.

"Are you on the policy?"

Part of the divorce settlement had been giving up health insurance. Todd's policy covered the children, and he was given a credit against the child support he paid. But Kelly had her own policy. "No, I'm not but—"

"Then we cannot discuss this with you. I'm sorry."

"But this is my child!" Kelly said, trying to sound forceful and confident.

"I'm sorry."

"Are . . . are you certain?" Kelly asked, partially hoping that the doctor was mistaken. She had enough on her plate to deal with. The unnecessary truth that Dr. Kumpoor had shared with her might just send her over the edge.

Dr. Kumpoor pursed her lips and raised an eyebrow as she looked toward the ceiling as if contemplating something. "Let's just say that, in my experience dealing with this type of treatment and your particular health insurance, I have never heard of them *not* reimbursing for treatment, Ms. Martin. They happen to be one of the *few* insurance companies that reimburse directly to the policyholder and *not* the facility providing treatment."

"That's—"

"Outrageous, I know," Dr. Kumpoor interrupted her. A pause. Or, rather, an intentional pause. "Might I suggest contacting someone, perhaps a lawyer, so that you could get your reimbursements back?"

Kelly couldn't even respond. She stood there, speechless, as she tried to digest this new bit of information.

The doctor took a deep breath and reached out, touching Kelly's arm once again. "I'm sure you have a lot to think about, Ms. Martin, and I am truly sorry to have been the one to deliver that news to you. However, I do need to move forward and proceed with the paperwork to transfer Zach to the facility."

Kelly opened her mouth to say something, but no words came out. She was still absorbing what the doctor had just told her. Was it possible that Todd had stolen all of that money from her? Could he truly be so evil? So bitter? And all of those years he complained about "giving" her child support and demanded that she reimburse him for every little nickel and dime that he spent on the children. Her pulse quickened as she grasped the extent of that man's vindictiveness. How dare he? Especially when he knew that she struggled to make ends meet so that the children didn't suffer any more than necessary from living in broken homes.

Sinking into the nearest chair, Kelly stared at the wall, seeing nothing.

First the scene with Debbie Weaver, and now the realization that her ex-husband had embezzled so much money from her. She could add another label to describe her ex-husband besides alcoholic: common thief.

CHAPTER 35

"He did *what*?"

Kelly sat across from Charlotte in the hospital cafeteria.

"Keep your voice down," Kelly whispered, glancing around quickly to make sure no one could overhear. She wasn't certain why. Surely no one would know whom she was talking about; however, she didn't want attention drawn to them. "What do I do now?"

Charlotte shoved away her half-eaten croissant in disgust. "You sue him."

"I can't afford a lawyer," Kelly countered. "You know that."

"Then do it pro se. I'll help you with the paperwork," Charlotte offered. "It's not that hard. Just Google the paperwork for filing an emergent order or motion to show cause. We'll request full custody and reimbursement of the health insurance money you paid."

Kelly shook her head. "It's not that easy."

"It *is* that easy," Charlotte insisted. "You paid it, he was reimbursed, and he kept it."

It would have been so simple to believe Charlotte. But Kelly knew otherwise. "I don't have any proof. The insurance company won't admit or deny that they reimbursed him since I'm not on the policy. And remember that the burden of proof's on the plaintiff." She made a face. "Innocent until proven guilty right?"

"That's ridiculous!" Charlotte inhaled sharply. "The courts can subpoena the records."

"That will take too long."

Charlotte frowned at her. "Look, Kelly, you can make up any excuse you want, but if you don't fight this . . . this crustacean, I'm going to really be disappointed in you. He has no right to profit from his son's medical treatment."

Charlotte's words echoed in Kelly's ears. Profiting from his son's medical treatment. "I just can't believe he would sink so low."

"Oh I can!" Charlotte responded far too quickly. "He's never forgiven you for leaving him. God forbid he accepts any responsibility." She drummed her fingers on the side of the table. "Faultless to a T, eh?"

"Always."

Charlotte's expression spoke volumes about what she thought of Todd Martin. "Well, don't you pay one dime toward this new facility. He can just pay it himself and get reimbursed."

But Kelly knew it wasn't that easy. Todd would fight her on the new facility for Zach. And then to expect him to pay out of pocket? He'd never do that. Not without a legal battle, and she just didn't have time for that. The hospital wanted to release Zach into the care of the facility within a few days, a week at the most. A chaperone would escort Zach to Arizona; no parental involvement was necessary or even recommended. But none of that would happen without the first month being paid for . . . and Todd's approval.

"One can only pray," Kelly managed to say.

Charlotte made a noise, almost as if scoffing. Kelly didn't need to ask what she meant. "Good luck with that," Charlotte said. "Some things even God cannot forgive."

"Now, now." Kelly gave her a stern look, even though she sometimes felt the same way.

And then an unusual silence fell between them. Charlotte wasn't looking at her but staring at something over Kelly's shoulder. Her eyes widened, and her mouth formed a slight *O* shape. Just from the change in her friend's expression, Kelly stiffened, suspecting she knew what Charlotte had seen.

Or, rather, whom.

"Is that . . . ?" Charlotte didn't finish the sentence, her eyes following a person who was, apparently, walking behind Kelly.

"Mmm."

Charlotte's gaze snapped back to Kelly. "Are you telling me that you knew? You knew that Debbie Weaver was here?"

Kelly made a face.

"Why didn't you tell me?" Charlotte hissed in a low voice.

"I forgot that you knew her."

Charlotte leaned back in her chair and stared at Kelly in disbelief.

"It's true," Kelly professed. "I know you don't run with that crowd anymore. I just forgot. And besides, she's here because of her daughter."

"Which one?"

"Molly."

"Is she all right?"

Kelly shrugged. She felt uncomfortable sharing too much information about Molly with Charlotte. After all, even Debbie Weaver was entitled to privacy.

"Molly's on the same floor as Zach," she admitted, making certain to lower her voice.

Charlotte leaned back in her chair, her mouth opening into a larger O.

"And, apparently, Debbie is blaming Zach."

At this, Charlotte's mouth shut and her eyes immediately narrowed. "What? How is that *even* possible?"

Kelly sighed. This *was* Charlotte after all. She knew that anything she shared with Charlotte would go no further. "Debbie claims Zach stole Molly's medicine out of her backpack when she slept over the other weekend." Saying it was one thing; believing it was another. "I don't think that's how it happened. I think it fell out of her backpack when she tossed it on the floor."

She could still see Michael Stevens smirking when he had mentioned Molly's name. She shuddered at the image, forcing herself to fight her anger at his impudent attitude about it. But then she remembered Debbie Weaver. No, Kelly would not be like Debbie. She would not pass around the blame any longer. It lay squarely on her son's shoulders. While he could claim that some of his problems were collateral damage from the divorce, that did not make up for this poor decision.

Charlotte still looked confused. "Even if it didn't happen that way, how would that be Zach's fault that Molly is hospitalized?"

Because it's easier to blame others than yourself, Kelly wanted to say, but stopped short, knowing that there was too much hypocrisy behind such a statement. She, too, had blamed others.

Instead, she sighed. "I suppose Molly didn't tell her mother that she lost her medicine and, well, got depressed. You know you can't just cold-turkey stop taking antidepressants. And then when Zach overdosed, she felt guilty. Maybe she presumed it was on her meds."

Charlotte appeared as stunned as Kelly had felt earlier that morning when Debbie had confronted her. "You've got to be kidding me. Tell me that's not true."

Holding her hands out, palms upward, Kelly shrugged. "I wish I could, but that's what she said to me this morning."

"To your face?"

Kelly gave a single nod. "Yes, to my face."

"Oh sweet mama." Charlotte leaned back in her chair and rubbed her cheeks. "I don't believe you."

Kelly understood how Charlotte felt. She, too, hadn't believed it when it happened. And yet, now she understood better. Condemning others made it easier to deny personal responsibility.

And then Charlotte added, "Is she out of her mind? I mean, seriously. How could she blame Zach for that?"

Kelly shrugged. "Parents will do anything to shift the blame to someone else for their children's flaws."

"I'm glad I don't have kids."

There were days when Kelly didn't blame her. The idea of passing through life with no one depending on her *did* sound appealing more often than Kelly liked to admit. Yet, she also knew that nothing replaced the good days, the kind words, and the occasional hugs, even if only from Fiona as of late. And then there were the memories. The images of her children's first steps and first words. Little Zach petting that large horse on the side of the road. Rocking her son to sleep when he felt poorly. Or simply standing in the doorway of his room, watching him sleep in his crib with his little arms tossed over his head, hands fisted, and his mouth sucking on a pacifier.

It didn't matter how brief those days were. Kelly wouldn't have traded any of the pain and agony of the past few years if it meant erasing those memories.

But Charlotte would never understand any of this. In some ways, Kelly thought that was a bittersweet blessing for her friend.

"And what kind of medicine was she taking?" Charlotte shook her head. "She's what . . . twelve?"

"Thirteen."

"Thirteen then! Whatever." She crumpled up her napkin and threw it on her plate, disgusted. "What's going on in *that* house that a thirteen-year-old needs to be on medication?"

Kelly bit her tongue.

"I mean, I know that Debbie would drive me to be on medication if *I* had to live with her." Charlotte scoffed. "I wonder what she's telling her country club friends about *this* little interlude in her otherwise picture-perfect life that she presents so well."

"No one's life is perfect."

Her thoughts immediately turned to her sister. They hadn't spoken since the aftermath of Heather's birthday. But she was another Debbie, caught up in the game of seeking validation through materialistic gain. It was more important to Jackie to surround herself with like-minded people than to even offer a shoulder of support to her own sister. Kelly knew the truth: the situation with Zach was too dirty for Jackie to get involved. The last thing Jackie wanted was for her loose-knit circle of fellow social climbers to have any fodder for gossip about *her*.

But Jackie was not alone.

The pressure that she put on herself was just as addictive as the drugs Zach had taken. Once someone stepped onto that track, they could do nothing but keep running, hoping to keep up—if not pass!—the others. It was a vicious cycle with plenty of people to keep her company on the journey.

As Charlotte and Kelly got up to leave, Kelly was struck by that thought. Was it possible that Jackie was an addict, too, only with a different drug of choice: prestige?

CHAPTER 36

The next morning, when she arrived at the hospital, Kelly hadn't expected to see Thomas waiting for her. She glanced at the clock on the wall. It wasn't even eight o'clock. Surely he'd be late for his work.

"Thomas!" Kelly managed to find a smile to spare for him. It wasn't hard to locate. "What a surprise!"

He didn't return the smile. "I hope you don't mind that I stopped in. I was . . ." He hesitated. "Well, I was waiting to hear how Zach's doing."

It took her a minute to realize that she had promised to call Thomas. Truth be told, she hadn't remembered. Calling anyone just wasn't a priority for her at the moment. But Thomas looked concerned, and Kelly felt terrible.

"I'm so sorry. I have no excuse, Thomas. I just forgot." Sometimes honesty was the best policy.

Her admission, however, was not met with a wave of the hand and *don't worry about it.* That surprised her.

"So?"

Kelly blinked.

"How is he?"

She felt like a fool and knew that the color flooded to her cheeks. "Oh! He's doing OK. Not great but OK."

Thomas nodded as he shoved his hands into his jacket pockets. That seemed to be his sign that he was about to leave. "Can you tell him I stopped by?"

Kelly stepped forward and, after the slightest hesitation, she placed her hand on his arm. "Thomas, wait. Don't leave just yet. I mean, if you can stay, would you?"

The thought of spending the morning alone suddenly didn't appeal to her. The previous day had wiped her out emotionally. Even talking with Charlotte hadn't helped her feel better. In fact, she had tossed and turned all night, switching from her fury at Todd over the insurance money to anger at Debbie for placing the blame for Molly's hospitalization on Zach's shoulders.

He pressed his lips together. "I suppose. If that's what you'd like."

She wondered if, perhaps, Thomas thought she hadn't called him on purpose. He had been attentive and supportive, more so than a former football coach should be. And then it dawned on her that, maybe—just maybe!—Zach was not the only reason Thomas was stopping by and visiting the hospital. And when she hadn't called, he might have thought she was not interested.

"I would like that," she admitted. She paused, feeling awkward. "I truly didn't call because, believe it or not, the last day or so was just . . . terrible. I can't even remember if today is Tuesday or Wednesday."

"It's Monday," he said.

"It is?"

He smiled and shook his head. "I'm teasing. It's Tuesday."

"See?" She waved her hand. "I would've believed you." Kelly took a deep breath, then exhaled, hoping that he could sense the pressure she had been under. "So it wasn't personal. Believe me."

"I believe you."

"Then maybe we could, you know, go . . ." Was she actually asking him out? She had never done that before, and she wondered how he might take it. She shifted her weight and bit her lip. "Uh . . . we could—"

"Grab a cup of coffee in the coffee shop downstairs?" He smiled and that made her feel better. "That sounds great, but only if you let me treat you."

Reluctantly, she agreed and wondered if this constituted a date. If so, who had asked whom? The thought that it might be considered one gave her a warm feeling. Besides Todd, Kelly hadn't been out with a man in almost twenty years. And, back then, men usually took her to restaurants on Friday evenings, maybe followed by a movie. She gave a soft laugh at the realization that she was now resigned to coffee dates in the early morning. Surely that was a sign of old age.

"What's so funny?" he asked as he held open the elevator door. He was smiling at her, and Kelly shook her head. But he persisted. "Come on. Tell me. Something struck your funny bone. What was it?"

Now she knew that her cheeks were turning pink. How could she explain this to him without embarrassing herself further? "I . . . well . . . I was just getting a kick out of going to coffee with you." She bit her lower lip as she stood in the elevator, facing the doors. "I mean, not that this is a date or anything, but, you know . . ."

He looked amused. "No, I don't. Educate me."

She ran her hand over her hair, a nervous gesture. "I mean, the last time I went out with a man was Todd, when we were dating twenty or so years ago. It just struck me as funny. How I'd never have drunk coffee then. Times have changed."

She couldn't look at him. Swallowing, she stared straight ahead, watching as the round numbers lit up over the door as the elevator began descending to the lower-level floor where the coffee shop was located. It finally stopped on C, and before the doors opened, she saw Thomas reach out and press the "Door Shut" button.

"Kelly."

She looked at him and caught her breath. He was staring at her, a serious expression on his face. But it was how he studied her face and settled his eyes on her own.

"Look, I know you're going through a lot right now," he said, his gaze never wavering. "And this might not be the best time for anything more than a"—he hesitated—"friendship to form."

She panicked. Trapped in the elevator and realizing she had made a mistake, she felt her neck heat up, and she wanted to reach out, tug at her collar. The humiliation of having made an assumption and then joking about it was too much. She wanted those elevator doors to open so that she could run and hide.

"I'm so sorry," she blurted out. "I didn't really think it was a—"

Thomas held up his hand and interrupted her. "If you'd like it to be a date, then it is, Kelly. I'm not going to say that I am not interested in something more; however, I suspect this is a time when you need a friend, not 'something more.' Just know that, when and if you are ready, I'm here. I'll be waiting. But if that day doesn't come, I'm OK with just being friends. I really do care about Zach." Another pause. "And you."

She swallowed and averted her eyes. He remained silent until she had no choice but to look at him.

"For now, Kelly, friendship is all I think you can handle."

Reluctantly, she nodded her head. He was right and, for that she wanted to thank him. She couldn't form the words, though. It felt too empty and expected. Instead, she moistened her lips and gave a simple nod. "I'd like that, Thomas. I really think I do. And I appreciate your thoughtfulness."

He tilted his head, pausing before he leaned over and, ever so gently, planted the softest of kisses on her cheek.

The gesture sent a wave of electricity through her. It was tender and kind, sweet and considerate. There was nothing pushy or intimate about the kiss. And yet, she also found it extremely exciting. She had never thought that she'd be remotely intrigued by a man again, not after surviving Todd. It was exhilarating, that feeling of eagerness about getting to know a man who, in turn, wanted to learn more about her. In fact, she wondered if Todd had ever been interested in anything about her. He had been much more absorbed in completing the whole picture: working man with wife and kids living in a nice house with a dog. He hadn't ever really been interested in *her*. Not as a person, anyway.

Thomas released the button, and the doors opened to a small crowd of waiting people. They stepped aside to let Thomas and Kelly through.

"Everything OK in there?" one man asked as they passed by. "Was getting ready to call maintenance."

"Button got stuck," Thomas said casually. "I think it's all right now."

Kelly dipped her head and walked behind Thomas, a small smile on her lips. She couldn't help but wonder what those people thought and, for the briefest of moments, she felt like a teenager again. There was something refreshing about feeling that way, as if God was giving her a second chance.

While she didn't want to jump too far ahead, race to rash conclusions, she couldn't help but wonder if God had placed Thomas in her life for a reason. With Thomas, she found herself thinking about more than Zach and Fiona. His attention and support were giving her the opportunity to think about herself for once. And Kelly realized that, despite all of the problems that she was facing, she needed someone like Thomas in her life, even if it remained what he had said: the formation of a new friendship.

CHAPTER 37

"Arizona?"

Kelly stood beside Zach's bed, focusing just on her son and not on her ex-husband. In fact, she did her best to forget that Todd was even there. She knew better than to look at him. If she did, she risked succumbing to the rage building inside of her. The more she thought about it, the more she wanted to confront him about having hidden the insurance reimbursement money. But she couldn't do that. Not in front of Zach.

"I don't want to go to Arizona," he said, turning his gray eyes to look at her. "Mom?"

"Look, Zach, I can understand feeling apprehensive about this, but I think it's for the best. You need to get away from Morristown. There are too many triggers here. Things that set you off and hinder you from getting clean."

Todd cleared his throat. "And it doesn't mean forever."

Secretly, Kelly hoped it did mean forever, if it kept Zach away from his father and Morristown.

Zach seemed to shrink further into the pillows of the hospital bed, suddenly looking much younger than a seventeen-year-old. "Which one of you are taking me there?" he asked in a timid voice, his eyes moving from his mother back to his father. "Dad?"

Sarah Price

"Neither of us," Kelly answered. "The facility's policy is for a chaperone to escort you—"

Holding up his hand, Todd interrupted her. "Now hold on a minute, Kelly. We didn't agree on that." He leaned over and touched Zach's shoulder. "I'm going to see about taking off work so that I can take you."

As usual, there was Todd rewriting the rules. "That's *not* their procedure," she reminded him in a sharp tone. "The facility highly discourages parents from doing that."

Tossing a sharp look at her, Todd scowled. "I don't care if they 'highly discourage' it, Kelly." *Kell-lee*. "I'm not having some stranger from a drug rehab fly my son to Arizona. We don't even know who this guy is."

Kelly clenched her teeth and took a quick breath. "Her name is Mary Thompson, and she's arriving on Monday so that Zach can leave on Tuesday."

"A woman?" Todd practically spat out the word as if he had just tasted spoiled milk. He shook his head vehemently. "Absolutely not!"

Kelly fought the urge to roll her eyes.

"I'll take you, Zach," Todd said.

"We'll discuss this later, Todd," Kelly replied. Oh, how he could get under her skin!

Zach frowned. "How long do I have to be there?"

Kelly knew there was no answer to that question that would make him feel better. Once again, she found herself realizing that she needed to speak the truth, even if it wasn't what he wanted to hear. "Until you are better, Zach," she responded, feeling it was the safest answer, even if it was noncommittal. "You simply cannot go on like this. You'll wind up dead, and none of us want that."

"I think you're being overly dramatic, Kelly."

She gave Todd a dark look but did not take the bait. No, she would not engage with him, not here in front of Zach. Despite what

238

she thought of Todd, she knew that Zach had to form his own opinions. One day, perhaps, he would learn the truth, that his father had contributed more to the problem than to the solution.

To her surprise, Zach turned to his father. "Dad, she's right."

Kelly tried to mask her expression. Had her son just defended her to his father? In any other situation, she would have pretended to clutch her chest in feigned shock.

Todd gave her another fierce look. "Maybe your mother's been here too much, telling you things." He returned his gaze to Zach. "Don't listen to her."

Just as Kelly was about to speak up, Zach did it for her. "You always told me that, Dad. But that wasn't right then and it's not right now."

"Zach—"

But Zach wasn't finished. "Dr. Kumpoor has been spending a lot of time with me."

Todd made a face.

"And she's made me realize that I have a lot of anger inside."

"How much time could she have spent with you, Zach? She's only been treating you for—what?—three or four days?" Todd gave a disdainful laugh.

"Maybe that's enough," Zach said. "At least to realize that I was headed down a dark path that could've ended up with me dead." He looked at his mother. "And if Mom hadn't found me, I probably *would've* been dead. By my own choice."

"Stop that, Zach. Don't talk like that."

But Zach insisted. "No, Dad. Don't deny it. Not if you want to help me. I tried to overdose on purpose. I didn't want to live. It was easier to give up than to fight on."

Kelly leaned down and placed her hand on Zach's shoulder. "I hope you realize that you have a lot of life ahead of you."

"I suppose that's what I have to learn," he said in a soft voice. "How to believe that."

"It won't be easy, Zach, but I'm here for you," she said and then, as if an afterthought, added, "Both of us."

He gave a slight nod of his head. "Thanks," he whispered.

His eyelids drooped just a little, and Kelly gave his arm a reassuring squeeze. "Sleep a bit, OK? I'll be back later this evening after I get Fiona situated."

Outside the room, Kelly shut the door behind Todd. He didn't wait until she had turned around before he attacked.

"How can you let him believe that crap?"

"What crap, exactly, are you talking about, Todd?"

"Whatever that Indian chick is feeding him!"

Kelly inhaled sharply. "If you mean the medical doctor who is treating our son . . ." Todd's transparency sickened Kelly, and she narrowed her eyes, glaring at him. "She's not feeding him crap, Todd. She's telling him the truth. A truth that you've been denying for years. Maybe it's time you start listening."

"What does she know about this?"

Kelly made a face, disgusted with the insinuation behind his words. "Why? Because she's a woman? Or because she's Indian? Give me a break, Todd, and get over yourself. She's a highly intelligent and well-trained professional. In just a few short days, she's managed to have a miniature breakthrough with our son, who, if you weren't listening, finally spoke about his problem and admitted that he was headed down a very dark path, one that no one wants their children taking, and most parents avoid discussing with them until it's too late."

Todd dismissed her with an absentminded hand wave and started to walk away.

Her anger rising, Kelly followed him. "I'm not finished with you, Todd Martin. Don't you walk away from me." She reached out and grabbed his arm. "I want to talk to you about all of those reimbursement checks you've been receiving and hiding from me."

He stopped walking and turned to face her. "What are you talking about?"

Kelly put her hand on her hip. "I know about the insurance money. You've been making me pay out of pocket for my share of the different rehabs, but you never told me that the insurance company reimburses you."

He stiffened and scowled at her.

"You've stolen that money from me."

"I pay for that health insurance policy. Nowhere does it say that you're entitled to reimbursements."

Kelly almost let her mouth drop at his words. How was it even possible that he might try to justify this? But nothing about Todd surprised her anymore. And today she was prepared. "Actually, you're wrong. Look at our PSA agreement. There's a section in there, section 7B, I believe. It specifically states that any health reimbursements must be distributed based on our percentages of contributions."

For a second, he looked flustered, rendered speechless by her words. Kelly felt a momentary sense of satisfaction that, for once, she had trumped him at his own game.

"You have two choices, Todd," she said carefully. "You can do the right thing and give me what I'm due, or I can take this to the judge. Either way, you will reimburse me."

"You think I will reimburse you." He practically snarled at her. "You take away my house and my children—"

"I paid you for that house, fair and square!"

"And you destroyed my life. I pay you alimony and give you child support—"

"You support your children! There's no *gift* there, Todd."

"I pay for their health care, so if there's a reimbursement, it's mine, not yours. You aren't due anything!" With that, he yanked his arm free from her grasp. "Now, if you'll excuse me, I have to get back to work.

You know, work? A real job? Something if you weren't so lazy you'd try to find. Then you wouldn't keep hounding me for money!"

He stormed down the hallway, leaving Kelly standing there, shaking with rage. Would his abuse ever stop, or would she always need to struggle to her feet after he pushed her to the ground, cutting her off at the knees with his verbal assaults and disparaging remarks?

CHAPTER 38

Like Tuesday, Wednesday turned into another day of surprises.

It was almost two in the afternoon when the security guard found Kelly in Zach's room.

"Ms. Martin?"

Kelly looked up from the book that she had been reading. "Yes?"

"There's a woman to see you in the waiting room."

For a moment, Kelly panicked. Was it Joan Stevens again? Had she come back? "Did you catch her name?" Immediately, she felt terrible for having asked. He was a security guard, not a secretary.

"She's a bit older," he said apologetically. "That's all I can tell you. Would you like me to go ask her?"

Kelly shook her head and set down her book. She gave him a kind smile. "No, but thank you. Surely you have better things to do than to run interference for the patients' families."

He gave her an appreciative look and backed out of the room.

Reluctantly, Kelly headed down the hallway toward the double doors. She felt a momentary wave of panic, praying that it wasn't Joan Stevens. After the previous days of surprises and confrontations, she didn't know how much more she could handle.

Taking a deep breath, she walked through the door and into the waiting room, where, to her surprise, she saw her mother sitting in the blue vinyl chair, clutching her purse on her lap as she looked around with wide, frightened eyes.

"Mom? What're you doing here?"

"Oh Kelly!" Her mother jumped to her feet and hurried over to where Kelly had stopped just inside the door. "They won't let me in to see Zach."

The frantic look on her mother's face almost made Kelly laugh. "It's not personal, Mom. It's their policy. Only immediate family, and just the adults at that."

"I'm immediate family."

"You're his grandmother."

"Isn't that immediate enough?"

The concerned look on her mother's face softened Kelly's response. At least she cared, and that meant a lot to Kelly. "I can ask, Mom, but they are really strict up here. The focus is on the patient, not the family. Surely you can understand that."

But from the look on her mother's face, it was clear that she didn't.

Kelly gestured toward a set of chairs in the room. "Let's sit and talk a bit, OK?" She guided her mother over to the seats. "I'm glad you came. I'm sure you'd rather be anywhere else."

"Oh, I had nothing else planned," her mother said. "Not until tonight, anyway."

Kelly took a deep breath. *Patience,* she told herself. "That's not what I meant."

"What did you mean?" Her mother looked genuinely confused, as if there could be no other meaning to Kelly's words.

"I meant that it must be hard to visit your grandson in the psychiatric ward at the hospital."

For a split second, her mother didn't say anything. She seemed startled by Kelly's admission, as if she hadn't known that was where Zach had been admitted. "I thought he was in intensive care."

"That was last week. They moved him here on Saturday." Kelly knew better than to add that if her mother had been a little more interested in Zach's condition, she would have already known that.

"Oh." She clutched her purse on her lap. "So, how is he?"

That's a start, Kelly thought. "Doing better. They want to send him to Arizona—"

"So far away?" her mother interrupted. "Why?"

"Well, if you had let me finish . . . ," Kelly said slowly, feeling her patience start to ebb away. "They have a facility down there, outside of Phoenix, that does equine-assisted psychotherapy."

"Equine?"

Kelly nodded. "Using horses to help patients suffering from depression. Apparently there's something about patients working with horses that creates a sense of calm. Patients tend to feel safe and talk more. They develop self-esteem and self-confidence, too. It sounds like a promising program."

Her mother, however, didn't appear convinced. "He doesn't know anything about horses."

"That's not the point."

"And I thought he was smoking that pot. Now suddenly he's depressed?" She made a face. "Seems like they're putting an awful lot of different labels on the child."

Kelly leaned forward. "That's the thing, Mom, he's *not* a child. In a few months, he'll be eighteen and, legally, that's an adult. But the last few years of drug abuse have left him behind. The doctor said it's as if, mentally, he stopped developing at fourteen, fifteen. He needs help getting caught up as well as cleaned up."

"I still don't know why I can't see him," her mother sighed, changing the subject. "He is my grandson."

"I don't make the rules here." It was the closest thing to an apology that Kelly would give her mother. If she truly had wanted to see Zach, she could have come to the hospital when he was first admitted.

And then she thought about what Thomas had said, that some people avoided car wrecks while others were drawn to them. Had her mother been avoiding the hospital because, like so many other people, she was in denial? Distancing herself from the wreck that was her grandson?

"Mom," Kelly said, carefully choosing her words. "You know that by avoiding the subject, it doesn't go away."

Her mother gave a little gasp and pressed a hand against her chest as if horrified at such a suggestion. "I'm not avoiding the subject!"

"You are." Kelly tried to keep her tone soft and gentle. "It's unpleasant, I know. But it's the truth. Zach is not just a boy being a boy. He's not like Eddie, smoking a cigarette instead of going to band practice. He's an addict. A drug addict. And he's depressed."

Her mother clucked her tongue and looked away.

"Seriously, Mom, you can't evade the truth." She paused, giving herself a moment to catch her breath and clear her thinking. She thought back to what the pastor had always said about forgiveness and addressing wrongs. Kelly knew that she needed to cleanse her own harbored feelings of bitterness. "And there's something else that cannot be dodged anymore. And that's the fact that I need you."

At this, her mother snapped her gaze back to look at Kelly. "And I'm here for you, aren't I? I'm always here for you."

"No." Kelly shook her head. "No, you haven't been. In fact, you haven't been here for me for a long time."

"Are you trying to hurt me, Kelly? Because if you are, you're doing a very good job at it."

Deflection. Once again. Like Debbie Weaver, her mother was deflecting the subject onto something else. Perhaps it was done subconsciously, as a self-defense mechanism. But Kelly could see it now. "Mom, I'm trying to tell you how I feel. If that hurts you, I'm sorry."

"You called me the other night, and I came over to stay with Fiona."

"Maybe I shouldn't have *needed* to call, Mom. Maybe you could've offered." Kelly took a deep breath and exhaled. "Why do you always wait for me to call you in order to help out?"

"That's not fair!"

Kelly held up her hand. If their conversation continued in this direction, it wasn't going to end well, and that was not her intention. She needed to redirect the focus onto her original point. "Look, I don't want to argue with you, Mom. That's not my purpose. But I'm telling you now what I need." She lowered her hand and placed it over her mother's. "I need you. My mother. I need you to be here for me and not just when I ask, OK? I need you even when I don't ask."

Her mother blinked back her tears. "You think you need me, Kelly. But you don't."

"I do," Kelly countered and gave a small laugh. "You have no idea how much I do."

"You never have needed me. You've always been my strong one, the one who I didn't need to worry about."

Her mother's words almost sounded like she was talking about someone else. "What on earth are you talking about?"

Once again, her mother wiped at her eyes, catching the last of her tears. "Oh Kelly, please. You've always been the fighter. Out of all three of my children, you were the one I knew would be the survivor, the one who could manage for herself. Why, do you think your sister could do what you've done? Leave Todd, do it on her own, and deal with what Zach is going through?"

Kelly frowned. "I don't think she has to worry about that. Her marriage is fine, she lives a good life, and Heather just about walks on water from the way Jackie talks about it."

To her surprise, her mother gave a little laugh and shook her head. "You see what you want to see, Kelly. But if you really looked, just a little beneath the surface, you'd be surprised to know that she, too, has problems. She's just a little more private about airing them."

For the life of her, Kelly couldn't even imagine what sort of problems her sister could have.

"And Eddie? Well, he's been laid off from his company. He's been out of work for almost a year. That's one of the reasons he hasn't been back to New Jersey to visit. He's embarrassed and, according to Sophia, depressed. He doesn't know what to do. They're living off his severance pay, but no one is hiring in his field down there."

Stunned, Kelly stared at her mother. "Eddie was laid off?"

"See? You think that everyone else leads perfect lives, but that's because they want people to think that. They're simply hiding in the shadows, too afraid to let other people know what's really going on."

"What about Jackie?" Kelly dared to ask.

"Jason's made some bad investments. I don't want to get into the details, but I've been helping them out until things swing back in their favor."

Mom would pay for it. That had been what Jackie had said to her two weeks ago, before Zach's overdose. Now Kelly knew that her suspicions were correct. Heather's private school tuition was being paid for by their mother.

"Why don't they just quit that club and put Heather in public school?" Kelly asked.

"Jason makes a lot of business contacts at the golf club, Kelly. He can't lose that right now if he wants to get back on track. And I didn't want Heather going to the public school. That's one of the reasons Jackie wanted Fiona over for Heather's birthday, so that she could meet some of Heather's friends. I was going to offer to pay for her to go to the same school, keep her away from Morristown High, especially after all that you've gone through with Zach." Her mother made a face and shrugged. "But then all of this happened, and I didn't get a chance to discuss it with you."

Kelly leaned back in the seat. If all of this was true, it certainly explained a lot.

"So you see, Kelly, I might not have been here for you, not the way you thought I should be." Her mother forced a smile. "But I thought you were handling everything. I should've known that even the people with the strongest shoulders sometimes need help with carrying the heaviest of loads." She moved her hand from beneath Kelly's and placed it on top, giving her a gentle squeeze. "I'll be here to help you. And you won't even need to call, deal?"

The warmth of her mother's touch sent a flurry of emotions through her. Kelly could only nod her head, fighting her own tears as she realized just how wrong she had been when it came to her family. She leaned forward and embraced her mother. Shutting her eyes and resting her head against her shoulder, Kelly let herself feel protected and safe, even if only for a few minutes, in her mother's arms.

CHAPTER 39

The papers that Kelly had printed out from the Morris County Courthouse's website were spread out across her kitchen table. Pages and pages of forms and instructions. Sighing, she leaned her head against her hand.

An hour earlier, Fiona had said good night, so Kelly had finally felt safe looking at the packet that she needed to fill out in order to reclaim the insurance money from Todd. She hadn't wanted to answer any questions from Fiona, knowing that shielding her daughter from this situation was imperative. Fiona's relationship with her father was already nonexistent. The last thing she needed was more fuel for the fire in that department.

Now, Kelly tried to make sense of what she needed to do in order to file the motion. She had even dug out her large plastic storage bin filled with too much paperwork from the divorce. Things could have been easier—with fewer dead trees—if Todd hadn't fought her every step of the way.

The china? Split it up.

The lawn furniture? Ditto.

Even the lawyers had eventually rolled their eyes at how every request had become an instant battle, which wound up tripling what the divorce should have cost.

And now this. Having to take Todd back to court to get her share of the insurance money?

The more she thought about it, the angrier she became.

How dare he, Kelly thought. He knew that she struggled financially, and yet, he had hidden the fact that the insurance company had reimbursed him?

Her phone rang, the low, melodic ringtone breaking the silence and her train of thought. She glanced at the clock, surprised to see that it was almost a quarter to ten. Immediately, she felt that sudden wave of panic that something was wrong. It didn't help when she saw that it was Todd calling her.

"What happened?" she asked as soon as she answered the phone. "Is he OK?"

"Huh?"

She shifted the phone to her other ear and held it there with her shoulder. "Zach. That's why you're calling, right?"

"No." A hesitation. "It's just . . . He's fine, Kelly."

Even though she was alone, Kelly narrowed her eyes. There was something about the way he was speaking, the syllables drawn out, the pause in the middle of the sentence. Her red flag went up and she began to fish. "Did you stop in to the hospital to see him?"

"I saw him."

"Today?" she asked.

"Yeah."

He was lying and she knew it. "You were? What time? I was at the hospital all day. I didn't see you."

Another pause. "Maybe it was yesterday."

Kelly pursed her lips and tapped her fingers against the papers on her table. "You've been drinking, haven't you, Todd?"

"What? Why would you say that?"

She rolled her eyes. His classic response. Whenever she asked a question that had an unfavorable response, he didn't give her a straight answer. Instead, he redirected it. He should have been a lawyer. At that thought, she glanced down at the paperwork again and realized that she probably would have to *hire* a lawyer to fill out all these forms for the motion. Was it really worth the money to go after him?

She took a deep breath. "Why'd you call, Todd? What's up?"

"I . . ." Another pause. "It's just that, well, it's tough going through this alone, Kell."

The use of her nickname made her cringe. Kell. Very few people called her that. And Todd had called her that only during the good times, the times that weren't surrounded by fighting or abusive name-calling. The times when he had let down his guard enough to convey to her that he did, indeed, care, even if he didn't always demonstrate it.

And yet, he could still steal money from her?

Her temper began to flare up, and she tried to calm herself.

"Don't you think . . . ?" He let his words linger, unspoken, and she thought she heard the sound of ice tinkling in a glass, as if he had paused to sip his drink.

"Our son's in the hospital after overdosing, Todd," she said in a flat voice, stressing the word "overdosing." How many times had Todd denied that Zach had a problem at all? At least now he couldn't do that. "He's struggling with addiction. And it's not just a teenage phase, Todd. So, don't you think you could put down the gin for just one night? Maybe two? Or, even better yet, maybe for good?"

"Why d'you have to be like that?" He cleared his throat, another telltale sign that he had been drinking. "You know, we had our good times, Kell. Maybe things would've been different if you hadn't left me. Maybe none of this would've happened with Zach."

She shook her head as if trying to shove away the memories of the too many times Todd had been like this when they were married. Always finding a way to blame her for everything. *If* she hadn't left him? Did he really think that he would've stopped drinking? That Zach wouldn't have found the dark side? As much as she despised that boy

Michael Stevens, Kelly knew that he had spoken the truth when he said Zach would've found it with or without his help.

Nothing would have changed if she hadn't left Todd.

And they both knew it.

"Look, I don't have time for this," she snapped, her eyes falling onto the paperwork before her. Part of her wanted to tell him that she was preparing to sue him, but she had learned long ago to never give him a heads-up. If she was going to follow through with the lawsuit, it was a much better strategy to spring it on him. "I'm in the middle of something. Maybe if you sober up at some point, we can talk like normal people, but I'm not doing this with you right now. Not like this."

She didn't wait for him to respond before she ended the call. *Go sleep it off,* she thought angrily. And then, before setting the phone down, she pressed the "Do Not Disturb" button, just in case he tried to call her back. Chances were that he wouldn't even remember calling her in the morning, and maybe that wasn't such a bad thing.

She shoved the legal papers away from herself. With all that she was fighting, the thought of taking Todd to court was just one too many battles for Kelly to face. Whether she went pro se or hired a lawyer, she knew that it would be a long and drawn-out process. She'd have to dig deep to discover what was paid and then try to prove that it was reimbursed by the insurance company. That meant phone calls to the facilities, gathering receipts, finding her own payments, and then trying to get the insurance company to actually discuss the claim with her—something they refused to do because she wasn't on the policy.

And, despite his sugary words spoken under the umbrella of intoxication, Todd would fight her every step of the way. He enjoyed fighting her because it kept him involved with her life. That was his goal, to remain involved. And that was the one thing Kelly didn't want.

No, taking him to court would create an enormous amount of stress at a time when she needed to be clearheaded so that she could focus on not just Zach, but also Fiona and herself. To be distracted from any of those much more important priorities was simply going to create an untold strain on her life, both personally and professionally. It was time for Zach to get to Arizona, Fiona to be a teenager again, and Kelly to return her attention to her work. Distractions? Pressure? Anxiety? Dealing with Todd?

No.

Abruptly, she shoved the papers away. She stood up and headed toward the stairs so that she, like Fiona, could retire for the night. No amount of money was worth enduring such unnecessary stress.

CHAPTER 40

"Kelly?"

She looked up and managed to smile at Pastor Russell. He was an older man with thinning gray hair and hunched-over shoulders. But he always exuded an aura of energy and positivity. That had been one of the reasons she had called and asked to talk with him that morning.

"Thank you so much for seeing me," Kelly said as she stood up and extended her hand to greet him with a handshake. "I know it's short notice and you're busy."

He tilted his head and gave her a look. "After all these years and what you've gone through? A handshake?" The pastor opened his arms and embraced her. "I'm so sorry, Kelly."

When she pulled away, she had to blink in order to fight back the tears. For a long moment, she couldn't speak for fear of crying, and she had told herself that she would not cry. She knew that if she started, she'd never stop.

"Come into my office." He gestured for her to follow him, and only after she was seated on the chair in front of his desk did he shut the door. "Coffee? Tea? Water?"

She glanced over her shoulder. "Water would be fine, thank you."

The pastor hurried over to a small refrigerator in the corner of his office. "So tell me," he asked as he withdrew a water bottle and held it out for her. "How is Zachary doing?"

Great question, she thought. But she didn't have the answer. He was opening up, just a little. Almost ten days without using any sort of drugs had seemed to help him clear his head. But that didn't mean he was better, not by any stretch of the imagination.

"I . . . I guess as well as can be expected." She took the water bottle from the pastor. "But I have to confess that I'm not here to talk about Zach."

He raised an eyebrow. "Oh?"

Swallowing, Kelly licked her parched lips. "I'm here . . ."

Why *was* she there? She wasn't entirely certain. All night she had lain awake, mulling over everything that had happened, starting with Zach's overdose. After the events of the previous days—confronting Michael, arguing with Debbie, hearing her mother's confession, and listening to Todd's drunken ramble—sleep was simply impossible.

It had been a long journey that she'd never thought she would take. And it wasn't just finding the tin of marijuana in Zach's room or all of the events that had unfolded since then. No. Everything had been snowballing for years. She had learned a lot about people—and about herself. And yet, she was just as confused as she had been before all of this began. That morning, when she awoke, Kelly knew that she needed to talk to someone. Needed to unload her mind in a supportive, nonjudgmental environment. And that realization had led her to call her pastor.

She twisted the top of the water bottle and took a small sip, the cold liquid cooling her nerves.

"I'm here," she began again, "to learn how to forgive, Pastor."

"Ah." He leaned back in his chair, the spring squeaking under his weight. He stared at her as if contemplating her request. "That's a mighty undertaking, Kelly."

"That's why I need your help." She leaned forward and set the water bottle on the floor by her purse. "It seems like I'm all alone, fighting this battle for Zach. No one cares, or maybe they care but they don't know how to show it." She ran her fingers through her hair and sighed. "I need someone to talk to, someone who isn't biased. Or uninterested because it's not their problem."

He remained silent, watching her thoughtfully.

"Zach's lost, Pastor. He's a lost little boy. I know he's seventeen but, mentally, he's just a scared child. For a long time, I felt that his father was in denial. That my sister only cared about herself. My mother pretended everything was OK. My best—and only—friend tends to focus on fixing everything. I had no one to *hear* me. To just listen to me and support me."

"You know that's not true."

Kelly sighed and fell back against the chair. Shutting her eyes, she gave a slight nod. "I know. I know it's not true. But that's what I thought."

"So what happened?"

She shrugged. "I guess I was only looking at things from one side and, slowly, I've been seeing it from a different perspective."

The pastor nodded his head. "That can be distressing, for certain. But it's a sign of spiritual growth."

Kelly wondered about that. She hadn't been too consistent with her attendance at church recently, and she rarely picked up her Bible anymore. Was she truly experiencing spiritual growth?

As if reading her mind, the pastor said, "Spiritual growth can come from within, Kelly. You don't have to sit in a pew to grow. But when you learn to practice tolerance for other people's situations, you are surely on a journey of growth."

"I suppose."

"And you speak about forgiveness. Releasing feelings of resentment against people whom you perceive as having harmed you is a lot easier said than done, isn't it?"

She almost laughed. "It is," she admitted.

The pastor nodded. "We're human and it's in our nature to hold grudges. Me, too, believe it or not."

Kelly smiled, feeling herself relax. She always felt better when she consulted with Pastor Russell. His easygoing nature and down-to-earth way of speaking were exactly what she needed.

"Forgiveness is not forgetting, nor does it mean condoning the wrongs that were done to you. Whether or not forgiving someone repairs the damage that was done, well, that's up to you. But if you can recognize the pain and release it so that it does not define who you are, you are well on your way to moving on and, frankly, that's the true definition of forgiveness. Releasing your anger and moving on."

"So I don't *have* to reconcile with people who have wronged me?"

The pastor shook his head. "If that were the case, we'd all have a lot of pent-up anger, don't you think?" He steepled his fingers together and pressed them under his chin. "Look at it this way: Forgiveness empowers you to let go. Negativity begets negativity. You need to release those negative feelings and focus on the positive. Count your blessings, not your problems. While that doesn't make the problems go away, it does put them into perspective."

"Such as?" she asked.

The pastor tapped his fingers together as if contemplating an answer for her. "Let's see." He paused, and then his eyes lit up. "Take a look at Zachary. He was in a bad place, doing things that were unhealthy for his mind, body, and soul, yes? That's a problem. But now he's getting proper care. That's a blessing. From what I understand, you've gotten Todd to agree that Zachary can go to this facility out west. That's another blessing. Sometimes, Kelly, God handles situations in his own way. We might not understand the why, but God gives you what you need." He paused to let the words sink in. "And remember, what you *need* is not always what you *want*. He is our father, and, as you know from being a parent, sometimes need and want are two very separate things."

"Sometimes it just feels like everything is coming down on my shoulders," she whispered. Her mother's words echoed in her ear: *Even the people with the strongest shoulders sometimes need help with carrying the heaviest of loads.*

"He will never give you more than you can handle." The gentle reminder stung.

"I don't think I can handle too much more."

"You'd be surprised what you are capable of." He gave her a warm smile. "Remember during your divorce? You didn't think you could handle some of the awfulness surrounding that, Kelly. How many times did you come to me? But you persevered and look what you've done. You've kept your home. Your daughter's doing wonderfully at school. And you've managed to stay on top of Zach's problem."

"Not on top," she corrected. "Two steps behind."

The pastor shrugged. "You might see it that way, Kelly, but I've counseled many parents who haven't been as focused on getting treatment for their children, and that's with both parents onboard. You've been dealing with Zach's addiction *and* Todd's denial. That's a lot for any single person to handle. You shouldn't be so hard on yourself."

Nor on other people, she told herself.

"Remember Jeremiah 29:11?"

Kelly gave a soft laugh. "How could I forget? You drilled it into me during my divorce."

"God has a plan for you," the pastor reminded her. "And he has one for Zach, too. Let God take care of things. Like any good parent, his plan will not hurt you. But you need to let go and let God."

"Let go and let God," she repeated, engraving those words into her mind.

"That's right. Let go of trying to control everything, and let God take care of everything. Turn it over to him. When you can do that, you'll see how many blessings you truly have."

More words of wisdom that she repeated over and over again as the pastor continued to talk. She felt better already and knew that God had just recharged her enough to continue fighting the battle that still lay ahead of her.

CHAPTER 41

"So let me get this straight." Charlotte wiped her mouth with the cloth napkin. "This place flies someone to New Jersey to pick up Zachary and escort him to Arizona?"

They were in Morristown, eating at a French Thai restaurant. Charlotte had insisted that Kelly leave the hospital and be pampered for once. Reluctantly, Kelly had agreed. And now, as they sat in the dimly lit restaurant, she knew that, once again, Charlotte had been right. Slowly, Kelly was beginning to unwind, feeling almost human again.

Almost.

"And your insurance company pays for that?"

Kelly nodded. "So I'm told." She still couldn't believe it.

"Good!"

Kelly glanced at the table next to them, watching as the waiter set down two large dinner plates before the man and woman. It was a Friday evening, and they appeared to be on a date. There was a sweet awkwardness about them. The cynical side of her wondered what secrets they'd eventually hide from each other.

"You're going after Todd for the money, right?"

Kelly returned her attention to Charlotte. That had been a question she had mulled over ever since leaving the pastor's office that morning. She had thought about it on the way to the hospital, while she had sat with Zach, when she had returned home to greet Fiona after school, and even on her way to meet Charlotte.

She just didn't have an answer yet.

Shrugging, Kelly responded with a simple "Maybe."

"Maybe?" Charlotte practically spat out the word. "How many thousands of dollars are we talking about?"

"A lot."

Charlotte frowned, her forehead wrinkling and her eyes squinting as she did so. "Did you suddenly find a money tree planted in your backyard?"

Kelly almost smiled. "Not exactly. I found something else."

"Oh gee." Charlotte leaned back in her chair. "This ought to be good."

"Forgiveness."

Charlotte rolled her eyes.

"I'm serious, Char. Listen, it's very empowering to forgive."

"That and a few thousand dollars pays the bills, Kelly."

This time, Kelly did laugh. "I spoke with Pastor Russell this morning. It was very clarifying. I feel like the weight of the world is lifted off my shoulders."

Charlotte sighed.

"Think about it," Kelly continued. "Harboring grudges is like a worm eating your soul. When you release that, there's a sense of enlightenment. I could file the paperwork to go after Todd, but that would just keep him involved in my life. And that's what he wants. Or I can release the anger and resentment, let him drown in his own slow spiritual death—"

"I highly doubt it's slow."

Kelly rolled her eyes. "You know what I mean. He stole that money from me. He denied Zach the best care possible. He contributed greatly to this problem, and he will have to answer for it at some point in time. In the meantime, I can look myself in the mirror each morning and know that I fought for the right things: my children." She took a deep breath and leveled her gaze at her friend. "There's no amount of money that can equal that."

"You're crazy."

"And, moving forward, I know that insurance pays. He can't fool me again."

"We'll see about that."

"But even if he does, Charlotte, what does it matter? The same with Jackie. She's been terrible to me and my children ever since the divorce. My brother, too. Not once has he picked up the phone to see how we're doing. I cannot focus my energy on resenting them any longer. It just steals my positivity and that's just not worth it. And my mother? I can't fault her for living in a bubble of neutrality. I get it. She's in her golden years, and who wants to be bogged down with all of this?"

Charlotte took a deep breath. "Well, it seems you're in a better place anyway. I don't want to take that away from you, even if I don't understand it." She reached for her water glass. "Or agree with it."

No, Kelly knew that other people might not agree with her. But she also knew that if God wanted her to have that money, he'd see to it that Todd did the right thing. If not, that was not in her control.

"Now, let's change the subject, shall we?" Charlotte said, far too casually to not be calculated.

"Good." Kelly wanted nothing more than to change the subject. "Talk about anything else. Please. I need a break from the depressing subjects of Todd and Zach, even if only for one night."

An odd expression crossed Charlotte's face, almost as if she was smirking. She leaned forward and gave Kelly a sideways glance. "A little bird mentioned that there's something you haven't been telling me."

"Such as . . . ?"

"Don't play coy with me, Kelly Martin." Charlotte sat up straight again. "A certain football coach? Hanging out at the hospital quite a bit?"

Kelly's mouth opened.

"Aha!" Charlotte pointed at her with her fork. "I knew it. You've been holding out on me."

"How on earth . . . ?" As far as Kelly suspected, no one knew about Thomas's visits to the hospital. She had no one to tell; that was for certain. At least no one other than Charlotte.

Dipping her fork into her *pad kee mao*, Charlotte arched an eyebrow. "Maybe you should lock your cell phone," she said before putting the forkful of noodles into her mouth.

"Fiona?" Kelly gasped. "She read my text messages?"

"Um hum."

"That rascal!"

Charlotte gave a little laugh. "So spill it, sister. Tell me about this football coach." She lowered her voice. "Is he cute?"

The heat rose to Kelly's cheeks. "Please, Charlotte. You sound so high schooler-ish."

"That's not even a word, Professor Martin."

"It should be." But secretly Kelly was pleased that Charlotte knew. For once, she had something good to share with her friend. "Well, Miss Nosy—"

Charlotte held up her hand. "Hey, I wasn't the one poking around your phone!"

"OK, then. Fair enough. If you must know, yes, he is rather attractive." She stressed the word "attractive." "Cute" was for puppies and babies, not grown men. "And he was at that meeting I had at the high school. Remember that?"

Charlotte nodded, her mouth full of food again.

"I don't know why, but he started coming to the hospital to check on Zach after he overdosed."

Swallowing her food, Charlotte dabbed at her mouth with her napkin. "He's one of those guys with a Superman complex."

Kelly laughed. "What?"

"You know. Superman." Charlotte waved her fork in the air. "Likes to swoop in and rescue the ladies."

"I don't think that's exactly it," Kelly said.

"Then enlighten me, Lois."

She couldn't help but smile. She had missed this, the casual, teasing banter between friends on a Friday night. When had she lost touch with this side of her friendship with Charlotte? Was that just another casualty of substance abuse? Lost friendships? Lost selves?

"I think he was genuinely concerned about Zach—"

Charlotte rolled her eyes. "Right."

"And, I don't know, we just became friends," she continued, ignoring Charlotte's interruption. "I mean, that's all it is right now anyway. Friends. I'm not in a good place to start *dating* someone."

"You say that like 'dating' is a dirty word."

She didn't want to remind Charlotte that, unlike her, she hadn't dated anyone in almost twenty years. And it wasn't like riding a bicycle—something that a person never forgot how to do. "But I like him," she admitted. "He's different. A gentleman. And, most importantly, he grew up with sisters."

Tossing her hands in the air, Charlotte practically shouted, "Hallelujah!"

Embarrassed, Kelly ducked her head, aware that several people glanced in their direction. Charlotte, however, didn't seem to notice, or, if she noticed, she didn't care.

"If I've told you once, I've told you a thousand times that you never should have married a man who didn't have sisters." Charlotte clucked her tongue as she shook her head. "That's a recipe for disaster, those sisterless men. Nothing but trouble. Too out of touch with a woman's needs."

Kelly laughed. If only Todd's problems were so simple.

"So this football coach. He sounds promising."

But Kelly wasn't about to think like that. "I'm not rushing anything. If it happens, it happens. Otherwise, I'm just glad to have a new friend."

"Hey, I'm not asking you to marry him, but I'd like to see you treated like a lady for once."

Now that was something Kelly could agree to. "Fair enough." She raised her water glass and held it out for Charlotte to do the same. "Here's to being treated like a lady," she said. "And, of course, to Zach," Kelly added. "May this new place be the one that helps him put the pieces back together again."

Their glasses made a soft clinking sound as they touched the rims together, and Charlotte nodded, adding a soft "Amen."

CHAPTER 42

"I don't want to go, Mom."

Kelly stood by Zach's hospital bed, staring down at him. He was pleading with her, his gray eyes wide and frightened. For a moment, she saw the whisper of a boy who used to come to her frightened about a monster under his bed or scary noises he heard outside of his window. She wished that she could envelop him in her arms, hold him on her lap, and rock him to sleep, comforting him the way that she used to when she chased away his fears.

But he was too old for that now.

"I'm sure you don't," she said at last. "But this will be a fresh start for you, Zach. Away from everything here that's holding you back."

"It's so far away."

Tell me about it, Kelly thought. He had never been away from home, not like this. Once he was in Arizona, he'd be too far for weekly visits. And while part of her welcomed the break from the drama and turmoil that Zach had wreaked on her home, the other part of her realized that, the next time she saw him, he'd be a man. Legally anyway.

"Dad never even let me go to sleepaway camp," Zach complained. "Remember how I wanted to go to baseball camp with Ben and James? Now I'm supposed to go to Arizona?"

Kelly gave a little laugh. "This is a big jump from baseball camp."

Zach shut his eyes.

"It's going to be OK, Zach." She reached down and brushed his hair away from his forehead. "You just need to concentrate on *you* for a while. Not to worry about school or me or your father or anything else, OK?"

Slowly, he nodded.

"And I've already booked tickets for me and Fiona to come for Christmas."

Zach's eyes widened. "Really?"

She had spoken to the facility earlier that morning and inquired about whether or not she could do that, see Zach over the holidays. While they felt a visit over Thanksgiving was too soon, they told her that Christmas would be all right. And, as soon as she got the green light, Kelly booked the tickets. "Nothing like a nice long weekend in Phoenix, right? As long as you're doing well, we can come to the facility for Christmas supper, and you can even come out with us on Saturday. Maybe we can go to the zoo or something."

"Not the zoo," he said, rolling his eyes. "Please."

She laughed. "OK, no zoo."

"What about Dad?"

Kelly fought the urge to cringe. She reminded herself of Pastor Russell's pep talk and managed to maintain her smile. "I know he'll visit, too. Maybe for Christmas." She paused. "I'm sure he doesn't want to sit home alone for the holiday."

"The four of us together for Christmas?" Zach made a face. "That would be weird."

"I agree," she managed to say in an upbeat, teasing manner. "But if he wants to come down, that would be fine. We'll make it work."

The sound of someone knocking at the door surprised both of them. Usually the doctor or nurses knocked once and entered. This time, however, the door remained shut.

Kelly glanced at Zach before she walked over to the door and opened it. An older man stood there and greeted her with a firm handshake.

"John Reynolds," he said. "I take it you are Zachary's mother?"

She nodded, still uncertain who he was. A social worker? A therapist? Or maybe even a volunteer? "I am. And who exactly are you?"

He gestured toward the room, a silent invitation to step inside. When she moved to the side, John entered and walked right over to Zach. "Hi Zach, John Reynolds." He extended his hand and waited for Zach to shake it. "I'm your escort for the trip to Arizona."

"Oh!" Kelly breathed a sigh of relief. Dr. Kumpoor had mentioned that an escort would be arriving that day, but the doctor had said that the rehab center was sending a woman. Kelly wondered if Todd had called to complain about that. Either way, Kelly felt better. *Something* was finally happening, movement in the right direction, and she prayed that it would help her son become the man she knew hid beneath the surface. "It's nice to meet you."

Zach, however, didn't look as thrilled.

John sat down in the chair next to him. "I want you to know, Zach, that I understand if you're feeling a little apprehensive. It might seem scary, leaving home and traveling so far away." He glanced at Kelly. "You, too, Mom." His gaze returned to Zach. "But you are going to a wonderful facility."

A hint of a smile crossed Zach's lips.

"And we do a lot of neat trips on the weekends. Bonding types of adventures."

Kelly stood back and let John talk with her son. She watched the exchange with curiosity. There was something about John, a certain magnetism, that Zach clearly felt drawn to. Kelly could see that right away. Unlike with most people, Zach warmed up to him and even asked him a few questions. There was most definitely a change in Zach. She knew better than to fool herself into thinking he was cured. No. That day was a long way off. But things were looking more positive than any of the other times when Zach had gone to a rehab.

"And Ms. Martin?"

She looked up. "Yes?"

John stood and reached into his pocket. He withdrew a folded piece of paper and handed it to her. "I don't know if you received this. Probably not."

Her eyes skimmed the paper. "What is this?"

"We don't like the clients to arrive too heavily loaded with things." He paused, leveling his eyes to meet hers. "Those are the items that Zachary may bring with him." He paused as if to emphasize his point. "And only those items."

"Got it," she said. "Maybe I should let you two visit a bit? I can run out and pick up what I need to." She looked at Zach to make certain he was comfortable being alone with John. "And your father said he wanted to stop by this evening after work."

Zach's eyes widened. "You're coming back, right?"

She nodded. "Of course. But later, OK? I want to give you and your dad some time alone." That wasn't necessarily the whole truth. She just didn't want to see Todd right now. Not after their confrontation the previous week and then his drunken phone call. She had successfully avoided him for the past few days, and she had a feeling that it was just better to keep it that way.

Kelly walked over to Zach and leaned down to brush a quick kiss against his forehead. For once, he didn't cringe or move away from her. That, too, was something new.

She smiled at John. "It was nice meeting you."

He nodded. "Likewise."

She reached down and touched Zach's arm. "See you later, OK?"

Outside in the hallway, she paused, uncertain whether or not she should shut the door. John was already talking to Zach, and, even though Zach appeared at ease, Kelly left the door partially open. Before she turned to leave the floor, she caught sight of a doctor standing beside a woman outside of a door down the hallway. Despite the distance, Kelly could see that the woman was Debbie.

For the briefest of moments, Kelly fought the urge to walk down the hallway and speak to her. She wanted to tell Debbie that she forgave her for the terrible accusations and things that she had said the other day. And then she remembered what Pastor Russell had said. Forgiveness did not necessarily have to be expressed. Just feeling it was enough. Letting go and letting God. Wasn't that what he had told her?

In her mind, Kelly wondered how Debbie would have reacted if she *had* walked down the hallway and tried to provide comfort. Knowing Debbie, it wouldn't have gone over well. No, she decided, forgiving Debbie did not mean that she had to repair the relationship. They barely had one, anyway. But Kelly's ability to release the anger and harbor no ill will toward the woman was more than enough to warrant her moving on.

And that's what she would do. Move on while God handled Debbie Weaver and her problems. For the moment, Kelly had enough of her own issues to focus on.

As she walked out of the double doors of the children's psychiatric ward, for the first time in a long time, Kelly felt as if the burden upon her shoulders was slowly lifting. Just enough to make her feel confident that God was going to take care of everything.

CHAPTER 43

Later that afternoon, Kelly was at the store buying the items that Zach needed to take with him: shampoo, deodorant, liquid soap, shower slippers, toothpaste. The list wasn't very long, but Kelly wanted to buy new things for his new start.

Standing at the checkout counter at the drugstore, Kelly felt the vibration of her cell phone in her back pocket. Thinking that it was Fiona, she grabbed the phone. She needed to pick her up at school, and from the way the cashier was moving—slowly!—she was going to be late. And she didn't want Fiona standing there, waiting for her.

But the message wasn't from Fiona.

It was from Thomas. Two words:

Call me.

Kelly frowned. The directness of the two words, "call me," sounded ominous.

Despite the feeling of foreboding, she forced herself to wait until she was out of the store. What emergency could Thomas have that impacted her?

Ten minutes later, after tossing the two plastic bags onto the back seat of her car, Kelly settled into the front seat and pressed "Call Back" on her smartphone.

It rang once and he answered, as if he had been waiting for her call.

"Where are you?" he asked, his voice breathless. Had he been running?

"Hello to you, too."

He paused, and she thought that he might backtrack to greet her properly. But he didn't. "Are you near the high school?"

"I am." She glanced at the clock. A quarter to four. "Is everything OK?"

It sounded as if he shuffled the phone against his ear. "I need to see you. Can you get here right away?"

Under other circumstances, Kelly might have made a joke about him "needing" to see her. But his tone did not welcome any such teasing. "Sure, I guess." She'd have to text Fiona that she might be late. "I'm five minutes away," she said. "Where shall I meet you?"

The drive took forever. Traffic through the streets of Morristown was heavy, typical for the late afternoon. Kelly clutched the wheel, her nerves on edge. What could possibly be so important? And why couldn't he just tell her whatever it was over the phone? The more time that passed, the more anxious she became.

He stood outside of the football house, waiting for her. He wore his burgundy jacket and, as usual, had his hands tucked into the pockets. He was pacing the sidewalk, his head hanging down and his shoulders slouched forward.

Something was definitely not right.

Kelly parked her car in a nearby spot and walked across the parking lot toward him.

He must have been deep in thought, for he didn't look up when she approached.

"Thomas?"

Startled, he stopped walking and turned to face her. His normally warm and welcoming face appeared drawn and tired. There was no color in his cheeks. He took the few steps to stand before her and reached for her arm. "Come sit down over here, OK?" Without waiting for her reply, Thomas led her to a low wall near the side of the building.

"You're starting to freak me out," she said as she sat down. "What's going on?"

He stood before her, his lips pressed together as if trying to determine how to tell her something. For the life of her, she couldn't imagine what it was that could cause him such distress.

"I wanted to tell you in person, Kelly."

Her eyes widened as she suddenly panicked that whatever he was going to tell her was bad, really bad. And still, she couldn't begin to think of what *he* could have to say that required such drama.

"It's Michael Stevens."

She caught her breath.

"He died today."

"Oh." It came out like a little poof of air.

"I just found out an hour ago, and I wanted you to hear it from me, not the grapevine." He knelt down before her and reached out to take her hand. It was a comforting gesture with no hint of intimacy. "It appears that he overdosed last night and, apparently, his mother found him earlier this afternoon."

For a moment, Kelly wasn't certain how to feel. A whirlwind of conflicting emotions hit her at once. *That could've been me,* she thought, which was immediately followed by: *I warned his mother; she didn't listen.* She remembered far too well the morning she had walked into Zach's room, just shy of two weeks ago, when she had found her son lying unconscious in his bed. If she hadn't tried to get him up for school, Zach might have died. Why hadn't Joan checked on *her* son earlier in the morning? Why hadn't she learned from Kelly's warning? Even more importantly, Kelly wondered what Joan was going through.

How did it feel to realize that her son would never come home again? No matter what Kelly had thought about him, she knew that there were no boundaries when it came to a mother's love for her child.

Kelly raised her eyes and met Thomas's. "I . . . I don't know what to feel."

He squeezed her hand. "That's all right, Kelly. You've been through a lot. It's OK to not know."

"But I should." She bit her lower lip. "I mean, I should feel something, right?"

He shook his head. "No, no, you don't have to feel anything."

"Relief that it's not Zach, I suppose," she said, more to herself than to Thomas. "But that's terrible. That's how people feel about someone going through a divorce or battling cancer. They feel relief that it's not them, although, in all likelihood, it could have been or, even worse, still could be one day."

He remained crouched before her, staring into her face and letting her think aloud.

"But I also feel sad." She blinked and met his concerned gaze. "It's a waste of a life, and, no matter how much I despised Michael, I didn't wish this on him. And yet, I warned his mother."

"You weren't the only one, Kelly," Thomas said softly. "She chose to ignore it. Sometimes it's easier to simply ignore your problems rather than fight them head on."

"Defense."

"It's a hard game to play," he admitted. "That's why many players sit it out."

Slowly, Kelly nodded. "Joan sat it out." She pictured the countless boys who often sat on the bench during the games, dressed in full gear, hopeful that they might get called into play. And yet, Kelly knew that some of those boys were secretly relieved. It was cool to be on the team but dangerous to be on the field. Yes, some of those players sat it out to avoid the danger.

"You know," Thomas said, his thumb gently caressing her hand. "You managed to save Zach, Kelly. You're one of those rare players who runs a great offense *and* plays a strong defense. You got him out of here, and, even though I've only known you a short while, I'm proud of you for fighting so hard."

"But I didn't!" She pressed her lips together, suddenly hating herself for having said that. Why couldn't she have just taken the compliment? "I could have fought harder earlier, Thomas. But I was too weak."

"You're not weak."

"Maybe not now," she admitted. "But why didn't I do more sooner? Why didn't I fight Zach's father? Research the insurance? Demand that the courts get involved? Zach will never get those wasted years back."

Thomas raised an eyebrow at her. "But he has all those years ahead of him now, Kelly, and that's something Michael lost. His future."

"I feel like I should cry."

"Then cry."

"But I don't *want* to cry. I feel nothing for Michael and his family." She hesitated. "Is that wrong?"

Thomas shrugged. "I can't speak about that, Kelly. You feel what you feel. I don't think there is any right or wrong in this situation."

"I need to go get Fiona."

He stood up and helped her to her feet, never once releasing her hand. "You sure you're OK to drive? I could take you to get your daughter."

She glanced at her car. "I have groceries."

He smiled at her. "That's not what I asked."

"Yes, I'm OK to drive."

He bent his knees just enough so that he was level with her eyes. "You sure?"

She nodded.

"Is it OK if I check on you later?"

He was still holding her hand. She found it comforting. "I think I'd like that," she said and gave him a soft smile. "And Thomas?"

"Hmm?"

She leaned forward and placed a light kiss on his cheek. And then, before she pulled away, she whispered, "Thank you."

A soft smile crossed his lips, and he gave her hand a gentle squeeze.

Yes! she thought as she slowly—reluctantly—extracted her hand. Standing before him, Kelly knew that something had just changed between them. Perhaps it was the shift from friendship to something more. His concern over her reaction to Michael Stevens had proven his true character, although she hadn't really needed proof.

And yet, she also knew that he wasn't about to rush her, to push her to that next level. She needed time, and, from what she could see, he was willing to give it to her.

"I better get going," she said in a soft voice. "I need to fetch Fiona and then I best go talk with Zach." Despite Kelly not approving, Zach had considered Michael Stevens his friend, and losing a friend, at any age, was difficult. However, she suspected that, under these circumstances, on the eve of leaving for rehab, it would be even worse if her son didn't learn about Michael's death in a compassionate way. While Kelly dreaded having to tell him the news, she knew that it would be better if he heard it from her, not someone else, and certainly not through social media or on the news. Telling him was something that she had to do. For Zach.

CHAPTER 44

An hour after dropping off Fiona at home, Kelly found herself standing outside of Zach's hospital door. It was closed, and she suspected that Todd was inside, saying his goodbye to Zach. The facility had been specific in providing instructions for the following morning. The guardian, John—and not Kelly or Todd—would sign the discharge papers and leave the hospital with Zach. It was better that way, they had explained. Sometimes tearful goodbyes made the patient fight leaving at all.

Even worse, Zach wasn't to know until morning.

Kelly had thought that the plan made sense. Now, as she realized that she would be saying goodbye to Zach for months, possibly a year, she wished that she could have more time. Sure, she would see him at Christmas, but it wouldn't be the same. Zach would be living in another state, far removed from Morristown, so that he could focus on his healing. It made sense, but that didn't soften the empty void that was beginning to form in her core.

She took a deep breath and knocked once on the door before pushing it open.

Sure enough, Todd was sitting beside Zach's bed. He still wore his suit and had certainly stopped in to visit on his way home from work. Kelly barely acknowledged him, trying to remember her conversation with the pastor, but still fighting her animosity toward him.

"Hey." She greeted Zach with a soft smile. "Things go OK with John?"

"He's pretty chill. I like him."

Kelly wanted to say something encouraging, to acknowledge Zach's positive reaction to the stranger. But she couldn't. For a moment, she just stood there, clutching her hands before her and staring at Zach, memorizing every little thing about him. Images of his baby face morphed into the more adult face that stared back at her, his gray eyes studying her.

"You OK?" he asked.

Another positive thing, she thought. Zach rarely cared about how anyone else felt.

"You don't look so hot," he added.

Todd stood up and stepped aside. "Sit down."

Without acknowledging him, Kelly brushed past him and took the seat. She cleared her throat, which burned and felt tight. Ever since Thomas had told her the news about Michael, she had tried to bury it deep within her. She didn't want to think about his mother discovering him. How had she reacted when she found him? Had he looked like Zach on that terrible morning? Pale. Lying unconscious with vomit in his mouth? Had Michael choked on it? Or had something else happened to him?

"I have to tell you something, Zach," she started, slowly enunciating each word. "And you need to be very brave."

She didn't have to look at Todd to sense his reaction. She was certain he wanted to tell her that she was being overdramatic or to chastise her for speaking in such a frightening manner. But Kelly didn't care. This wasn't about Todd. This was about her son.

As he sensed the seriousness of what she was about to say, Zach's eyes widened. "What happened, Mom?"

She took a deep breath, letting the air fill her lungs. As she exhaled, she shut her eyes and said a quick prayer that God would guide her to pick the appropriate words. Finally, she opened her eyes and met Zach's concerned gaze. "It's about Michael."

"That kid?" Todd commented somewhat casually.

Kelly ignored him.

Zach, too, focused on Kelly, not his father. The color drained from his already-pale face. "What is it?"

Reaching out, Kelly took Zach's hand. She held it in hers, just loosely, and stared at his fingers. *When had he started biting his nails?* she wondered. *When had they become calloused, losing that soft silkiness from his baby years?* She clutched it and lifted her eyes to stare directly at him. "Michael died."

Zach blinked once and frowned. "What?"

Even Todd shifted his weight and moved closer to the bed.

"He overdosed, Zach." She paused and slowly added, "On drugs," even though it wasn't necessary. But she wanted to drive home the point. Drugs had killed his friend. "I hate to be the one to tell you this. I know that you were friends. But I wanted you to hear it from me."

As he sank back into his pillow, Zach's gaze drifted to the wall. "Michael?"

The expression on his face, a mixture of disbelief and grief, hurt Kelly's heart. She knew that she couldn't protect her son from this, just like so many other painful things that Zachary had experienced in his short life. Oh, how many times had she tried to wrap Zach in her arms, shield him from the evils of the world? But with every day that passed, Zach had grown, as children always do. And at each stage, there were dangers that Kelly simply could not predict, but this news hit so close to home, making it even more difficult to comprehend.

"Dead?"

He whispered the word so softly that, had he not looked at her again, she wouldn't have realized that he had spoken at all. Just that one word. But it said so much. It spoke of fear, uncertainty, sorrow. It also spoke of disbelief, and Kelly wondered whether Zach was trying to convince himself that, maybe, her news wasn't true.

She didn't respond. Instead, she held his gaze.

"He's only seventeen," Zach said, his eyes wide and face still pale. "His mother loves him."

Kelly swallowed, trying to erase the image of Joan Stevens's face from her memory. Oh, what pain that woman must feel! Such a sense of loss. No mother ever should bury a child. Even worse, to have to do so not from disease or an accident, but from the child choosing to use and then abuse drugs? If avoided, addiction was preventable. Unfortunately, once the addict got caught in the dark web of substance abuse, the outcome was far too predictable.

"Yes, Zach, his mother loves him. And she is most certainly distraught beyond either of our comprehension." She grabbed his hand and, leaning down, she squeezed it. "It's something I never want to feel, Zach. And it's why we are blessed that you are sitting here, in the hospital, and leaving soon for Arizona. Don't you see that?"

He blinked at her as if he didn't understand her words.

"That could've been you," she said forcefully. "In fact, if you hadn't been here already, it very well would have been you. You might have been together, Zach. Maybe he had bad drugs. Maybe you would've taken them, too."

She thought she saw him take a sharp breath as he shut his eyes.

"You have to take this seriously this time, Zach," she continued. "You have to kick this." She paused, waiting for him to open his eyes and look at her. "We cannot risk losing you, Zach. You see, I love you, and I don't ever want to feel what Michael's mother is feeling right now. I don't want to be Joan Stevens, a mother who has to pick out her son's coffin, his burial suit, his tombstone."

Zach scrunched his eyes closed, but not before a single tear rolled down his face.

"I can't be Joan Stevens," Kelly said. "I would not survive that level of pain. The loss of either of my children would be far too much to bear. So you see? You have no choice, Zach. You must go to Arizona and focus all of your energy on healing, on becoming healthy again, on learning how to live. Because if you don't, I can assure you that I *will* be a Joan Stevens, standing on the edge of her son's grave as the coffin is lowered into the ground, watching as each shovelful of dirt buries more than just her son; it buries her, too."

"Stop it, Kelly," Todd said in a hoarse voice. "Please."

She ignored him and kept her focus on Zach. Tightening her hold on his arm, she softly said, "I don't ever want to be like Joan Stevens, Zach."

He swallowed. She saw it as well as heard the effort. Slowly, he nodded, never taking his eyes from hers. "I . . . I probably would've been with Michael," he admitted.

From behind her, she thought she heard Todd react. For a moment, it sounded as if he might be crying, but she knew better than to become distracted from Zach.

"I don't want to die, Mom." Another tear fell from his eye. "I . . . I don't want to be like this." He stopped talking, pausing as if trying to gather the strength to speak.

She waited patiently for him to collect his thoughts.

Finally, he gave a determined and slow nod. "I . . . I want to get better." Another pause. "I want to learn to *live*." He pressed his lips together and furrowed his brows.

It was enough. Kelly shut her eyes and took a deep cleansing breath. *Thank you, God,* she prayed, *for putting your hand upon my son. Please guide him on this journey, no matter how long and troublesome it might be.*

Just as Pastor Russell had told her, she had let go and let God. And, as he always did, God had shown the wisdom of doing just that.

From behind her, she heard the sound of a strangled sob coming from Todd. She almost glanced at him, but refused. If he was coming to his own senses, realizing, perhaps for the first time, that his son had truly almost died, so be it. He, too, was in God's hands now.

"Mom?"

She opened her eyes and reached over and brushed a lock of hair away from Zach's forehead. "Yes?"

"I . . . I just don't think I know how to live. How to live a normal life." He frowned. "I don't think I know what normal is anymore."

"You'll learn how to live again, Zach. You'll find a new normal." She smiled at him. "I have the faith."

"Don't give up on me," Zach whispered, his lips trembling.

Leaning over, she pulled him into her arms, embracing her son as if he were a small child and not almost a grown man. She could smell the scent of shampoo on his hair, and it brought back the memory of the days when she used to bathe him as a baby. His giggles, his arms waving, his bright gray eyes watching her. And when they were finished, she would swaddle him in a warm, fluffy towel and hold him in her arms, rocking him while singing a lullaby.

And, with that memory fresh in her mind, she held him and whispered into his ear, "I'll never give up on you, Zach." She tightened her hold. "Never."

EPILOGUE

The doorbell rang, and Kelly called out that she'd get it. She hurried to the front door, shooing the barking dogs into the kitchen before she paused in the small foyer to look in the mirror. She had turned the foyer light down, just enough to complement that orange glow from the candles that burned on the front table. In the dimmed lighting, her reflection appeared more youthful and soft. She reached up, pushed her hair behind her ear, and gave her cheeks a quick pinch.

All morning she had fussed over what to wear. Even while she had been cooking, she had tried to inventory what was in her closet. When was the last time she had gone clothes shopping? Some dresses were too small, others outdated. She made a mental promise to spend at least a few hours over the weekend cleaning out her closet. She owed that to herself.

When it finally had come time to get ready, she had settled on the old reliable black dress. *No one can go wrong with that,* she reasoned, especially when she complemented it with a single strand of pearls at her neck and small pearl earrings.

Now, one final look in the mirror and she took a deep breath.

Ready, she thought.

"Welcome," she said as she opened the door.

Thomas stepped inside and greeted her with a chaste kiss on the cheek. When he did, she caught the musky, clean scent of cologne on his skin. He had dressed up for the evening, his khaki pants and white button-down shirt looking freshly starched and ironed. And his shoes appeared brand new, which struck her as funny. Had he, too, been worried about what to wear?

He held out a bouquet of orange and red flowers and gave her a sheepish smile. "Happy Thanksgiving."

Taking them, she knew that a blush covered her cheeks. When was the last time anyone had given her flowers? "I'm glad you could come," she managed to say.

He leaned over and whispered, "I'm glad I was invited," into her ear. And that, too, furthered her blush.

Oh, how he loved to do that to her.

Over the past few weeks, they had met at least once a week for coffee at the Starbucks in Morristown. Casual meetings. Friendly meetings. Every day, she received a text from him. Sometimes it was a simple check-in message; other times it was an "I'm thinking about you." Those messages made her blush, a warm feeling engulfing her and a smile emerging on her lips.

It was nice to be thought of.

And then, just two weeks ago, Thomas had surprised her by inviting her out to dinner. It was time, he had told her, and she hadn't thought twice about saying yes.

At first it was a dinner. Next it was a concert at the Mayo Performing Arts Center in town. Nothing too fancy, nothing too serious. But she found herself feeling more and more comfortable in his presence outside of the shadow of Zach.

And now, she was taking the next big step: introducing him to her family.

She glanced toward the living room, where Fiona, Charlotte, and her mother were playing a game of Scrabble. She could hear Charlotte bickering with Fiona that the word "gherkins" wasn't a real word.

"Let's hope you feel the same way after meeting everyone."

He didn't move away from her but, instead, reached out and let his hand brush hers. "I'm a football coach," he said in a low voice. "I'm always ready to play defense."

She gave a soft laugh. And it felt good. How long had it been since she had felt liberated enough to laugh at a teasing joke like that? "Then, if you're all geared up and warmed up, let's go meet them."

Thomas hesitated, taking a quick look over his shoulder to make certain that no one was at the end of the hallway. Then he stepped closer to her and leaned down, gently brushing his lips against hers. He let them linger before he pulled back.

"What was that for?" she asked, breathless from the unexpected kiss.

"Good luck," he whispered. "Every good football player has *something* they do for good luck before jumping in the game."

She tilted her head and smiled. "Has it worked in the past with your other girlfriends?"

"I'll let you know after supper." He winked. "First time I tried it."

She couldn't help but laugh. "Oh you!"

He reached his hand for her and entwined his fingers with hers. "Let's go meet the other team." He started walking in the direction of the living room, gently pulling Kelly with him. She followed, pausing only to set the flowers onto the side table outside of the kitchen door. And then, together, they joined the rest of her small family in the living room, a time for fellowship before sharing the Thanksgiving meal.

ABOUT THE AUTHOR

 Bestselling author Sarah Price, a former college professor, began writing full-time after she was diagnosed with cancer. She is the author of two previous works of women's fiction: *Heavenly Blues* and *The Faded Photo*. Additionally, she has written more than twenty romance novels, including the Amish Christian novels *An Amish Buggy Ride* and *An Empty Cup*. Drawing on her own experiences as a survivor of both breast cancer and domestic violence, Sarah explores the issues that touch—and shape—women's lives. She splits her time between living in Morristown, New Jersey, and Archer, Florida, with her husband and two children. Follow her at www.sarahpriceauthor.com, on Facebook at FansOfSarahPrice, or on Instagram @sarahpriceauthor.

21982318671520